SPARK

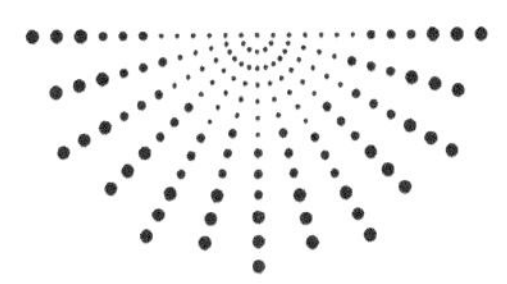

EMMA GRACE

CONTENTS

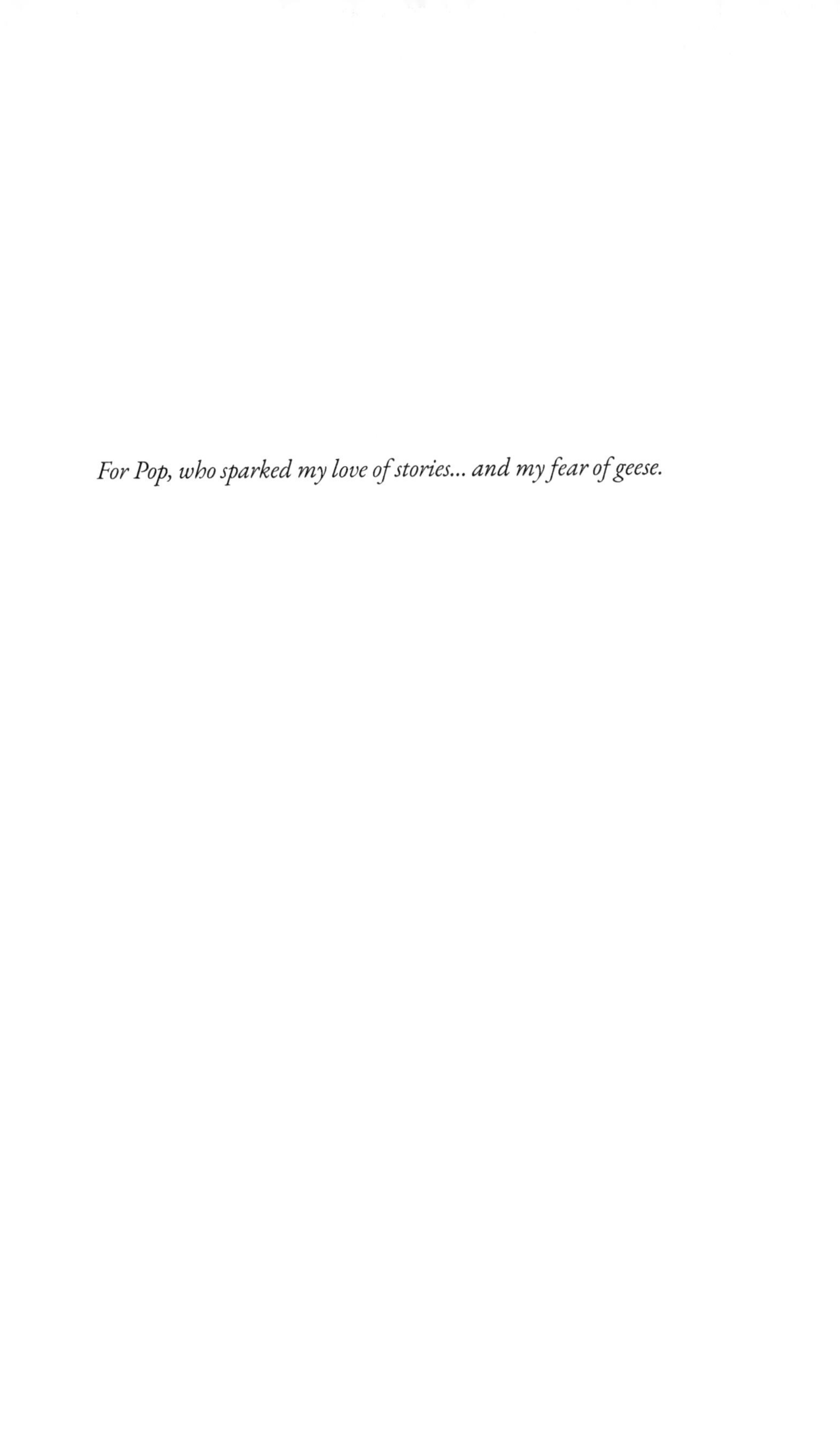

For Pop, who sparked my love of stories... and my fear of geese.

CHAPTER ONE

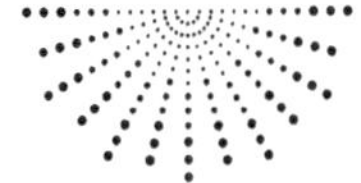

CHRIS

IT IS SHOCKINGLY easy to die. Step off a curb without looking both ways, choke on a piece of chicken, or fall through the ice of a frozen river. One bullet, one blade, or even one wrong choice, and it's over.

Sometimes there's no choice at all. Sometimes you die before you even know you're alive. That's what happened to my brother.

My mother had her first ultrasound when she was eight weeks pregnant with me. My sister was a toddler, and my parents were ready for their second—and final—child. But instead of one heartbeat, there were two.

Having three children is not permitted in Carcera, the place where I was raised. My parents would have to choose, before birth, which one of us to give up. Ankou, the presiding government, would harbor the offered child. My parents knew that whoever they gave up would be gone from them forever.

They told me that at my mother's second ultrasound, there was no other heartbeat, just the one. Just mine.

My mother told me that the relief was immediate and all-consuming. They had lost a fetus, yes, but they had not lost a child. My mother's body had made the decision for them. Her child would not be offered to Ankou any more than she was.

For the longest time I puzzled over my should-have-been-twin. Did my mother absorb him? Did *I?* I always imagined that I would've had a brother, and he would've looked just like me. I wonder who would've been older, and who my parents would've chosen to keep.

My lost sibling was just that—lost. He was missing, not dead, but not alive either.

Sometimes it feels like Katie, my best friend, is in the same place.

Try as she might, I don't think Cecilia, my trainer, understands. Ever since we lost Katie, we've been meeting for coffee on Friday nights. In the Underground, the resistance military I now call home, therapists are beyond hard to come by. Trainers like Cecilia take on that role. Every Friday night I try to tell her what it feels like to lose the other half of your soul, but I always fail at getting her to understand that, too.

Tonight is our third meeting. I order peppermint tea that I won't drink with credits that I don't have, and Cecilia gets a black coffee that she'll sip through pursed lips when she doesn't know what to say.

"So," she says after we take our usual seats. "How's the week been?"

"Fine."

"Ashborrow, really?" She arches one manicured eyebrow towards her close-cropped hair. "Come on. You're better than that."

Awful, I want to say. *The third-worst week of my life, right after the second-worst week of my life, which came after the worst week of my life. And I'm an orphan. I'll always be an orphan.*

"It was okay," I say instead, trying to keep my voice level. "Ava is home and staying with us. No one's heard from Amy." I try not to choke on the lump in my throat.

"I haven't heard from her either, if that makes you feel better," Cecilia offers.

It doesn't, but nothing will. "Thank you. Ava's doing okay. She still takes heavy painkillers, so she's groggy a lot. Noah is keeping an eye on her, and his stitches are healing up nicely. He's lucky that thing didn't cut clean through his cheek, really. I–"

"Ashborrow, I asked about *you.*"

"I'm okay. My head's all better and the scrapes have healed up nicely.

I eat my greens and shower every day, which is more than can be said for a lot of people around here."

"How's your brain? Because I have to be honest, you're physically in a great place, but not everything seems great up there." She taps the side of her head with one long finger. "You're trying to keep tabs on everyone else, but you're neglecting yourself. I think you need to give yourself time to grieve, to not worry about your squadmates so much. They're okay, but you're not, and that's understandable. Your girlfriend just died."

"She wasn't my girlfriend." I have to force the words through my teeth, ignoring that other, horrible word entirely.

"You told me you kissed her?" She says it like a question, when, in fact, I did tell her that. I told her it was the best day of my life, that Katie had tasted of mangoes and cherries. For once, her skin had been warmer than mine.

"I did. I was gonna actually ask her out when we got home. I even had a little thing of chocolates for her, the ones you can get once a month. Dark chocolate, her favorite. I gave them to Ava as a 'welcome home' gift instead."

The seconds pass as she searches for the right words, sipping her coffee. I don't even fake it with my tea, the blue mug sitting idly on the carved-up table. *Mitchell,* it says in a child's handwriting, carved in by a pen or a pair of scissors. Everything here is salvaged from the Surface, raided from abandoned cities and pillaged from Border towns that have been "liberated." Towns like Carcera, which still sits ensnared by a wall of Ankou-guarded stone.

Finally, Cecilia finds her voice. "I'm sorry. I know she meant a lot to you."

I almost laugh. "A lot? She meant way more than a lot, Cecilia. I would do anything, literally *anything,* to bring her back. To hold her hand, to hold..." My throat grows tight. "Her, just once. It's killing me, not to see her every day. I actually think it might be killing me."

She takes another sip of her coffee. "Can I tell you a story?"

I nod, voice too cracked to speak.

"In training, as you know, it's easy to fall for your squadmates. Well, a few years ago, a young couple decided to get married, even though they were still in a high-risk squad and had some time left before they could age out. They got married and were surprised with a beautiful baby boy, so the wife, having done her required years of service by then, was excused from training. But her husband wasn't quite finished, and one day was called to the Surface. When he walked out the door, he never walked back in.

"His wife was devastated, of course, but she carried on. What else was she supposed to do? She applied for a training position and sometimes springs her toddler from daycare to come to work with her. And she misses her husband every day, but the grief can't consume her. People die all the time, especially here. People we love die, too; they're not immune just because they're loved."

I pause for a moment, taking it in. "I'm sorry about your husband," I finally say, trying to ignore the hideous jealousy gnawing at my stomach. At least she got to get married.

"Oh, it's alright. I have Tucker, and they're so much alike, I'm not sure I could handle both of them."

"He likes that show with the talking pigs, right?"

Her face breaks into a smile, and she nods thoughtfully. "Yeah, Tucker loves animals. I wish he could see real ones, on a real farm."

"We'll make sure he does."

"He won't."

"Why not?"

"He's dying, too."

I stare at her tight posture, regal nose, tight curls that sit like a crown on her dark skin. The picture of leadership, of composure, telling me that her only child is dying with all the emotion of a marble statue. Only the slight quiver of her bottom lip gives her away. "What?"

"You heard me. He's dying. It's cancer. He has a bit of time left. Now we're just trying to keep him comfortable."

"But he looked so healthy, just a few weeks ago... with Noah."

"I know." She pauses. "I know. My point isn't to upset you. My point is that we all lose people we love. Ask anyone in this room and they'll tell you they've lost someone, they've felt the world implode around them just like you are right now. You aren't alone in this. I still use present tense when I talk about my husband, about how he likes oranges and the color purple. He isn't gone, not to me. I still wear my ring. I still love him, because that's what grief is. We don't have to stop loving them just because they're gone, and they don't stop loving us, either. I hope one day that the love you have for her stops killing you and starts keeping you alive."

I VISIT Sam after leaving the coffee shop even though it's getting close to curfew. She opens the door quickly and slips into the hall, shutting it behind her.

"What's up?" she asks, pulling her dark red cardigan tightly around her and frowning. "Is everyone okay?"

"Yeah, we're all fine," I say. "Do you know about Cecilia's son?"

"Yeah. She told you?"

I nod, suddenly unable to speak for fear of choking, and hang my head so she can't see my face.

Sam opens her arms, and I fall gratefully into them, trying to ignore how much I wish she were Katie. All I want is her; all I've ever wanted was her.

I pull away before I can start crying. "Thanks."

"How are you doing?" she asks, leaning back against the doorframe and readjusting her cardigan so the missing button is hidden. "I'm sorry we haven't gotten to talk much."

"It's fine. I'm doing alright." I force a small smile across my face. "How are you holding up?"

She sighs heavily. "It's been tough, but we're alright. Amy's in a lot of pain."

"They, uh, from the hip, right?"

She nods. "Yeah. The whole bone was shattered, at the ankle and the knee."

"Sam, I'm so sorry."

"I—*we*—know."

Is there anything I can do to make it up to you? I sign, too choked up to speak.

She shakes her head and replies in sign. *No, but thank you. Just...* She pauses with her hands still raised, weighing the words in her palms.

I'll be here if you need anything, I sign.

Thanks.

See you at training?

Yeah. I'll be a little late, gotta get her to PT.

I offer another tentative smile. *See you tomorrow.*

See you then. She gives a small wave and disappears back into her room, careful not to open the door too wide.

I am left wishing I could walk in like I used to, in a time when they left the door cracked if they knew I was stopping by. I always asked Amy for advice, considering Sam and Katie are (were?) so similar. She was the one who told me to kiss her on Farewell Night, that if I didn't do it then, I might never work up the courage, and it would kill me to always wonder what would've happened if I'd just been brave. And now Amy's leg is gone, and that's killing me, instead.

Antoinette Latrodectus stares as I walk down the hall. I glance over at her, but she quickly looks away.

Other people, at least those who know what happened, look away when they see me, too. I don't mind too much—they do that because they feel awkward. I don't blame them; most people our age have never been on a mission that went that wrong. One of us nearly paralyzed, one an amputee, one permanently scarred, and another gone. Sam and I are the only ones to come out of it unharmed, if you don't count scrapes, bruises, and my minor concussion. We were lucky.

The gash on Noah's cheek is still healing. The stitches are out now, but he'll have a thin scar running from his ear to his chin. He's okay with it—seeing Ava and Amy put things into perspective for him. Besides, Ava told him she thinks the scar's going to be hot.

Ava's injury is right in the middle of her back, slightly off to the left. She's lucky—if it had hit her spine she might have died and at the very least would have been paralyzed from the waist down. She's still in a wheelchair for the time being but is in relatively good spirits. She's a tough cookie, as my mother would've said. Says? I think I'm more at peace with using past tense for her.

Amy was not as lucky as Ava or Noah. She was shot three times in her left leg. One bullet shattered her ankle bone, another tore apart her kneecap, and the third went clean through her thigh. It is because of good surgeons and sheer luck that she is still alive. The doctors said that there was too much nerve and tissue damage for her leg to be saved—she was bleeding out. She hasn't spoken to anyone but Sam even though she came home from the hospital three days ago. I haven't seen her since she was comatose. Maybe that's a good thing.

Before I know it, I'm home, but I don't want to go inside. Ava is going to be in bed, Noah in his nest of blankets on the floor. The two of them have been sleeping a lot since we got home; I don't understand how.

Every time I close my eyes, I see Katie vanish into the stairwell, watch as that last little smile graces her beautiful face. I see her dead in a thousand different ways—stabbed, shot, clubbed into a pile of meat and bone fragments. Sometimes I just see her standing in front of me, and even that is enough to wake me in a cold sweat.

I gather my courage before opening the door. Just as I predicted, they're both out cold. I check my watch: 8:27. The curfew bell hasn't even sounded yet.

I sigh heavily and get cleaned up, taking a hot shower and changing into sweats. Instead of getting into bed, I sit on the bathroom floor, just like I did not so many nights ago with Katie. If I close my eyes, I can almost feel her, soft and strong at the same time.

Cecilia told me there was nothing I could've done to prevent what happened from turning out the way it did. I could've stopped her, though. I could've gone to get Sam and Amy instead of letting her do it. She would be sitting here right now; she would still be alive. She would be the one meeting Cecilia on Friday nights, but I wouldn't want this pain to be hers to bear, either.

Maybe I could've fought my way out of there with Sam and Amy, and we could all be together right now, whole. Maybe in another world she's sitting on the bathroom floor with me, her head on my shoulder. Maybe there's a place where no one had to die for us.

Someone knocks softly on the bathroom door, jarring me out of my thoughts.

"Just a sec," I say.

"Chris, you alright?" Noah asks.

"I'm fine, hang on."

I pick myself up and open the door, shivering as the considerably-cooler air hits my skin. Noah is rubbing one eye sleepily and leaning against the doorframe, hardly keeping his own two feet under him.

"You okay?" he asks. "It's late."

I check my watch. "It's 9:14, it's not late."

"Oh."

"What's up?" I frown; Noah is rarely this muddled. He jumps between sleeping and waking in an instant. He hardly even remembers his dreams, but now he is stuck in one, blond hair tousled as if he's been unconscious for days.

"I miss her," he murmurs.

I sigh and open my arms. "C'mere. I miss her, too."

He leans into me, and I rub his back as he talks. "We never got a funeral notice."

"They don't do funerals for people who are never found. I asked Cecilia about it; they need proof."

"But we *know* she's dead."

"Yeah, we do. They need her body to make the firework, though. It's the way they do things here."

"Bullshit."

I laugh a little. "Yeah, I know. C'mon, let's get some sleep."

He nods and pulls away, walking over to his pile of blankets.

"Here, take my bed tonight," I offer. "You've been on the floor for a week—it's bad for your back."

"You sure?" he asks.

"Yeah, you need it. Get some rest."

"Thanks. Goodnight, Chris."

I settle on the floor and stare up at the green light of the smoke detector, resigned to watching it all night as sleep evades me. "Goodnight, Noah."

I DREAM ABOUT KATIE AGAIN. This time she is standing in a dimly lit hallway, shadows cast across her face. She wears a red dress, and her hair is long again, like it was when we were kids. She extends a soft hand to me, slender fingers outstretched.

"Let's go," she whispers. Her voice is all around me, echoing in my head. "We can't be safe down here. Let's run."

I try to respond, but I can't open my mouth. My hands are bound to my side, and I can't reach her. I can't even sign my answer: *yes, yes, you're right. We have to go.*

Her gorgeous hazel eyes melt, and her strong shoulders droop like deflated balloons. "You won't come with me?"

I try to step forward, to scream that I will, that I always will, no matter where we're going. That I'll go anywhere with her, for her.

"Alright. It's your choice. I have to go, though. I'll see you soon."

She turns away. I blink, and she is gone.

<hr>

WHEN I WAKE, there is bile rising in my throat. I stagger to the bathroom and barely make it in time to fall onto my knees and heave the contents of my stomach into the toilet.

I wipe my mouth and flush the toilet once I'm done, blowing my nose repeatedly. My head falls to rest against the cool porcelain, and I'm too exhausted to get water for my burning throat. I hiccup pathetically and, not for the first nor the last time, wish I were home. If Carcera can still be considered home. My mother would be there; she'd get me a glass of water. My stomach aches with missing her, and Mel, and *my* bed. I miss things being mine.

I find the strength to rinse my mouth and stumble back to my now-empty bed. My stomach lurches as I curl up facing the wall. The last thing I want to see right now is Ava and Noah cuddling. Every night they fall asleep separately but always end up in the same bed halfway to morning. He jumps up when the alarm sounds every day so I don't see, but I wake in the middle of the night all the time.

It's a relief to be back in bed—the rough cement floor has given me a seizing, almighty backache. I have to give Noah credit for starting every night down there, and for being mobile enough to leap up so quickly in the morning. I need to go back to working in the hospital, make some credits, and buy a damn rug.

I draw the blankets high around my shoulders and try to ignore the pain in my chest and stomach. My intestines seem to seize with each shuddering breath, and I cannot stop shivering. My body groans in protest at every movement, especially now that I've pulled all the muscles in my neck and jaw.

I fall restlessly in and out of sleep so much that it's difficult to tell where dreams end, and thoughts begin. I am caught in the middle ground, the place between sleep and consciousness that is paradoxically comfortable and lonely.

Cecilia told me last week to write a letter to say goodbye to Katie, but I don't know how to say goodbye to someone I never said hello to. She's been there forever; our first meeting is a hazy, distant wisp of a memory.

I'm afraid to sleep again, scared to see her but more scared that I won't. I start writing, if only in my head.

Katie, love.

No, not like that.

My dearest Katie.

Nope, Katie wasn't that formal. Better just stick with her name and go from there.

Katie, hey. It's me. Been a while, hasn't it? I miss you. That's probably obvious. We all miss you, especially Ava. She sleeps in Noah's bed so she isn't alone—your room's been empty since that night. She wears Noah or Sam's stuff; none of us have the courage to go back in there. Some things are too much, you know?

Of course she knows, she's Katie. Sometimes I feel like she knows me better than I do.

So, how've you been?

Get it together, Chris.

You don't have to answer that—it was a dumb question. I hope you're doing okay, wherever you are. It's been rough here without you. You're probably wondering what happened, if you can wonder anything.

We ran to the roof just like we were supposed to. We hid behind that garden wall, thinking you were right behind us, but you weren't. Sam and

Amy finally made it up and I was so scared that I... well, that's not something you probably want to hear about right now. I'm sorry.

I really wish you were here. You'd make it all okay, or at least it would feel like that. I could share a room with you so Noah and Ava could have their privacy. You should see them. He's done a great job of taking care of her, making sure she gets to PT and takes her meds on time. I wish I had been there more when she was in the hospital, but I went to the library and finished those books we were reading, and then I read some more. It's easy to get lost there—the endings are always happy. I thought we kind of earned one after everything, but I guess not.

I pause for a moment to gather my thoughts. Where is this going? Why am I still thinking about it? I don't want this, any of it. I want her.

Katie, let me just tell you how beautiful you are. I don't think I ever really told you, but God, you're absolutely stunning. Even on your sweatiest, grumpiest days, you are so infinitely beautiful. Your smile can turn my worst day into my best. Hearing you laugh is enough to make my whole week, and when I get to be the one who makes you laugh, forget it. That's the best feeling in the world, to make you happy.

Do you remember when we were eight and I scraped my elbow on the playground and you kissed it, even though it was against the rules, even though blood scared you? I wish I'd properly thanked you for that. You've always been so strong, Katie. I admire that about you.

Why did Cecilia tell me to do this? I haven't even written anything down and already my heart is breaking. It feels like losing her all over again.

Then I'm five months younger, shivering in the January cold with her by my side. We stand in the back of a crowd of mourners, beneath a sun that holds no warmth at all, ready to bid farewell to two of our own who did nothing but speak up.

I'm telling Ava, Noah, and Katie that it's selfish to cry at one's own loss, that the deceased is the one who has it the worst. Katie and Noah are arguing in the harsh way they always do, voices strong but shoulders soft. They'll be fine in moments, the way siblings are.

If I could go back to those kids we were five months ago, I would tell them I was wrong. There's no need to argue; I was being silly.

It's not selfish to cry at one's own loss. That, I now know.

CHAPTER TWO

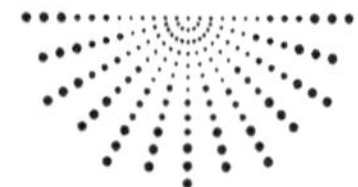

THE NEXT MORNING is as normal as all our other ones, now. Noah leaps out of bed and helps Ava sit up in a practiced pull. She takes her pain meds as he washes up, and then he helps her into the bathroom as I get dressed and make our beds. I brush my teeth last, then race down the stairs to get a morning workout in, trying to beat the elevator down. I meet them at the door to the dining hall a little out of breath; Noah informs me that I was only thirty-four seconds behind.

We juggle our trays, helping one another get to our usual table. Sam walks into the dining hall as the three of us eat fruit salad and talk about today's classroom studies. For the first time since before we went to the Surface, she is joined by Amy.

I spot her first but try not to make a big deal out of it, looking quickly away. My heart leaps into my throat, trying to make a run for it, and my hands immediately begin to sweat. Noah sees my face and turns around, mouth falling open in surprise, and of course Ava reacts the same way. I swat at them both, but they still gape like fish.

Sam and Amy make their way over to us with bowls of fruit and slices of peanut-butter toast. It is the first time we've seen Amy since she was in a coma. There's a magenta blanket draped over her lap, hiding what isn't there, and the bags under her sunken eyes look like they've been painted on permanently. The sight makes my stomach heave.

"Hey, guys, thought we'd join you for breakfast," Sam says cheerfully, white smile and ice-blue eyes wide. She slides over her chair so Amy can park next to her.

"Yeah," Amy mumbles as she maneuvers into her spot. "Dammit, I forgot a fork. Sam, can you grab me one?"

"You can grab it," Sam replies, sitting down. "It's not far."

Amy gestures pointedly to her lap, but Sam only shrugs.

"You can do it, Amy."

Amy huffs out a breath as she wheels away.

As soon as she is out of earshot, we all turn to Sam, plastered smiles falling. Ava finds her voice first. "Forced public outing?"

"She's gotta get down here sometime. She's gotta leave anyway for PT, why not half an hour earlier? Plus, this way I'm not late," Sam explains, taking a bite of toast.

"You don't think this is too big of a first step?" I ask worriedly, trying to hide my selfish nerves. "I mean, she wouldn't even let *us* see her, and this is peak breakfast time." The dining hall seems to hum around us as plates clatter and soldiers laugh, the cavernous ceiling swallowing the noise and belching it back down to us.

"She's gotta do it at some point. I'm sick of bringing every meal up to the room. Trust me, guys, Amy's tough. She's fine."

Amy returns and parks herself crookedly between Sam and Ava. "There. I got it. What do I get, a sticker?"

"Nope," Noah says. "You only get a sticker if you learn how to do wheelies."

I shoot him a frown, but Amy smiles. "I'll keep that in mind."

He grins smugly at me, a 'told you so' kind of look. The scar grins with him, and I force myself to stay seated.

"So, Amy," Ava tries. "Sam said you crochet now?"

Amy shrugs and picks at her cantaloupe. "Yeah, I tried making a scarf. Kinda crooked though."

"There's a program I heard about where you can donate anything you knit or crochet to soldiers going on long missions in the winter. I figured I'd give it a shot. My mother had me take Home Ec. back in

Carcera. They taught us how to knit, and I gotta say, I wasn't too shabby. Maybe we can get together and work on it sometime? They give you some extra credits; we could go on a shopping trip if you want."

Amy shrugs again. "Sure, I guess we could do that."

Ava grows quiet. No one speaks, but Noah shifts uncomfortably in his chair, and Ava's knife screeches across her plate. I miss the tired, easy silence that used to follow us after a long day in the gym.

After everyone finishes eating, Sam stands. "Alright, I'll meet you boys down in the pool."

"I can wheel myself, it's fine," Amy says quickly. She seems to shock even herself, black eyes wide with surprise. "Ava, wanna go together?"

"Yeah, sure," Ava says, grinning cheerily. Her cheekbones cut through her once-round smile. "We can work out together."

A semi-genuine smile lights up Amy's face for a fleeting moment. "Yeah."

Sam offers to return their trays so they can head down to PT. Ava takes the lead, and the rest of us watch them go.

Ava's physical therapist said that she'll be strong enough to use a walker soon. She should be back to full training within another month or two. Amy, however, will be working in another squad until she ages out. It's either that or take up a service job. Theoretically, she could be moved to Level 7 for a job in the food production labs, but we all know Cecilia won't let that happen. Amy belongs here in Level 8, with the rest of the squad. With Sam.

We know very little about the rest of the Underground—only that we are in Level 8, which houses active-duty military. We are comprised of long-range sniper squads, tech. squads, search and rescue teams, and close-combat squads like mine, Squad #5609. Of course, there are service jobs, too—food service, maintenance, and trainers—but most other positions—like the librarians, hospital interns, and Activity Center staff—are all part-time or volunteer-based. I used to work in the hospital on Sunday nights to earn some extra credits, but it's been hard to be there since losing Katie. I don't want to watch anyone else die.

"It's like watching our kids go off to school for the first time." Noah laughs briefly, pulling me out of my thoughts. "Like they don't need to hold our hands anymore."

"Yeah, except they're our girlfriends," Sam replies dryly. Her face darkens for a moment, then returns to normal. We pack up in silence and then head for the pool.

"Hey, Sam," I say as we wind through the tight hallways. "She did really well for that being her first time out of the dorm."

She sighs. "Yeah, she did. I just wish that there was more that I could do for her. I miss her."

"She may not be herself for a while," I reply. "You just have to give her time."

"I know. Everyone keeps saying that's normal. Doesn't stop me from missing her, though."

We walk the rest of the way in silence and split up at the locker rooms.

"Ava has nightmares a lot," Noah says quietly as we get changed. "That's why I always end up next to her. Once she wakes up, she's scared to go back to sleep, so... ya know..."

"I get it," I say. "You're good. Just sleep up there with her if it'll help you both. As long as you're not... ya know..."

He whacks me with his towel. "Hey man, she's still outta commission. Once she's good to go though, I can't make any promises." He winks, and I roll my eyes.

"Ugh, gross."

"At least we're not sucking face in a supply tent while some poor guy's waiting for his morphine."

The silence is absolute, stunted only by the ticking of a clock reminding us that we are late.

"Chris, I'm sorry, I..." he says, cheeks flushing scarlet to match his scar. I watch the heat creep down his long neck as he stammers out an apology. "I just kinda forgot, I didn't mean—I'm sorry."

"Noah, it's okay," I reply as gently as I can, although my stomach is clenched like a fist. "I forget sometimes, too. It's... nice, until I remember."

He nods. "I know what you mean."

The fist in my gut clamps tighter with jealousy as I think of him holding Ava, feeling her heart beating right next to his. *Do you?* I think as we lock up our dry clothes. *Do you, really?*

I clear my throat after a moment. "Alright, we should head out there."

Noah beelines for the door. "Yep. Sam's probably waiting for us."

I follow him, grabbing a towel on my way. Two other squads are already in the pool, but Cecilia is nowhere in sight. Noah and I exchange a confused glance as Sam jogs over to us.

"Do you know about Tucker?" she asks, voice hushed. I nod, but Noah shakes his head. "Tucker has cancer. He came down with a fever last night. Cecilia took him to the hospital, so we're under the supervision of Squad 5613 for workouts. I don't know this guy's name, but he seems like a hardass, so be good."

Noah's mouth falls open in shock, and he blinks hard. "Wait. Is he okay?"

Sam sighs. "I don't know. He's just not doing well today, that's all I know."

Noah nods, shoving his mouth closed in a grim line. I pat him on the back—Tucker likes him best out of all of us.

"Are you 5609?" A squat older man asks, voice gruff and slightly muted by his salt-and-pepper beard. He seems to be perpetually chewing something, and his breath washes over us like an acrid cloud.

Sam nods sharply, shoulders rounded back. "Yes, sir. Our trainer is absent today, and we've been put under the command of Squad 5613."

"That's me. Come."

Noah and I glance at each other as we follow him to the deep end of the pool. Sam holds steady, braver than the two of us combined.

"Alright," he says. "I'm not learning your names, you can deal with it. Get in, do your thing and warm up, then we'll see how well you've been trained in the water. You'll be working alongside my guys today."

We slip into the water and float for a few minutes to get acclimated to the cold, like Cecilia taught us. Next, we each dive to the bottom to pop our ears and warm up our muscles.

After a few minutes, he stops us. "Alright, everyone warm up a few laps. One for each stroke, let's move!"

Noah and I stare at Sam in unprecedented horror; what are *strokes*?

Sam leads the way after a moment's hesitation. She signs *follow* as she passes us in the only "stroke" we currently know. We follow her without a hitch, arriving at the other end of the pool with relative ease and speed. The three of us stand in the shallow end.

"You two are gonna follow my lead, okay? We haven't done as much swimming as these guys. It's okay. I'll take the heat for any mistakes we make—just do what I do and don't draw attention to yourselves."

She pushes off hard from the wall before either of us can protest, staying under for as long as possible. Noah pushes off next, and I follow him.

This new stroke is painfully awkward—we have to pull our arms up over our heads and scoop the water behind us. I can't see Sam, so I have to take what I can get by watching Noah, of all people.

The next two strokes are even worse. By the end, I'm officially the idiot of the pool, and gasping for air, too. Even Noah looks better than I do, and he's supposed to be the klutz.

When we return to the wall, the trainer glares down at us. "That was, without a doubt, the *worst* butterfly I have ever seen in my life. Who the hell taught you, a sloth?"

Noah and I glance at each other; what the hell is a sloth?

"I have half a mind to tell you to get your asses out of the water and transfer you to a long-range squad, and be-*lieve me,* I would, you're just not technically mine. I honestly have no idea how you three screwed up that bad. What's this bitch been teaching you, how to get killed?"

Sam uses the diving platform to pull herself out of the water so fast it's a wonder she doesn't slip.

Before Noah or I can stop her, she's in the guy's face, dripping water all over his t-shirt.

"My trainer is *not* a bitch. She has done everything in her power to keep us safe, but accidents happen, idiot. Don't speak about things you don't understand."

I finally come to my senses, pulling myself out of the pool and putting a dripping hand on her bare shoulder. "Sam, calm down, let's just—"

"She doesn't care about you, smartass. All she cares about is getting paid so she can try to keep her son alive."

I let her go.

"How *dare* you say that! That's her *baby*, you have no *idea* what that's like."

Usually Sam is dry rage, cracking like lightning, not a dam. But now there's water in her voice, and I don't think it's from the pool.

"And you do? Listen here, you little—"

"I do!" Sam yells, voice thundering around the room. "I do know what it's like to lose a child, but I don't expect you to, because no self-respecting woman would ever even look your way, let alone screw you."

"Sam, let's go," I say quietly. "We're pissing people off."

His squad is treading water not far from us with murder gleaming in their eyes, and I really don't want the three of us to be in the middle of a fight. Not with people who are supposed to be on our side.

"Fine," she spits, glancing back at the man with a gaze full of venom as she walks to the locker room. "And just so you know, I'd die for our freedom. That should be what matters, not if I can swim the freaking butterfly."

I help Noah out of the water, mutter a quick apology, and practically run to the locker room. We change quickly, barely drying off before we throw our clothes on and flee.

Sam isn't waiting for us in the brightly-lit hallway, which is strange. She's normally the first one out here after a swim. No one is around, so Noah briefly opens the door, keeping his head turned toward me and his eyes shut.

"Sam!" he shouts. "You okay?"

"Fine!" she yells back. "Just getting cleaned up. Give me a minute."

Noah and I glance at each other. Sam doesn't ever really 'get cleaned up.' She usually just braids her hair if it isn't already—which, today, it is—and gets changed. She's faster than we are.

We stand in the hallway for another minute or two, half-expecting someone to come out and finish the fight we started. Sam finally emerges with her head bowed, damp curls covering her face.

Noah reaches her first. "Sam, what's wrong? Are you alright?"

"They found my tattoo," she mumbles, shrinking away from the hand Noah places on her shoulder.

"What tattoo?" I ask.

She lifts her shirt up to reveal a number tattooed over her belly-button with the letters "BM" above it.

"What does that mean?" Noah asks. "Are you hurt?"

She looks up at us, revealing a blackening eye and split lip. "Can we talk about this at home?"

"Jesus, we have to get you to the hospital," I say. "Can you walk?"

"Yes, I can walk, you dummy. I'm fine, I just need some ice. There's an old machine down the hall from my room—I'll fill the toothbrush cup with it."

"Do you need stitches?"

She touches her lip gingerly and winces. "Can we please just go home?"

We walk quickly back to her room, thankful that the halls are empty, and that Amy and Ava are at PT. Noah fills her toothbrush cup with ice while I dab at her bloody lip with the edge of a towel.

Sam sits on the toilet lid while she explains the whole story, holding the makeshift ice pack to her cheek.

"So, these girls, they must've been in the pool when I yelled at that guy, cause they were soaking wet. Three of them came in while I was changing and called me out on it, so I said he had no right to talk about Cecilia like that. One of them stepped up to me, got in my face, and called me..."

She sighs and winces as she shifts, and I wonder about her ribs, hoping they're not bruised or worse.

"They called me birthing scum. I was only half dressed, so they saw my ID number from... Orihya. That's where I'm from."

"When we turned fifteen, we were allowed to apply for a position outside the mines. That's what everyone did—we mined precious metals, gold and copper, mostly. Everyone worked there, and everyone died by 55. Positions outside of the mines were extremely rare, mostly just teachers and doctors, and the only other option when I was fifteen was Birthing Mother. That was how all babies were born in my town; I never knew who my birth mother was. No one did. They told us that being a Birthing Mother was an honor, that we could do things all on our own time. We would receive our own homes, friends and family could visit whenever they wanted, and we would never be Matched. All we had to do was have babies, which... I didn't know how to do back then.

"I was one of two girls chosen. I was taken out of the mine one day and never went back, thank God. My parents were proud of me, hell, *I* was proud of me. I went through tons of tests–blood work, hormone checks, the works. They wanted us to start as young as possible since the chemicals in the mines can damage your fertility when you're older. To be chosen meant I was strong and healthy, which was more than could be said for most of my peers. I was given a new home on the other side of town and thought it would be good.

"They took me to my new house, and it was nice. All I had to do was live there, alone, for the rest of my life. It seemed like a small price to pay for not being Matched. They said they'd send over a fertilization kit once I was settled."

"Sorry, a what?" Noah asks, and I'm thankful for it. Women's bodies were never discussed in Carcera, especially not by men.

"They were going to send me some sperm and I would... God, I'm not saying it."

"Oh... *oh*," Noah says, eyes widening. I try to suppress a grimace.

Sam purses her lips, nodding. "Yep. Anyway, on my fourth night there I heard the front door open. I tried to call the guards, but all they said was that he was supposed to be there. He came upstairs and told me what we had to do, and if I put up a fight, he would..." She takes a deep, shaky breath.

"Sam, it's okay, you can stop," I say gently.

"No, it's fine. He raped me, that's what happened. I didn't sleep a wink after he left, just sat... sat in the shower for hours. In the morning, I found a pregnancy test on the kitchen counter with instructions. I knew better than to tell—even if I was brave enough, who would believe me? And even if they did, what would they do?"

"My first two babies were healthy. I got to hold them for a little while before they were assigned to their families. My boy had wispy black hair, and the other, the girl, she was bald, God bless. But they both had... *bright* blue eyes, the clearest you've ever seen. They were strong.

"My third was born a full ten weeks early. I stayed in the hospital with him for the three days he was there, but there wasn't anything they could do. His lungs just couldn't work. They blamed me, said it was my fault. Accused... accused me of trying to abort him, kill him on purpose. I didn't; I would never. I loved him."

She clears her throat, hardening back into the granite pillar that she always is, shoulders tall and chin lifted to the sky that we fight for every day. "I'll spare you the details, but they made sure I'll never have kids again. That's why I was so ready to leave when we were taken over by the Underground. I was eighteen then, and I had my third when I was seventeen. They also sent me back to the mines with no recovery time. I have no idea what happened to my first two, but they probably didn't survive the Purge Bomb."

"Purge Bomb?" Noah asks.

"Yeah. Ankou will bomb a city that's been taken over by the Underground to try to stop us from recruiting more people. They really only do it if they've lost total control of the city, kind of a last resort. It's partly how Pevidere got destroyed, but that was just as they were trying to build the Border in the first place."

I lean back against the wall, glancing at Noah and then at Sam. "So, let me get this straight. You've been... assaulted, at least three times, had three children, lost one to a premature birth and the other two to Ankou. You can never have another child, even if you wanted to. You've lost your whole family, and your girlfriend is struggling with PTSD and the loss of her entire leg. How the hell are you holding it together, Sam?"

Tears spring into her eyes, but she laughs anyway. "I'm not."

CHAPTER THREE

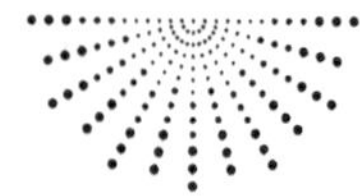

W HEN WE PICK Ava up from PT later that morning, she is smiling in a way that she hasn't for a long time.

"He gave me a cane to use in the room!" she beams, brandishing it above her up high and nearly hitting me in the face.

"That's great!" Noah presses a kiss to the top of her head. "I'm so proud of you."

"Thanks." She grins as a blush creeps into her cheeks.

We meander to the dining hall, letting Ava decide the pace. Noah smiles at me in the elevator, and I try to smile back, but I can't.

After lunch, all of us head down to classroom studies, Amy included. She doesn't ask about Sam's face, but wheels herself even through the tightest halls instead of asking Sam for help like she usually would.

Cecilia isn't waiting for us in our assigned room. Instead, there is a note on the blackboard: *Teach yourselves. Sam's in charge. In the hospital with Tucker. Meet here tomorrow morning.*

As we take our usual seats, Sam perches on the table at the front of the room. "Alright, I have no idea what she wants me to teach you about that you don't already know. I guess we'll do World Knowledge in sign. You people are getting rusty."

Before she can continue, there is a knock at the door. Noah hops up to open it, beckoning two younger soldiers inside. A better word for them would be 'students.'

"Um, hi," the girl says, pushing her bushy curls away from her eyes as she takes a tentative step inside. "We're looking for Cecilia Adder?"

"She's not here today," Sam says. "What's your name?"

"I'm Kelawren Monroe, and this is Griffin Hobbs," she explains. The boy gives a small wave when she says his name. "We've just been assigned to Squad 5609, this morning, actually. The Head Trainer told us to meet her here after lunch."

"Well, that's us, welcome to the club," Sam says. "Cecilia will be back tomorrow. Have a seat; we're practicing sign."

They move to sit down. Griffin pulls out the chair that used to be Katie's.

"We leave that one empty," I say, an accidental bite in my voice that makes even Sam wince. "Sorry. A friend sits there."

He scurries to the back row to sit next to Kelawren. Guilt gnaws at my stomach, but that's *her* seat.

"Alright," Sam says. "Why don't we all introduce ourselves, do some icebreakers, ya know? I'm Sam, I'm nineteen. My favorite skill is hand-to-hand combat, but I also like to swim. Sometimes I use sign if I'm having trouble hearing in a loud place, because I have hearing damage from when I was younger. Who's next?"

"Hey, I'm Amy, also nineteen. My favorite color is yellow, and I used to like running, but... yeah."

Noah and Ava introduce themselves next, then I do.

"My name's Chris, I'm seventeen. My favorite skill is long-range shooting, but I also enjoy working on the heavy bags. I like to read— mostly murder mysteries, sometimes sci-fi."

The two newbies are up next.

"Hi, I'm Kelawren, but my friends call me Kela. I have one sister, and I'm sixteen years old. My favorite color is purple, and I love to dance." Ava's dark eyes, usually muddled with a frown these days, light up like the first day of spring.

"I'm Griffin, everyone calls me Grif. Kela's family adopted me a few years ago; she's like my sister, so we know each other really well. I like pop music and sketching comics. And I have one question: who's the friend that sits in that chair?"

Well, at least he's curious.

I glance up at Sam—she gestures to the space next to her, an invitation to tell the story. I sit beside her on the table at the front of the room, hands a little numb. This is the first time I've had to introduce her. These will be the first people who know her only through stories, who never get to see her smile for themselves. The first people, in the world, who I know but she doesn't.

I keep it brief, not confident in my ability to talk about her without weeping. "It belonged to a friend of ours who... died, recently. Her name is Katie, and Noah, Ava, and I grew up with her. We escaped our Border, Carcera, together. She means a lot to all of us and I—*we*—leave it open out of respect. I'm sorry. I didn't mean to snap at you like that."

Grif gives me a soft nod as Kela stands abruptly, chair screeching against the floor. She strides over to me on long legs and hugs me with a fierceness that stuns my eyes into drying up.

"I'm sorry about your friend," she says. "She must've been a wonderful person."

"She was," I say, clearing my throat and giving her a small smile as we take our seats again. Talking about Katie makes me feel like I've been put through a paper shredder and glued back together by a five-year-old. My heart shatters further as I realize that I used past tense.

I WRITE my letter to Katie after dinner that evening. When I'm done, I decide to be brave and visit her room, to drop it off.

I borrow the key from the drawer in our dresser that Ava's been using and slip out, pausing outside of Katie's door to gather what's left of my courage.

Her room smells faintly of sweat; I can practically feel the dust gathering in the air. I flick the light on, and even though this room barely looks different than my own, it still hurts to see. Memories flood every corner. I can almost see her stepping out of the bathroom, can almost hear her laughing at one of Noah's terrible jokes. She's almost here, just barely out of reach.

I pull her bed away from the wall, trying not to get distracted by how the sheets still smell like her, like lemon and lavender. Damn, I miss that.

Our names are still bleeding on the wall, slightly faded and smudged by the bed sheets. Chris and Katie, frozen in time together.

It hits me out of nowhere—I actually killed someone that night. Back in that hallway, when I was fighting to keep her safe, keep us *all* safe, they were soldiers. Now, sitting on Katie's bed for the first time since we slept here together, I remember that they were just men. They had bedrooms, too. They were like me, like my father, doing what they were told.

Up until the few days before he died, my father did exactly what he was supposed to do. It was when he decided to stop that everything went wrong. Most people don't know that the explosion at the factory where he worked was orchestrated by Ankou, and that he was part of the reason why. In fact, I am the only one to know this to its full extent, although I'm sure my mother had her suspicions.

My father overheard two soldiers and his boss talking about the trains one day. He wrote it all down in a journal that I memorized after his death and eventually smuggled here, to Level 8.

March 19th, it reads. *Caleb and two soldiers whispering in the lounge today. One of the soldiers said that new trains needed better locks on the cargo doors. I listened from the other side of the door. He talked about the Underground—people who don't live within a Border who have been attacking our supply trains. I didn't think people like that could exist—was Victor Castellano right? The government is supposed to keep us safe here. That's what my father taught me, what I'm teaching my children. Is that the truth?*

March 20th. Spoke with Caleb today. The soldiers noticed me listening yesterday. Being investigated for treason. I hope they understand I didn't mean anything by it. I played dumb, said I didn't hear anything, just saw them having a conversation so I left. I talked to Jen about it, and we agreed not to tell the kids. 13 and 11 are too young.

March 21st. They're going to take me into custody tomorrow after work. Caleb told me to run, use my card to get through the Border, find the Underground. My card is here with me, but I can't leave my family. The kids are too young for me to leave them, and far too young to come with me, out in the cold. I don't even know if the Underground is real. Haven't told Jen, not sure I will. I love her so much.

I remember March 21st with astonishing clarity. We ate dinner as a family and then played board games instead of going off to relax on our own. My father seemed especially fond of us that night.

On March 22nd, at approximately 12:14 PM, the train manufacturing plant was blown to pieces. No one walked out of the inferno, not even those who went in to try to save those already inside. My cousin Trevor died that day, too.

I never learned this for sure, but there must have been far more going on than my father knew. He mentioned Victor Castellano, who said things about the outside world that were bizarrely accurate with seemingly no source. If my father and Caleb both knew and trusted what Victor was saying—which was kept extremely secret, and I only knew from Ava, his niece—I have to do the same. It also makes me almost certain that those words were being spread inside the manufacturing building to more people than just my father. The government, probably fearing Underground spies, blew it up.

Sam essentially confirmed this when she told us about the Purge Bomb. Ankou doesn't care, and he never will.

192 people were killed because they knew something the government didn't want them to know. They wanted my father dead for overhearing a conversation. They killed 192 just to shut them up when they weren't even talking yet, to kill spies that may or may not have been there. So, how badly are they losing to the Underground?

There is red spray paint on Katie's bed sheets that mimics blood. I pull out her letter, freshly written in black pen and folded in crisp lines. I contemplate reading it aloud but decide to spare myself. Besides, she already knows what I want to say. Katie always knew what I was thinking before I did.

I tuck the note underneath the mattress and stare at our names again. There used to be two of us; we were a pair. Where one went, the other followed, always. I briefly wonder if this is what losing a limb feels like.

When looking at her name becomes too painful, I push the mattress back against the wall and step into the bathroom.

Katie's hair gel is still on the counter, and so is her toothbrush, marked with a 'K' in blue pen, her handwriting. I contemplate pocketing it to get that letter tattooed on my wrist, and then wonder how many initials I'll have inked on my body over the course of my life, especially spending it here. Will N.G. be next, for Noah? Or S.S. for Sam?

I redirect by fixing the toothpaste cap, which wasn't tightened properly. We left so fast that the last person in here didn't even close the medicine cabinet.

I straighten her toothbrush on the counter, bristles facing inward towards the sink. I close the medicine cabinet, straighten the towels, turn the light off.

Before I leave, I flop down on Katie's bed and stare straight up to where the smoke detector blinks green. This is what she saw every night before she went to sleep, what she saw the last night we were here. The last night she was alive.

I could feel her heartbeat under my ear as I fell asleep that night. Her chest rose in opposition to mine, so it was like we were motionless, suspended in an instant that could've—should've—lasted forever. Every day I kick myself for sleeping when I could've been with her.

I inhale deeply, as if what's left of her can be absorbed into my body, so that I can be made up of cells of my own, cells of my almost-twin, cells of my almost-girlfriend.

All the best things in my life have been almosts.

I WAKE up to a loud pounding on the door, startled by the fact that I had fallen asleep at all.

"Chris!" Noah yells frantically. "Sam needs us right now, get your ass out here!"

I jump up so fast that my foot gets caught on the box spring and I sprawl across the floor. A string of curses pops from my mouth as I stagger to my feet, wincing at the pain in my ankle, and throw open the door.

"Jesus, what happened to you?" Noah asks, taking a step back to look me up and down. "And why were you in there?"

"Took Ava's key, wanted to clean the place up, fell asleep," I lie. "What's wrong?"

"It's Tucker," Noah says. "He died this morning."

I barely knew him, but it *hurts*. Noah's voice is muffled as if speaking through a layer of cotton. "Sam needs us to meet in her room. I just told Ava, she's already on her way there. And for the love of *God,* don't go anywhere without telling one of us—I've been running around like a freaking chicken with my head cut off."

"Its head," I say stupidly. "You're supposed to say 'its head.'"

"Who cares? A kid just *died*," Noah says. "Come on, we have to go."

I follow him to Sam and Amy's room, vaguely aware that we're jogging. We make it in what seems like no time at all, ignoring the 'please knock' sign. On any other day, in any other moment, being granted the pleasure of ignoring that sign would've brought the widest smile to my face.

Ava and Sam are sitting cross-legged on the bed, Amy in her wheelchair. The three of them are all crying, but Sam quickly composes herself when we walk in, swiping the tears off her face like an embarrassed child. I want to tell her that it's okay, that I cried today, too, that I cry every day, but she clears her throat before I can.

She doesn't bother with a hello. "Cecilia's taking a personal week to prepare for the funeral, so random subs will oversee physical training. She put me in charge of classroom studies. We're just teaching the newbies sign, but since they've lived here their whole lives, they'll probably already know it."

"What?" Noah asks incredulously.

Sam starts to explain again, voice raspy, but he cuts her off. "No, what happened to *Tucker*?"

"He was already very sick. The chemo didn't work, so Cecilia decided to let him go at home. This morning, he woke up with a fever, so she took him to the hospital for pain meds. He fell back to sleep on the way and didn't wake up. He died around noon."

"He was four," I say, running my fingers through my hair. "Christ, he couldn't even read yet."

"He would've started kindergarten in a few months," Sam says, voice thick. "I met Cecilia in the hospital; she was still there after dinner. I have her address, so I'll be checking on her this week. I think it's a good idea if we each write her a letter expressing our condolences."

"I agree," Ava says, wiping her eyes and taking a shuddering breath. "When do you want them done?"

"Tomorrow afternoon, if you can," Sam says.

"Why... why couldn't they save him?" Noah asks. Ava stands shakily, leaning on the handle of her wheelchair, and tries to stop his pacing. He brushes her gently away. "I mean, there was a kid back home who had leukemia when she was eight and they fixed her like it was a common *cold*."

"We don't have the technology of Border towns," Sam says. "We don't have the money, the equipment, or staff. They tried their best, but we just don't have the resources."

"He was *four*!" Noah shouts. Ava jumps back and stumbles over a shoe, but he doesn't seem to notice. "How can we be unable to save a little boy? He couldn't even read, for God's sake. He still had Velcro shoes because he didn't know how to tie laces."

"Noah, that's what we're fighting for," Ava says, reaching out tentatively, leaning heavily on her wheelchair. "That's why we keep fighting, so that kids like Tucker have a better chance. They tried their best. You know that."

"Well, their best wasn't good enough for him, was it?"

Sam shakes her head. "It wasn't. That doesn't mean we get to stop trying. Hell, we should be trying even harder now."

"Well, I'm sick of people dying. I'm done with losing all my friends. I'm tired of it. It's not *fair*." His voice cracks, but his face doesn't change.

"It's not," Ava says. "Nothing is."

Noah nods, and Ava nods, and we all nod because we don't know what else to say. A little kid died before he learned how to tie his shoes, and if that's not something to render us speechless, then nothing is.

CHAPTER FOUR

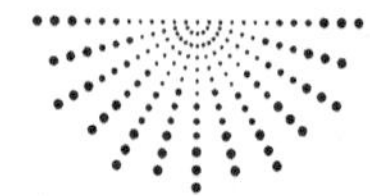

W E   S P E N D the next morning in classroom studies again, where Sam teaches all of us basic sign. Going back to letters and numbers is so boring that I start to nod off a couple of times.

Noah and I sign to each other discreetly to pass the time, genuinely happy for the first time in what feels like forever. It's like being a kid again, sitting in a boring algebra lesson, passing notes when our teacher turned her back.

"You two act like the rest of us don't know sign and can't see your hands," Sam says loudly. She stands with her arms crossed and one manicured eyebrow raised, sounding about ten years older than she actually is.

Our cheeks blush as we lower our hands beneath our desks, where I continue to sign even though Noah can no longer see. Happiness has become an almost foreign feeling these days. I try not to think about how much better this would be if Katie were here, how good she is at cracking jokes in sign. My hands are too clumsy to be any good at it, but hers are quick as lightning.

"Chris, you with us?" Sam asks. I snap back to find my whole squad staring at me, even the two newbies. Kelawren has a nervous look on her face, lips pinched together.

"Yeah, I'm here," I lie.

Sam frowns at me but continues teaching. She'll make a wonderful trainer once she ages out: kind but not soft, fun but not lenient. She knows just when to push and exactly when to back off.

I make a mental note to eventually ask her if she's considering it as a career, but then remember that we have to survive this, first, and we have a lot of years to go.

We head to lunch early, finding a quiet table in the back.

"So," Griffin says, stabbing a fork into his pasta. "What's Cecilia like?"

We let Sam answer him. "She's a hardass. But she does everything in our best interest, so it's good."

"Is it true that her husband died?"

We glance at each other awkwardly, unsure of what to say.

"Yeah," Noah finally says. "He died a few years ago, though. We never met him."

"Sucks," Kelawren says. "I heard she has nipple piercings."

It shocks me how routine this seems for her, how relaxed she is about someone dying young. Noah and I stare down at our food, trying not to imagine our trainer's pierced nipples.

"Nope," Sam replies, repressing a laugh at our stunned expressions. "No nipple piercings."

"Well, how do you know? Have you *seen* them?"

"No, shut up." Sam laughs.

"Ooh, I've got a question, Ava," Grif says suddenly.

"Yeah?" Ava says, looking up from her burger, which is dripping mustard, her new favorite condiment.

"Are you and Noah, like, a thing?" He gestures to my increasingly uncomfortable best friend.

Her tan cheeks flush. "Oh, yeah. We're together."

"Chris, anyone for you?" Kela asks. The others unanimously flinch.

"No, not for me," I say quickly, trying to brush off the stabbing pain in my stomach. I push away my food. "You guys mind if I meet you down there? I wanna go visit a friend real quick."

"Want me to go with you?" Noah offers.

I stand and grab my tray. "No, it's alright, I got it. See you later."

I wander through the library for a couple of minutes, pulling random books off of shelves and skimming through them only to put them back again. After a solid twenty minutes of browsing, I decide to call it quits and head to the weight room. Getting there a few minutes early won't hurt—I can warm up on my own and enjoy the peace and quiet.

I pass the children's section on my way out, and a familiar figure catches my eye. I pause and turn towards her, shocked.

"Cecilia?" I say.

My trainer turns to face me, arms full of books. Her eyes are puffy, and she wears a long orange cardigan over her usual dark tank top and leggings. I don't think she's slept. "Hey, Chris."

"I'm so sorry," I say. "Sam told us what happened."

"Thank you," she says, offering a sad smile. "I'm shelving these to help out the librarian. She's too busy to do all this."

I know that's not true, because the librarian has been chatting with a friend at the front desk for the last ten minutes, but I don't say that. Instead, I say, "Want a hand?"

"Sure. Thank you."

I take half the books from her and begin shelving them. *The Littlest Dinosaur* and *How Do Dinosaurs Eat Their Food?* go right next to one another.

"He was a dinosaur fan?" I ask, hoping to take some of the ache away, as she's done for me. We have different-shaped holes in our hearts, but they are holes, nonetheless.

She laughs shortly. "Oh, yeah. Couldn't wait to get to the Surface to meet some. I never had the heart to tell him that they went extinct millions of years before he was born."

I make a mental note to ask her what she means by that later, because my parents told me that dinosaurs were a myth, but now's not the time.

"He sounds like he has quite the mind," I say instead. "I mean, curious. Inquisitive."

"Ohhh yes," she replies with the knowing nod of a mother who has heard nothing but questions from her child. My mother had the same look. "He loves my husband, though. If nothing else, I'm glad they're finally together."

"Boys and their fathers, right?" I don't know what to say, other than that.

"Yeah. Where is yours now?"

I shelve the last book slowly, pausing for a moment with my fingertips hovering over the spine. *Goodnight, Moon.*

"Wherever they are, I guess," I say finally. "He died when I was eleven."

"I'm sorry," she says.

"Thank you."

She turns to go. "I'll be back next week. Mind if we skip coffee this Friday?"

"That's more than fine," I say. "Take all the time you need."

"Thanks. See you next week."

As she walks away, a thought pops into my head. "Cecilia!"

She turns around, one finger already raised to hush me for yelling.

"Tucker... he was very lucky to have you as his mother."

She nods, purses her lips, and leaves without another word.

We find the funeral notice tucked under our door one evening less than a week after Tucker's death. It reads:

> *To celebrate the life of Tucker Adder*
> *Please meet in the dining hall at 8 PM*
> *Thursday, May 27th*
> *Formal wear is appreciated but not required*

"We have to go," Noah says immediately, pulling out his suit jacket. "She'll need us there."

I nod, staring at my suit in the closet, clutching the invitation in my hand. The last time I wore that suit...

"Hey," he says, breaking me out of my thoughts. "It's already 7:30, we gotta get ready."

"Yeah, yeah," I say, running a hand through my messy hair. "It's... what's the weather up on the Surface?"

"Warm," he says. "Bring some water."

"Okay."

Within twenty minutes, we are meeting the girls in the dining hall. They look lovely despite the somber occasion, while Noah and I have wrinkled shirts barely covered by our dusty jackets. My hair refuses to be tamed even by gel, but I can't bear to cut it. Katie likes it longer.

Cecilia arrives not long after we do, wearing a plain black dress and boots, always ready even in her worst moments. Sam offers her a hug, but the rest of us give her gentle pats on the shoulder instead.

"C'mon, we gotta get going," Cecilia says quickly, leading the way into the tunnel. We pause several times for Amy and Ava, but no one says anything. Guilt claws at my stomach.

Shortly, we are in the car and on our way. One trails behind us, and before I can ask, Cecilia answers. "Those are his doctors and nurses. Most of them were able to take the evening off to come. They... they're wonderful people."

I nod, placing a hand on her shoulder and trying to give her whatever strength I have left.

Just as Noah said, the night air is warm. The last trails of a sunset streak the sky, painting it pink and purple as the clouds puff down like burnt marshmallows. The grass whispers in a soft breeze that cools the back of my neck as we roll through with the windows down. I can smell the oncoming rain.

The cars drive on for another few minutes, then stop at a clearing in the grass. A wide swath has been cut, enough for about twenty people to stand comfortably on solid ground. Cecilia is the first one down, and she lowers the ramp for Amy and Ava.

I stand beside the waist-high grass, marveling at the feeling of it against my outstretched fingertips, at the soft earth beneath my feet. Already Ava is choking back tears, on her feet but leaning heavily against Noah. He supports her as if she is no weight at all.

"Thank you all for coming," Cecilia says once we're all gathered, clearing her throat. "I know many of you, my squad, didn't really know Tucker, but you remember how he was in the classroom. Thank you all for always making him feel so included in our work, especially you, Grim. He really... looks up to you."

Noah swallows hard, and visibly gnaws at the inside of his cheek to keep the tears at bay. Ava takes his hand gently, rubbing the smooth skin of his thumb with the pad of hers. She places her cane down to lean against him, and the sight nearly shatters me.

Cecilia continues, and I turn my attention back to her. "Carla, Josephine, thank you for always making him smile, even on transfusion days. And Dr. Ramirez—I've never seen anyone work so hard. You gave us months when we should've had weeks, and for that extra time I will always be thankful."

Tucker's doctor, a tall man with large, spindly hands, nods silently. The two nurses, both middle-aged, both a bit plump, hold onto one another. They remind me of my grandmother, gone since I was six, and I briefly think that they must give the best hugs.

"Tucker... he was the light of my life," Cecilia continues. "Still is, really. He loves farm animals and cream-cheese bagels, and coloring pictures of dinosaurs. He can't wait to meet one someday. I never had the heart to tell him they went extinct so long ago... but I know that wherever he is now, his daddy is taking him to see one, because there's gotta be at least one dinosaur petting zoo in heaven." She smiles through the tears, but her shoulders begin to crumble. One of the nurses puts an arm around her as she sucks in air. "He was... he was so brave. You all know that, of course. He was only scared of needles the first time and boy did he let us all know how mad he was. But after that... he went to every appointment braver than I did. He took every round of chemo like a champ, he really did. He's his daddy, through and through. My tough guys."

A small sob escapes her lips, and Sam flinches. I put an arm around her, letting her lean into me. She holds Amy's hand, who holds Ava's, who holds Noah's. He and I stand on either side of the girls, exchanging a glance over their heads.

I remember putting an arm around Mel on the bus ride to her Matching Ceremony, letting her worries hang in the air in front of us, unable to quiet them but at least strong enough to hold them at bay for a moment. I wish I could do the same for my friends.

"Sorry, sorry," Cecilia says breathily, voice shaking. She clears her throat, straightens, presses her shoulders back. "He's a great kid, but he isn't mine to keep. No kid ever is." Her eyes flick over to us briefly. "We can't keep them forever, no matter how much we want to. No matter how hard we try. He taught me more about being a mother than any book could've, more about love than anyone else could've. I just hope that wherever he is now, he's with his father. The two of them were peas in a pod, I swear. I'd... I would give anything to have the two of them back, but that... that isn't what God has in store for my family.

"I don't want to stop talking now, because if I do that means we have to send him off, and I don't want to, yet. I'm not ready to do that."

I feel Ava's chest hiccup with a sob all the way through Sam and Amy–that's how much we're leaning on one another. Sam's cheek is pressed against my shoulder, and Amy's head is buried against her stomach. Noah is on Amy's other side, holding her hand, and the other arm wrapped around Ava, almost fully supporting her.

I want nothing more than to fall to my knees in grief, to be held, but I'm the one holding.

"Ceci, it's time," Dr. Ramirez says softly, reaching into the car and pulling out a small velvet bag. He places the firework and lighter on the soft ground and returns to her, putting a hand on her shoulder. "C'mon."

Cecilia heaves a shaking breath and walks to the firework. The nurses flank her, each with a hand on her arm, keeping her grounded.

"What...?" Ava murmurs, having forgotten the paperwork we filled out on our first day.

"His ashes are in there," Sam says from my shoulder, wiping an eye and quickly wrapping her arm around Amy again. "They'll light it, send him up. It's about freedom—he's no longer confined to a Border, or the Underground, or even to the Surface."

Ava doesn't reply, but I think of the helicopter that took us on our mission, how we soared above anything that could hurt us, but I'd never felt so trapped. And then I think of the ride back, of Sam's screams ring-ing, ringing, ring—

"I can't watch," Ava whispers, burying her face in Noah's chest. He wraps his arm tighter around her, letting her hide against him as Cecilia kneels beside her son. She strokes the firework as if it were his cheek, as if he could still feel her.

The sight makes me miss my own mother so much it hurts. I almost can't breathe; if it weren't for my holding Sam, I would run. It's unbearable.

"I love you, baby," Cecilia murmurs, lighting the tail of the firework and stepping back. We watch as it whistles upwards and explodes into a thousand orange sparks. He paints steaks across the sky, illuminating the clouds and wildflowers and grass for just a moment. And then he floats back down to us, reduced to a smoke trail joining the atmosphere and ash that settles in the dirt. He comes back to us, to her. How could a boy ever leave his mother?

***

THE NEXT DAY finds us all in target practice using airsoft guns to fire at makeshift "people." The trainer we're working with—a hard, grizzled man of at least fifty—has installed fake blood bags on them, designed to explode when our bullets make contact.

Grif and Kela have amazing aim, but I spend the first half of the morning working with them, anyway. I have little interest in firing a gun again, even if it is fake.

"You!" the trainer eventually barks at me. The scar slashed across one of his beady eyes is an ugly purple. "Are you going to stand there all day or actually get some work done?"

"Sorry, sir," I say, finding the cracked, dirty floor suddenly quite beautiful.

I step up to the line with my rifle clutched across my chest. The metal hums beneath my fingers, seemingly charged with electricity.

"I've got you," Noah murmurs from my right.

"Thank you," I say quietly, catching a glimpse of his black shoes just behind me.

I raise my gun and line up, clicking the safety off and taking a deep breath, just like Cecilia taught me.

One, in, two, out. I sniffle hard, chilled to the bone by the damp air down here. *Three, in, four, out.* I miss the sunlight, and the way Katie laughs. *Five, in.* Laughed. *Six.*

Despite the few weeks away from this, I'm still a clean shot. The head of the target directly across the room from me explodes in a spray of red and suddenly I can hear her screaming again.

"Chris, what the *hell*!" Sam screamed as Amy tried to stagger forward on a leg that was barely there. The night air was hot, stiflingly hot, and I tasted blood in my own mouth.

"No, no, I—"

Amy's demented shrieking drowned out whatever I was going to say as she fell to the concrete roof, clawed hands scrabbling at her shattered leg. Noah was lifting her before I had even moved from behind the garden wall, tossing her like a ragdoll into the waiting helicopter, blood spraying everywhere. Sam leapt in beside her as she writhed on the floor, crouching down and trying to stem the flow with shaking hands, whispering "No, no, no," all the while.

Then it all went silent and still. Sam and Noah were staring at me with the eyes of terrified children. Amy and Ava were lying in the helicopter, one contorting on the floor as she howled in pain, the other limp and hauntingly silent.

"Get in!" Sam yelled, sitting in a pool of her girlfriend's blood.

"*Katie!*" I screamed, as if it was the only word I knew.

"Chris, we have to go!" Noah shouted, extending a hand.

I looked back at the door, and then he was dragging me to the helicopter as guards began streaming out of the stairwell. I leapt inside with him, held the door shut as the pilot dropped us off the edge of the roof and we surged into the air, gunfire spraying behind us.

"No, no," Sam was saying as Amy's moans got softer and softer. "Amy, *Amy!*"

I had only heard a shriek like that once before—when my mother realized that my father was gone.

"*Chris!*" Noah shouts, bringing me back to the training room. My hands are clenched so tightly around my rifle that they cramp when I uncurl them, letting the fake weapon clatter to the floor.

"You okay?" he asks, voice falling as he puts a gentle hand on my shoulder.

He must see the look on my face, because his grip tightens and he steers me to the trash can in the corner of the room, where I let up breakfast and some of last night's dinner. He rubs my shoulder with one hand as I choke.

"Shit." I cough the remaining bile out of my mouth once I'm mostly done.

"You're okay," he says, helping me stand upright again. He swipes at his mouth, and I do the same, coming away with spit on the back of my hand.

"Oh, gross," I shudder, spitting once more into the trash can. "I, uh—"

"Want me to come with you?" he asks, nodding towards the door. The rest of our squad is trying to look busy, and a few people from the other squad we're working with are outright staring. My neck grows hot, and another wave of nausea comes over me as my chest tightens.

"Yes."

We slip into the hallway; Noah leaves his gun at the door. He walks me to the bathroom, where I wash my face and rinse my mouth with cold water. The boy staring back at me in the mirror is gaunt and tired, with dark bags under watery blue eyes that seem to float just a little bit in his head.

"I'm sorry," I say when I step back into the hall.

"Why?" Noah asks incredulously, eyebrows shooting up under his blond mop.

"Because," I say slowly, trying to figure out exactly what it is I'm sorry for. "The whole thing. I shouldn't... shouldn't have done what I did." I swallow hard, choking down a lump in my throat.

"Chris, we are *children*," Noah says, catching my eye. "You hear me? Children. And they threw us into a position we never should've been in, without the proper training. You were trying to keep us safe. And not one of us blames you."

"I do."

The silence is deafening as I watch the hard line of his brow crack. "Chris—"

"Don't," I say quickly. "Just don't, Noah."

He nods, looking away. "Alright. Well, we're here. I... I'm here. If you need me. I've got to get back in there, but you... you take some time. As much as you need. I'll cover for you."

"Thanks," I say, already wondering how I'll explain this.

"I'll tell them you've got a stomach bug, if you need," he says, as if reading my mind.

"Yeah, that would be great. I think I'm gonna take off."

"Where to?"

I shrug. "Home, maybe. The library."

He nods. "Okay. Well, I'm here."

I swallow hard, still tasting bile. "Thank you, Noah. I am, too."

He cracks a now-rare smile. "Yeah, you are."

I SPEND the rest of the day in the library, and the evening, too, lost in the world of fiction where I'm not someone who lives in a place where the sun doesn't rise.

The next day they announce at breakfast that there's a Scouting mission taking place in a few weeks, and it's up to squads 5600-5610 to fill all fifteen spots. Only twelve people volunteer, not one from my squad, and I'm randomly chosen to fill one of the remaining spots.

Kela and Grif try to take my place, but the prerequisite is at least four months of training, and by then they'll barely have four weeks.

"I can't believe we can't go," Kela grumbles at dinner. It's the same mantra she's been chanting all day.

The seven of us sit at a table in the corner, two brooding, one ghost. Amy barely eats these days, so it's no surprise to see her mute and limp, but watching Kela and Grif push their food around rather than wolfing it down is a strange sight.

"I've lived here my *whole life*," Kela continues, stabbing at her potatoes. We heard that line earlier, too.

"Well, you haven't been training as long as we have," Sam says. "I've been in for over a year now. These guys have been here almost six months."

"Doesn't mean my parents haven't taught us stuff," Kela says.

"She's right," Grif adds. "The Monroes have taught me a lot, and we learned all about the Surface in school."

"If you *really* want to go, you can take it up with the Head Trainer," Sam says. "Don't count on getting the answer that you want, though. Once he makes up his mind, there's no changing it. Besides, this is just a Scouting mission anyway. Chris is just gonna go look through Pevidere for two days, find nothing, and come home."

"Then shouldn't we get warmed up with that?" Kela asks. "I mean, neither of us have ever been to the Surface. Shouldn't we go on a simple mission first before going to actually *kill* people?"

"She's got a fair point," Ava says. Ever since Kela's been around, Ava's been questioning everything. Normally that would be frustrating, especially as she and Noah bounce off one another, but I'm just glad to see her talking again.

Sam shrugs. "It's just the way it is. And honestly, the Surface is no different than the Simulators all you guys use in school. I tried one. It was spot-on."

"Simulators?" Noah asks, taking a bite of salad.

"We use Surface Simulators to help us prepare," Grif says. "Puts us in all kinds of scenarios that we would encounter up on the Surface. That way we don't get there and totally freak. We used them in school, but they have them for rec, too, if you guys wanna try some."

"I'm down for that," Amy says, a pleasant surprise. Usually just one word is a miracle, let alone four. Guilt swallows me immediately after that quick rush of joy, because it's my fault that she's a still-breathing ghost most of the time.

We finish quickly, scarfing down our dinners so we can get to the Activity Center before curfew. Kela leads the way, taking us to a rocky outcropping all the way in the back of the cavern.

"Kela! Hi, honey," a tall man booms from behind a counter. They look exactly alike; I wonder briefly if I look anything like my father. I don't remember his face like I should. "How's it going? How's your training?"

"Hi, Dad!" she says, giving him a hug. "This is my squad. Ava, Chris, Noah, Sam, and Amy."

"Good to see you, son," Mr. Monroe says, hugging Griffin. He turns to the rest of us. "Nice to meet you all. Are they being good?"

"More than good, sir," Sam says with a professional smile. "Your daughter's a real natural with sign, and Grif is the straightest shot I've seen in years."

"Good to hear," Mr. Monroe says, giving Kela a firm clap on the shoulder. His hands are the size of dinner plates, firm as stone, and dark as the night sky.

"They've never done a Simulation," Kela chirps, looking up at him.

"Oh man, you're all missing out," he says, reaching behind the counter with his mammoth hands. He pulls out a small container and hands us each a tablet about the size of my thumbnail. "Chew this, you'll be good to go. This one's on me. It only lasts about ten minutes; best to start with a short one. Some people say it makes them 'feel funny.' My girl's never had a bad reaction to it, right, Kela?"

She smiles and pops the tablet into her mouth. "Grape this time. I'm a fan."

"So, what exactly does this do?" I ask hesitantly, eyeing the tablet in my palm.

"Essentially, it's a full-body hallucination," Mr. Monroe explains. "It tricks the receptors in your brain into believing that you're on the Surface, filling all of your senses with the experience of being there. The labs did a lot of work to make them realistic and safe for those of us who were born here."

I nod, place it on my tongue, and chew it carefully, the chalky texture instantly coating my throat in a sickly sweet, vaguely grape flavor. I try not to gag.

"So, we'll be absolutely tripping for ten minutes?" Noah asks. "And then it just goes away?"

"I'll give you a tonic to get you fully out of it," Mr. Monroe says. "You'll have full thought processes and everything, but you'll feel exactly as if you're on the Surface. You'll most likely be able to hear us, as well. Auditory hallucinations are harder to produce."

My stomach knots in a mixture of both excitement and anxiety as we spread out around the room to avoid bumping into each other.

Kela goes first, a hushed, "Woah. That... never gets old."

When I blink next, the world changes into a vast open plain. Grass rustles around my hips, the big blue sky opening around me. I suck in a breath, shocked at how real it is. The wet dirt squishes beneath my shoes, smelling of spring days that are just warm enough to convince your mother you don't need a jacket.

I step forward, grass swaying in the breeze, trying to ignore my scratchy throat and pounding heartbeat. I search for comfort in the rough grass and bluer-than-blue sky, but find none. The vastness makes my heart quicken further.

"Noah?" I say, reaching out. I need to see him, or anyone. "Noah, you there?"

"It's beautiful," he replies, but I can't see whatever it is that he can, because the world is beginning to spin.

"I don't feel good." I sink to my knees in the grass as gravity pulls me down. I know that there is concrete under my legs, but all I feel is mud. My mouth tastes like iron, and I groan, doubling over as my stomach clenches. My head grows hot and fuzzy, and when I look up at the sky, my vision dances with dark spots.

"Noah!" I tilt sharply to the right, falling onto my side as my chest heaves. The sea of grass ripples around me as a strong hand lands firmly on my shoulder.

"Chris, it's okay," Noah says from somewhere far away, worry edging his voice. "It's not real, you're okay... *Are* you okay?"

I've never felt this bad in all my life. There's bile caught in my chest, burning as I gasp and fight for every breath. My ears ring incessantly, drowning out everyone and everything else.

"Where...?" I gasp, unable to ask for the one person I want. Where is she?

"We're taking you to the hospital, you're having a reaction," Mr. Monroe says, voice thundering directly overhead. His hands roll me onto my side, and the mud squelches beneath my ear.

I shouldn't hear that, I think. *Oh, Ankou, am I stuck out here?*

"Chris, you're gonna be fine," Kela says. "Just stay awake with us." Panic laces her voice even as she tries her hardest to suppress it.

A sense of falling comes over me as my vision swims and fades, blue blue blue into blackness, warmth. I reach out with one hand, hoping to find someone familiar. A hand grabs my own and I can tell it's Noah's; I feel the scar on his palm from when we were kids and I stabbed him with a pencil. What a demented game we played.

It's the last thing I think before his hand slips away and I do, too.

CHAPTER FIVE

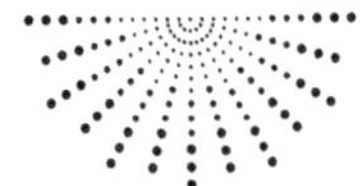

The cool darkness gives way to a warm light behind my eyelids, and the ringing finally yields to hushed voices and rustling curtains.

I groan as my body comes back to life, every inch of me aching to the bone.

"He's awake!" Noah shouts, and I recoil. One of the girls hushes him sharply, and he whisper-yells instead. "Chris, hey, welcome back!"

"Give him a moment to breathe," Ava says. "He almost died."

"He did not," Sam says from my left. "He just had a bad reaction."

"He went into anaphylactic *shock*," Ava hisses from my right. "His heart nearly *stopped*."

"It... what?" I mumble, refusing to open my eyes against the too-bright lights.

"Chris, hey, buddy," Noah says, voice suddenly going soft. "How're you feeling?"

I shake my head slowly, swallowing hard to bring some moisture back into my mouth.

"Should we get a doctor?" he asks. A gentle hand brushes my forehead, pushing my sweaty hair away from my eyes. It's Ava's; I know because her nails graze against my skin, and her touch is the softest I've ever felt.

"I'm okay," I murmur. "Tired…"

"Yeah, you had a rough time out there," Ava says, voice strained. I reach one throbbing hand up to search for hers. She takes it firmly, sending shockwaves of warmth through my arm that push the ache away.

"We couldn't see you," Noah says thickly. "When the paramedics got there, we still couldn't. By the time the Simulation wore off, you were already gone."

"I've never seen Noah run so fast in my life, not even for a burger." Sam laughs dryly. "Is there anything we can get you, Chris?"

"Water?" I ask, trying not to sound needy but still desperate to be rid of this horrendous cotton-mouth.

"Sure thing, be right back," Sam says. A chair scrapes, and I watch her shadow move from behind my eyelids. The curtain rustles, and I assume she is gone.

"Chris, are your eyes alright?" Noah asks worriedly.

"Is bright," I say, the words unintentionally slurring together. My lips are numb and tingly, like the time I got Novocain at the dentist when I got a cavity filled. I only opted for that once, though. Later, I discovered that the needle was scarier than the actual procedure, so I always went without. I used to joke it was the only badass thing I'd ever done, but I guess that's not true anymore.

"Here." Ava turns off the brightest of the lights. "That better?"

"Yeah," I say, cracking my eyes open. My vision swims, but I still see them, my best friends, hovering around me close enough to make the air feel thick. For once, I don't mind the lack of personal space.

Ava smiles sweetly, and it's like watching the sunrise. "Welcome back."

"That was… scary," I mumble. Tears spring into my eyes that I am powerless to hide, and then they are doing the very thing I wanted most: sitting on either side of this too-small bed with me, each holding one of my hands.

"I'm glad you're okay," Ava says quietly, rubbing circles onto the back of my hand with her thumb. I momentarily wish for a third arm so that I won't have to let go of either of them when Katie gets here, but then I remember that she won't be walking in to make this better, and my heart shatters all over again.

"Here," Sam says, returning with a small cup of water. "You need help?"

I shake my head and gently take the cup from her, tipping the water into my mouth. "Thank you," I say, handing the cup back to her.

"I'm gonna go update Kela and Grif," she says, patting my knee awkwardly. "I'll be back in a little bit."

"Thanks," I say as she hastily slips through the curtain.

I drift in and out of sleep for a while, trying to get away from the perpetual ache I feel all over. My nose tingles from the oxygen cannulas in my nostrils. I am mostly asleep, wishing Katie were here, and my mother, and Mel.

"Chris, hey, doctor's coming in," Noah says eventually, pulling me into consciousness.

Opening my eyes is easier this time, and I don't feel as queasy as before. I sit up slowly as the ache begins to dissipate, save for where it hovers around the IV on the inside of my elbow.

The doctor slips through the curtain with a clipboard on her hip. She's young, nearly as young as we are, with a tan face and dark, warm eyes. Her hair is tucked under a maroon scarf that matches her scrubs, which are an inch too short in the leg, revealing pink socks under her sneakers.

"Hi, Christopher. How are you feeling?" she asks kindly, pulling the curtain shut behind her with a gentle hand.

"I've been worse," I say, voice dry and scratchy.

"You don't have to lie, it's alright," she says, chuckling softly. "My name is Dr. Maher. I'm gonna be the one keeping an eye on you tonight. I heard you had a bit of a scare with a Surface Simulator, correct?"

"Yes," I say, tears springing into my eyes. I clear my throat and try again. "Yes. I'm not sure why, though."

"No worries, that's what I'm here for." Her smile is radiant, but her eyes are distant the way that all Meliors' are. "Do you know what anaphylactic shock is?"

"Yes. I was on the medical track in school."

She lowers her clipboard. "Wonderful. What about your friends here?"

"Both engineers," Noah says. "Or, were gonna be. Then, you know."

"Of course," Dr. Maher says, nodding thoughtfully. "Well, Chris, let me get a set of vitals real quick, and then we'll chat about it."

She gets to work, using an old-fashioned blood pressure cuff and a stethoscope with a bit of rust on it. Sitting up makes me wince, so Noah helps tug me forward enough for her to listen to my lungs.

"Well, other than slightly low blood pressure, you're doing great," Dr. Maher says as she scribbles everything on her clipboard. "And that will rebound in no time, as I'm sure you know. Otherwise, you're perfectly healthy."

"So then why did... *that* happen?" Ava asks with a touch of fear in her voice.

"Surface Simulators are pretty new technology," Dr. Maher explains. "We've recently discovered that, especially with people from the Surface, there can be some adverse side effects. Typically, that's just hay fever—itchy eyes, runny nose, the works. Some people get mild hives. I'll be honest and say that we've never seen anaphylaxis with them, though.

"A lot of families have been here for a few generations and have been exposed to different chemicals and such that you guys haven't. We think that one of the hallucinogens in the Surface Simulators can trigger allergic reactions in people raised on the Surface, but we aren't sure which one."

"So, people just try them and hope for the best?" Ava asks, shifting uncomfortably in her seat.

"Unfortunately, yes," Dr. Maher says regretfully. "I'm going to personally ensure that there's a medical kit in the Activity Center, though, stocked with an epi-pen and other necessary medications. That should prevent anyone from having as severe a reaction as Chris."

"You took one for the team, buddy," Noah says, punching me lightly on the arm.

"He really did," Dr. Maher says, glancing at her clipboard. "We are going to keep you for the night just for observation. No need to worry, though. If your friends would like to stay, they're more than welcome. Is there anything you guys need?"

"Could I get some ginger ale, if you have it?" I ask. "Or just something to settle my stomach?"

"How about a low dose of Zofran?"

"Oh, God, that would be amazing."

"I'll have one of the nurses bring it around." Dr. Maher flashes her sunshine smile again. "Nice meeting you all. I'll check back in a little bit."

She slips through the curtain again, pulling it softly closed. As soon as she's gone, Ava bursts into tears.

"Ava, hey, it's okay," I say quickly, reaching out to her. She sits on the edge of the bed, throws her arms around my neck, and weeps. I hold her gently, and Noah sits on her other side, rubbing her shoulder.

"You almost... died," she sobs, sniffling hard. Her chest heaves against mine.

"Almost, not quite," I say, trying to be brave even though I'm scared, too. "I'm still here, it's okay."

"We would've lost you, too." She sits back and wipes her eyes only to crumple into another sob. Noah wraps his arms around her from behind, and I sit up to meet them.

"I'm alright," I murmur to both of them, burying my face in Ava's shoulder. "It's okay. You're not gonna lose me, I promise."

"That was so awful," she says, voice shaking. "You sounded so scared, and there was nothing I could do..."

"Even if you could see me, they would have pushed you away. What matters is that we're all here, we're all okay. I'm not going anywhere." It nearly kills me to realize I said 'all' as if we're not missing a quarter of our family.

Ava carefully elbows her way out of our embrace, wiping her eyes. "I love you guys."

Noah and I echo her words, attempting smiles that somehow become genuine.

"Can we stay?" Noah asks me, his brown eyes resembling a pleading child's. For a moment, I see Owen looking up at us, asking—no, begging —for another cookie.

"Only if you really want to, I don't mi—"

"We're staying," Ava says stubbornly, and I know there's no use arguing even if I wanted to.

"Thank you." I shift so that they have more room. The three of us get as comfortable as possible in the limited space we have, just happy to be alive and together.

I LEAVE the hospital in the morning with nothing but a Band-Aid on my leg from the epinephrine shot and a cotton ball taped to the inside of my elbow from the IV. It's the last training day before Cecilia comes back, but I get a pass on working anyway. We go up to our room first to grab clean clothes and extra painkillers for Ava—sleeping in a hospital bed with two mostly-grown men did a number on her back.

I sit on the edge of the pool while my squad gets drilled by a trainer who barks orders at everyone, including people he isn't training. No one seems to mind. I'm starting to think that maybe all trainers are like this, and Cecilia is just the exception.

After about an hour, I wander into the locker room with the idea that I'll get in the water and just take my time. Maybe I can take some heat off the rest of my squad. My skin crawls watching them get verbally abused while I just sit around. I should at least suffer with them.

Noah jumps out of the water as soon as he sees me. "Uh-uh, buddy, no way."

"I'm *fine*," I protest. "Seriously, I can do this. Tomorrow's Sunday, anyway. A whole day off."

"The doctor said a full day," Noah replies. "Please, just sit this one out. I know you're bored, but *please*. Ava's at PT; she should be done soon. You can go pick her up."

"Noah, she's a *grown woman*," I say, raising an eyebrow. "Seriously, pick her up?"

"Just, go hang out with her, I don't know," he says. "She'll be done before Amy. Go do some digging for me."

"Digging?"

"Ya know, see if she likes me." He winks and raises his eyebrows twice.

"You know she likes you," I joke, punching him in the arm and retreating to the locker room. Within fifteen minutes I'm standing in front of the PT Tunnel, even though I took it slow up the stairs.

While it's a place I never want to have to visit on the regular, I have to admit that the PT Tunnel is pretty cool. It used to be subway tracks, but walls were built most of the way up to create different rooms. The arched ceiling has long lights hanging from the bedrock, mismatched as all things here are.

I know which room Ava's usually in, so I knock quietly. She opens the door with one hand, the other leaning on her cane.

"Chris, hey," she says breathlessly. "What are you doing here?"

"I came to hang out once you're done," I say.

"Ah, come in," she says, backing away from the door. I follow her inside and sit down in one of the chairs, trying to look busy as I thumb through an ancient magazine.

Her appointment is soon over, and she is granted the privilege to use a cane in the hallways. The wheelchair is still ideal for moving around in the dining hall and over long distances, but it should only be another few weeks before she won't need it anymore. We both smile at that.

For once, Ava accepts my offer to push her in the hallway.

"Glad to be back on your feet more?" I ask as we take the elevator up to our room.

"You have no idea," she replies.

We drop her cane off and head down to the Activity Center, which is more barren than I've ever seen it. We meander to the coffee shop for drinks and settle on a bench in front of the sad, cracked fountain.

"So," I say, taking a sip of my latte. "What's the deal with you and Noah?"

She laughs, setting her tea down as it cools. "You know what the deal is with me and Noah. We're dating, I guess."

"You guess?"

She shrugs. "Well, yeah. He never *officially* asked me out, you know."

"I didn't know that."

"It's not set in stone, but yeah, we're together. Our lips are friends. I don't know."

"Your *lips* are *friends*?" I laugh.

"Yes!" She giggles, a sound so welcome that it's like fresh air. "I don't know. I wish he asked me out properly."

"Why don't you do it?"

"Mayyybe."

"Well, do you like him enough to do that?"

She nods. "Yeah, of course. I just... I can't explain it well, but I have a *different* relationship with him. I look at him and it's like the sun is coming out. I'd do anything for him, hell, I'd cut off all my fingers and toes for him if I had to. Not sure why I would ever have to, but I would." She laughs a little.

"I see you guys in bed at night," I say. "No... finagling, okay?"

She laughs again. "No finagling, got it."

"While I'm in the room."

"While you're in the room."

"Or on my bed."

Her face falls. "Oh, Chris..."

I choke on my drink. "What?"

"Kidding!" She shoves my arm. "We haven't finagled on your bed. Yet."

"Gross," I groan. "But seriously. He really likes you, you know."

"I would hope so," she jokes, then grows serious. "He really does?"

"Yeah, he really does. You mean the world to him. I bet if he needed to cut off all his fingers and toes for you, he'd do it no questions asked. You guys mean a lot to one another."

"Thanks," she says. "I hate to ask, and if you don't want to talk about it, that's okay, but—"

"Forget digits, I'd hack off an arm."

The fountain trickles sadly in front of us, dripping yellow water into a grimy bowl.

Ava sighs with all the weight of the world on her lean shoulders. "She would've done the same for you."

THE NEXT FEW weeks miraculously fly by. Cecilia returns like nothing ever happened, and although I offer to talk about it over coffee, she politely refuses. I still look for Katie around every corner, even as I learn to live with the mind-numbing ache.

I survive by pouring all my waking energy into work. I PR on all my lifts and runs, then do it again.

One day in the weight room, Cecilia decides to set us up against a few other squads, one of Scouts and one of combat, like us.

"Alright, it's just a little friendly competition," she explains, despite the fact that all the squads are huddled up like they're strategizing for war. "Just try your best and we'll see what happens."

"You got it, boss," Sam says, a devilish grin on her face. "Are we doing this by weight class, or—"

"Nope, just gender," Cecilia says. "Too much effort; Art didn't feel like it."

Art is a giant hulk of a trainer who towers over everyone, with two tattoo sleeves and an eyepatch. He barely speaks, preferring to grunt.

Sam only grins harder, a wicked expression that makes Noah flinch a little. "Perfect."

We start out on deadlift, her best lift. One of the girls from the Scout squad pulls 225, so Sam pulls 235. The other girl pulls 240, so Sam sets up for 245.

"C'mon, Sam," Noah says. He and I are standing right in front of her. She locks her feet in, dusting chalk off her hands. It puffs around her like a cloud, and she looks up at me as she takes a deep breath. I nod at her.

She grabs the bar and sets her hips, flipping her head back to get her hair away from her face. It cascades around her bare shoulders like a broken halo, and her gray eyes find mine again as she rips the bar off the floor.

Her eyes bore into me as she locks out; the cheering and shouting from Cecilia and Noah—and even some people from the other squads —go silent as we stare at one another. I feel microscopic under her gaze, studied like a sample on a slide. She holds the bar at her hips for a moment, chin lifted in victory, and then lets it crash to the ground, staring at me all the while.

We move on to squats next, my worst lift. I do poorly, but Noah excels, with freakish hip mobility and a long torso but short legs.

Last is the bench press, my favorite. Some of the Scouts go first, weeding themselves out early. They don't do much upper body—trained to run, their legs are strong as hell, but they neglect their arms and chests.

My first lift moves like a hot knife through butter. 155, usually towards the end of my session.

When I stand, Noah and I look at each other.

"Dude. He grins. "More weight?"

"Hell, yeah," I say. Someone has a speaker blaring, and the music is filling me with fire.

I sit out of 165 and watch a few more people fail that weight. I've never pushed more than 170.

Noah sets 175 on the bar for me when it's my turn again. I lie back and set myself, looking up at him.

"Go get it," he says.

I grin, then close my eyes for a moment. When I open them again, I think of her pushing Preston Harper off.

The weight moves like it's a feather, and then I'm on my feet and my squad is cheering, even Sam. I get a hug from everyone except Cecilia, who offers me a clap on the shoulder instead.

Three other guys fail out of 175, so it's just me and one more trying for 185.

"That's usually my warmup," the guy says to me as Art puts the weight on the bar. He has short, dark braids and a white scar on his pulsing chest.

"Same here," I say quietly, eyes locked on the bench.

I go first, being the newer member of the Underground. Noah and I go through the same routine, and Sam's thundercloud eyes burn holes in my hands as I grab the bar.

I think of Katie, of kissing her for the first time. I think of the way she didn't tell me about Preston until months later, of how by the time she left here, she would've been strong enough to push him off. I think of her smile.

Noah lifts the bar off the rack for me, helping me position it over my chest. I nod at him to let it go, and then it's just me. The music is blasting from the speaker, but all I can hear is her. *Up,* she says.

I lower the weight, letting it graze my chest. *Up.*

A monumental effort, feet pressed into the floor, lips shoved together. I exhale as hard as I can, pushing with everything I have. *Up.*

Then I'm re-racking the weight and Noah is tugging me off the bench and cheering, and I'm laughing with him. This time, even Cecilia hugs me.

The other guy isn't done, though, and the gym falls silent for his attempt. The weight hovers an inch or two above his chest, and then comes falling back down.

***

BEFORE I KNOW IT, Cecilia is handing me the report papers for my "volunteer" Scouting mission. I'll be on the Surface for two days and one night alongside fourteen other soldiers I have yet to meet. Sam's been on one of these missions before—she says it's a nice break and a chance to get to know other people.

I wake up at the usual time, but there is a different sense of urgency this morning. Noah and Ava both check my bag to ensure that I don't forget anything. I almost leave my toothbrush behind accidentally. It wouldn't kill me to go without it; I have no way to bring toothpaste with me, anyway, but Ava goes on and on about the importance of dental hygiene, so I shove it in my bag for her sake.

I eat breakfast with my squad, where Sam gives me last-minute tips. I try not to get too preemptively homesick at the thought of leaving them. When they leave for training after a barrage of hugs, I feel painfully isolated. My palms sweat as I tear a paper napkin to shreds, trying not to bite my fingernails. Hayden from down the hall is sitting calmly at his own table, but I don't recognize any of the other soldiers who are coming with us.

The Head Trainer gives a speech about sticking together and providing for the Underground. I try not to be angry with him—it isn't his fault that Katie isn't here anymore, but anger bubbles in my chest anyway. He finally stops, and we head through the tunnel to the loading dock.

I hop into a car with a driver and six other soldiers I don't know. Sam said the ride is only about forty-five minutes; we should be there by 9:00.

I gel my hair along with another boy on the ride, and the girls braid one another's tightly in place. The train they form is vaguely familiar, and then I remember how Ava, Katie, and Mel used to make these lines, trying all kinds of crazy hairstyles on each other. They even braided themselves together, once.

The ruins of Pevidere are just as magnificent as I remember; the buildings cut into the clear sky like jagged knives. I didn't notice last time how pines grow in some of the streets, or the way the wind whispers through the buildings. I shiver as the breeze makes my hair stand up. I hop from the car and extend a hand to those behind me. One girl smiles at me from behind her bangs, but I offer nothing more than a polite smile back. I try not to think about Katie, about how the last time I was here, she was here, too.

Once all of us are on the ground, one of the grizzled drivers leans out of his window. "Alright, five of you head along the eastern streets, five to the west, and the other five stick to the middle. Tomorrow afternoon we'll be right here to pick you up. Sweep up and back, then camp together at the far end of the city, along the bridge. It's not a big place, so don't expect any trouble. You find any lost people, bring them with you—we'll have an extra car if that's the case. Try not to drug 'em. Everybody got it?"

"Yes, sir," we all say quickly, a chorus of teenagers ready to be alone. It reminds me of when my mother and Melissa would leave me home alone and I would walk around naked because nobody could stop me (except for that time Noah was sitting in my living room unannounced and we could barely look at one another for a week).

The cars pull away without another word, leaving us to divide ourselves into groups. The brunette who smiled at me comes to stand with me, Hayden, and another boy.

Another girl I don't know joins our group, which is the first to be completed. She has red hair so bright it glows like fire and expressionless

Melior eyes, faraway even when she's looking right at you. Something about her is familiar, but I can't place her.

"We're heading to the eastern streets," Hayden says to the others, gesturing to the five of us. "See you guys tonight. Be safe!"

We turn and move out, quickly leaving the large group behind.

"You guys wanna deep-sweep the buildings?" the brunette asks.

"Yeah, we should," Hayden says. "We've got almost twelve hours of daylight left and we only have, like, four streets to clear. May as well try to find some supplies if we can. I bet the hospital is empty, so we can try to get some medical supplies from there. Maybe even earn a few extra credits if we bring enough home."

"We can get extra credits for this?" I ask.

"Yeah," the brunette answers. "The Head Trainer doesn't like to broadcast it, but if volunteers bring home enough useful supplies, he might give them a few extra credits. Sometimes he does, sometimes he doesn't."

"Huh, cool."

"So, what do you guys do?" the redhead asks as we enter the first tall building. It's been blown to pieces; most of the interior walls are gone, and daylight streams through gaping holes. There's a fern growing through a crack in the dusty floor. "Well, I know what you do, Ruda," she adds, grinning at the brunette.

"Duh," Ruda answers, flashing a prize-winning smile to the rest of us. "Maeve and I are full-time Scouts, boys."

"Oh, cool," I say. "My name's Chris. I'm close-combat."

"Same here," the not-Hayden guy answers. "I'm Aaron, by the way."

Other than exchanging names and pleasantries, we don't talk much as we sweep the first few buildings. I find a green piece of glass that's been smoothed down and pocket it to give to Ava if I don't find anything nicer for her.

"Who's Ava?" Ruda asks when I explain what I'm doing. By now we're on our fifth building; it must be at least 11:00. My stomach growls, but I know we're not breaking for lunch until noon, so I don't say anything.

"A girl in my squad," I say simply, even though she is so much more than that.

Ruda nods. "Somebody special, or just a friend?"

"Just a friend," I reply, peeking into another room. This building looks like one of the offices back in Carcera, only much taller. Looking out the window is enough to make me dizzy. "My girlfriend, uh, isn't here anymore."

"God, I'm sorry," she says. "That's terrible."

In another place I would say, "You have no idea," but I can't with people from the Underground. It's hard to tell who's lost someone close to them; better to assume that they have, rather than that they haven't. Most of them—*us*—have.

I nod, offering to take the top floor by myself. No one protests, so I jog through quickly and head up to the roof. I'm half-expecting someone to be standing on the sun-soaked concrete, but no one is. A strong breeze offers some relief from the heat gathering under my uniform as I stand alone in the middle of the sky.

The view is remarkable. The mountains cradle the city in their lap, slowly reclaiming the brick and steel, and a churning river runs along the edge of the mass of industrial rubble. I spot the highway where we're supposed to meet tonight and wonder what it was like when Pevidere was alive. We are both husks, remnants of what was. Unfinished sentences and days long gone that have not yet been crossed off of desk calendars.

I admire the view for another moment, trying not to think of her admiring it with me, the way the wind would tousle her short hair and she would hastily pat it back down as if it would stay put for more than a moment. I begin my long descent. Along the way, I allow my mind to drift to Ava and Noah, Sam and Amy. I hope they're alright.

I'm so lost in thought and the constant rhythm of my walking that I don't notice how the next set of stairs is steeper than the previous ones. One wrong step sends me tumbling down the entire flight without enough time to even shout in surprise.

The concrete digs into my face, creating fine scrapes that couldn't sting more if I poured salt into them. I land so hard on my back that even my vest can't stop the air from being knocked from my lungs.

I wait for a moment, gaping like a fish and trying to take stock of my body. Nothing seems broken or sprained, but I feel blood trickling down my left arm, and my cheeks burn from the shallow cut, helmet effectively useless because I didn't tighten it properly this morning. *Idiot*, I think as I regain my breath. *Another concussion and you'll be out of training for weeks.*

I groan and pull myself to my feet, yanking my helmet back on properly and tightening the chin strap as much as I can.

The rest of the group is waiting for me outside, sunbathing on a large pile of rubble. Ruda is lying with her helmet and shirt off, arms splayed out overhead, exposing lean triceps and a tattoo of a bird in flight.

"Hey, welcome back," Hayden says. "We were beginning to think you got lost."

I half sigh, half laugh. "I fell down the stairs."

The smiles fall from everyone's faces. "Oh crap, you alright?" Aaron asks, hopping down from the massive cinderblock he's sitting on.

"Yeah, yeah, just a little banged up."

"Your arm is bleeding," Ruda says, sitting up and waving me over. "Here, I have the med kit. Sit down for a moment, I'll patch it up for you."

"It's fine, really," I say, feet staying firmly planted. "I'm okay."

"Just let me clean it out," she protests, waving me over again as she pulls out the red med kit. "It's not even going to hurt that bad."

"I'm not scared of it hurting," I grumble, walking over to her anyway. What I really want to say is, *I barely even know you and you're not wearing a shirt,* but I don't, because my mother did not raise a rude son.

Ruda cleans up my arm with an alcohol wipe and then wraps it snugly. I contain a wince by clenching my other fist. She gently presses on the bandage for longer than she has to, a few extra fingers lightly brushing against the exposed skin of my arm. I'll have to patch my uniform when I get home—Ava will finally get to teach me how to sew. She's been badgering me and Noah about it for months. Back in Carcera, we would just take our ripped clothes back to the depot and exchange them, but resources are too few to replace what can be mended.

I practically leap to my feet and readjust my pack as soon as Ruda starts zipping up the med kit. "Ready to go?"

Everyone nods. We decide on one more building before lunch and split up to get it done more efficiently. The girls will take the upper ten floors, while Aaron, Hayden, and I get the bottom ten plus the basement. I can't help but enjoy how easily we work together—every legitimate decision so far has been a unanimous vote.

"So, do you know if we're actually looking for anything?" Aaron asks. We're in an old dentist's office now; there's still a pile of plastic bibs on a counter.

"People, I guess," Hayden replies. "Anyone hurt, any Border town refugees. If we find any hostiles, we're supposed to kill them. I just..."

"I don't want to, either," Aaron says. "Whatever we can do to avoid that, I want to try."

"Same," I say, pleasantly surprised that they wouldn't be ready to eliminate a threat without a second thought. "So, were you guys... are you Meliors?"

"Yeah," Hayden says, glancing over at Aaron. "Both of us."

"Oh, cool," I say. "So, have you ever... you know? Had to."

"No," Aaron says. "The opportunity comes along less than you'd think. Have you?"

I am tugged back to the momentary resistance under my knife, then the release of flesh parting, the seizing gasp of death beneath me. The way his eyes found mine and I whispered, "I'm sorry, I'm sorry, I'm sorry," as life left them.

"Yeah." I open a drawer and peer inside. "Hey, do we need tweezers?"

"Sure," Hayden says. "Can't hurt."

We finish up the building and fly through the rest of the day, eating our sandwiches as we meander through the bombed-out streets, clambering over piles of rubble bigger than my mother's house. We don't find a single living being, not even a bird. I don't mind though—I can enjoy this warm summer day in relative peace, even if the silence is a little eerie.

CHAPTER SIX

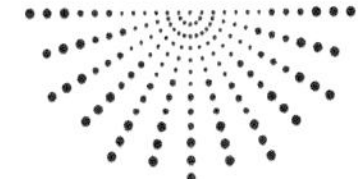

OUR GROUP IS the first to arrive at the highway that evening, so we gather wood for a large fire and collect water from the nearby river. It feels as though I've gone back in time six months, only now I can feel my fingers. I wish my squad were here to experience wildflowers growing through the asphalt, a rainbow of white, orange, and purple.

Ruda and I volunteer to fill and treat the group's canteens. "So," she says, picking her way down the steep embankment to the river. "You seem like a survivalist. Who was your teacher back in school?"

"I didn't have a survival teacher," I reply, following her path to the water. "I'm from a Border town."

She nods slowly. "Oh, okay. So, you taught yourself all this?"

"All what?"

"The survival stuff. How to light a fire, how to treat water. You know, all that." She waves her hands in the same way that Ava does, and I find myself wanting to smile.

"Oh, I kind of learned it in school, but most of it was just experiential," I say, shaking the grin away from my face and kneeling next to the water. "I already knew how to use matches, cook food to kill bacteria, all that. It's just kind of everyday stuff. Plus, I had some medical training, so I had some extra knowledge about first aid and sanitation."

"You're a doctor?" She kneels next to me and uncaps a canteen.

"No. I was going to be."

"That's really cool."

"Thanks."

"You'd make a good-looking doctor."

I glance sideways at her. "What?"

"Doctors, ya know, the white coat, the stethoscope," she muses. The canteen she's filling bubbles with water, dribbling onto her slender fingers. "It suits you."

"Uh, well, thanks," I stammer, ashamed that my cheeks are so hot.

She looks at me with a half-smile, more of a smirk, really, but without the attitude that it usually comes with.

We finish filling the canteens in silence, hanging them around our necks and dripping water all over our chests, laughing about it.

"This is gonna sound really lame," I begin, already kicking myself. "But no one's ever called me good-looking before."

Her eyes widen. "Really?"

"It never really came up, with the Matching and all."

"Not even your girlfriend, once you got here?"

I shake my head. "Nope. We didn't have the time to... get used to talking like that."

Ruda sits down with her back against a log, and I mirror her, listening to the gurgling stream and hum of insects.

"I'm sorry," she says earnestly. "I didn't mean to come across as too flirty."

"No, it's totally fine," I say quickly. "A compliment's a compliment. I appreciate it. And for the record, you'd look good in the white coat, too, although I think combat clothes are more your style."

"I do love my Kevlar." There's that little smirking smile again, and my heart drops into my stomach, and I really hope those piercing black eyes can't see what's in my head.

I stand abruptly before this develops into something I can ruin, almost tripping in the process. "We should be getting back. I'm sure the other groups have arrived by now, and—"

"And you don't want this to get more pleasantly uncomfortable than it already is?" she guesses, starting up the hill. Her voice is so filled with confidence that it almost doesn't matter what she's saying.

"Well, yeah," I say, taken aback by her nonchalance. We walk the rest of the way in silence, as if I wasn't confused by her and she wasn't flirting with me. Was she flirting with me?

The evening passes quickly. Dusk falls, and we light small fires along with the large one, adding hot water to freeze-dried food that actually isn't terrible. One group found berry bushes in their chunk of the city, and they brought plenty to share. For some Meliors, this is their first time eating food grown on the Surface. There is joy and laughter, and talk both big and small as we get to pretend that we are regular people on a camping trip. Just for a few hours.

Long after dark, we finally bed down and leave only one fire smoldering, assigning the youngest boy, Rick, to watch it. Ruda explains that giving the youngest person the first shift on his first mission is an important tradition. She does this as she settles into her sleeping bag, which is right next to mine.

Everyone falls asleep except for Rick, Aaron, and me. Aaron and I sit with our backs against a fallen log facing the twelve others, who sleep in clumps. Rick stares into the trees with his gun in his hands, shoulders wired tightly to his neck as the forest comes alive for the evening, cicadas screaming and crickets joining in. His jaw ticks with every hoot of the owl nesting not far off.

"So, who is she?" Aaron asks me, nodding at Ruda.

I glance over at him. "Ruda, duh."

"No, no, I *know* that. I mean who is she to *you*?"

"Oh, a friend, I guess," I say. "I mean, I just met her today."

He raises an eyebrow for the briefest of moments. "Only a day and you're already this close?"

I laugh a little at the absurdity of it. "We're just friends, that's all."

"Well, you should get to know her better. I grew up with her; she's awesome. Plus, I think she likes you."

I shrug. "Yeah, I mean, she's great. I just don't know what I would do if it went *that* way."

"You and... well, you've done this before, right?"

"Yeah, but there was no *flirting*. We just fell into it, totally natural. There was nothing... artificial, about it."

"There doesn't need to be anything artificial about this, either. Just fall into it."

"Can that happen with more than one person in your life?"

He shrugs, staring into the smoldering embers. Whatever heat they'd thrown off is long gone, and the sticky air is almost chilly on our bare skin. "I don't know."

I have a thousand questions about life in the Underground (what was it like to learn about the Surface in a textbook? Was it hard to leave your parents, like it was hard for me? When did you first experience death?) but I'm too shy to ask them. Instead, we stare into the remnants of our fire and swat gently at mosquitos.

I eventually settle into my sleeping bag, mesmerized by the swirling stars as my vision drifts in and out of focus. I am vaguely aware of Ruda rolling over, but I'm already too asleep to see if she's awake.

In the moment before I fade, I realize that tonight is the first night I have simply thought about Katie with sweet affection, not missed her with the desperate ache that lights my ribcage on fire. Then, I'm gone.

THERE IS a girl in my arms when I wake in the too-early hours the next morning. The sky is the cool blue of 5 AM and the fire has long since gone out, dew gathering on the charred logs. Her hair is in my mouth and her perfume smells of vanilla. Warm skin presses against mine.

I don't know how she got here, or when, but I know that I don't want her to move. So instead of doing the right thing and delicately untangling myself, I wrap my arms tighter around her and bury my face into her shoulder. Ruda stirs just slightly, pressing into me, making me question all the things I've ever been told about being cautious with women. My mind is still half-asleep, but the rest of me is fully conscious, and suddenly I find myself kissing the back of her neck as if I've done it a million times before, the way I always wanted to kiss Katie.

"Chris," she murmurs, coming awake in my arms. "What...?"

I break away, breathing softly against her neck. "Do you want me to stop?"

"No," she whispers, pausing for a moment before settling back against me. "No."

I kiss along her hairline, down to her collarbone, across her shoulder. She sighs happily and holds onto the arm I have wrapped around her, and I am amazed at how well our bodies fit together.

"Chris."

I pause, resting my forehead against the smooth skin of her shoulder. "Mmm?"

"The others will be waking up soon."

"Alright."

"I'm sorry," she whispers, pushing out of my arms and slipping gracefully out of my sleeping bag. The air that hits me is freezing in her absence; a shiver runs down my back.

I blink myself to full consciousness. "Ruda, uh, I..."

"You alright?" She pauses, crouched beside her sleeping bag, curled up like a spring.

"What time did you get into my bag?"

"Half hour ago."

"Why...?"

She flashes that half-smile expression at me. "I was cold."

Ruda falls asleep again, but I can't. Instead, I roll up my bag and walk down to the river for a bit. I know that I shouldn't be off by myself, but sometimes it feels like I never get the chance to be alone anymore, and I can't let this perfect morning pass me by just because everyone else is still asleep.

The light bounces off the bubbling river and dances through the trees, turning the leaves to gold. It is magic. I take off my boots and socks and wade into the chilly water, shivering as it laps at my ankles. Small minnows dart around my feet as I roll my pants up and wade in up to my mid-calf, squishing the earth between my toes. I can smell mud and ferns, the scent pungent, ripe, and absolutely wonderful.

A branch breaks from the other side of the river while I'm studying the little fish, and my heart drops. I stand hunched in the river like an animal being hunted—my gun is back with the group, and they're all too far to help me, even if they're awake by now.

After another moment of tense almost-silence, a young girl steps out from the trees. She can't be more than ten years old, with sticks in her matted brown hair and piercing green eyes that are far too old for her round face. Her nightgown, too small and vaguely pink, is muddy and tattered. Red scratches and mosquito bites freckle her knees and bare feet.

We stare at each other for a moment, trying to guess what the other will do first. A few seconds pass, and then she raises a hand and gives a small wave, a childlike gesture that is the last thing I expect. I straighten up and wave back, still unable to move my legs. From this far she almost seems ghostly. I wonder where she lives, or if she has parents. I wonder, albeit briefly, if this is a trap sent by Ankou, designed to lead us into an ambush. I wonder if this girl belongs anywhere, or if she's lost, too.

Aaron shouts from up the hill. "Chris! Where are you?" I turn towards the sound of his clumsy feet breaking branches, and when I look back, the girl is gone. I wonder if she was ever there at all.

***

By late afternoon I'm back home, toting a small orange rug that I think Ava will like for the bathroom and a gray lampshade for Noah, his favorite color. The rest of my group salvages similar items—Hayden snagged a poster of an underwear-clad woman with a beer can, and Maeve found an empty jar she wants to use for her art supplies. Ruda brings home a pearl bracelet and gives me her room number before we part ways. I promise to keep in touch even if I'm not sure I can make good on it.

I strap the lampshade to the back of my pack and take my time ascending the stairs,

When I walk back into my room, it looks like a bomb has gone off. Knitting needles and colorful yarn are everywhere, along with all kinds of makeup that I didn't even know existed.

Ava leans out of the bathroom with a paintbrush in her hand.

"Chris!" And to my complete surprise and utter joy, Amy leans out at the same height as Ava.

I stop dead in my tracks, staring at the girl with one leg who appears to be standing. Actually, really *standing*, the way she would've been if it weren't for me.

"Hey," I say stupidly. I have one hand in my pocket, turning the green piece of glass over and over in my palm, the rug tucked under my other arm. "Long time, no see."

Ava walks over to me as fast as she can, only limping slightly without her cane. She stops in front of me. "Shrink," she commands, and I do, and she plants a firm kiss on my cheek. "Missed you. What's this?"

I crack a smile. "Missed you, too. Figured you'd like this for the bathroom, since you always complain the floor's so cold. And I got you this." I hand her the glass.

"Oh, it's beautiful," she marvels. "Chris, thank you. Come here, I wanna show you something." She practically drags me to the bathroom.

"Ava rigged this so I can do my makeup closer to the mirror," Amy says. "We have one set up in my room, too." Two elastic bands stretch from the towel racks, creating a kind of sling to hold her close to the sink. "I can balance pretty well; this just makes it a little easier."

"I love it," I say, beaming earnestly. "Amazing."

I glance around at the chaos that has become our room, and I have never been happier to see such a mess. Pretty soon Ava won't even need a cane, and Amy can get a prosthetic, and they can go forward. With a pang I remember that going forward means leaving her behind, and I resolve to remain on the bridge, one hand on hers and the other stretching forward to Ava, and Amy, and all the rest.

CHAPTER SEVEN

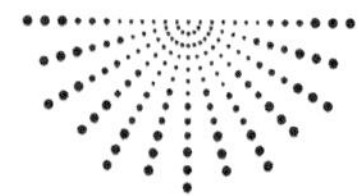

RUDA CALLS me a few days later, having gotten my number from a friend of a friend of a friend. We decide to get coffee together. It's one of the scariest moments of my life.

I pick Ruda up from her dorm, where she lives with her older sister Mina, and the two of us head to the coffee shop in awkward silence. I can tell she thinks about holding my hand by the way the back of hers keeps brushing mine, but neither of us makes the move. I'm simply not brave enough yet.

You idiot, I think. *You were brave enough to consider making out with her in the woods surrounded by other sleeping people but not holding her hand in an empty stairwell? Oh, Ankou.*

I shake my head to clear it, remembering what my mother said about holding the door for girls and pulling out chairs, and then wonder if Ruda is that kind of girl, because she seems used to sleeping in the woods, not having an awkward, stuttering, sorry excuse for a boy pulling out her chair. But at the bottom of the stairwell, I hold the door anyway, because that's what my mother and Mel taught me, and Ruda murmurs a quiet "Thank you."

She gets a latte and I get my usual tea, and we sit at a high table by the window.

"So," she says. "Close combat, right?"

I take a sip of my drink and nod. "Yes, ma'am. And you're a full-time Scout?"

"Yeah, I am."

"So, you're up there a lot, then?"

"Pretty often, yeah. Maeve goes on a lot of the volunteer missions, too. I average about one short mission a month, a longer one every two to three."

"What's it like, being up there so often?"

"Well, you get to know all the drivers really well." She laughs a little. "It keeps life interesting. I have to be good at everything, so my training is really varied. I spent time learning medicine, too, so I can stitch wounds, set bones, the works."

My heart skips a beat; could I do this, too? Is the life I wanted not all that far away, after all?

"So, yeah. It's a lot sometimes, and it can be really stressful, but I wouldn't trade it for anything. Seeing every season, almost every month, is pretty rare for people like us."

"Have you ever saved anyone?" I ask.

She takes a sip of her tea. "I did, once. There was a little boy we found in the middle of nowhere. I mean, there was just nothing as far as we could see, absolutely nothing. We had been dropped off at the ruins of this farmhouse to look for supplies and make sure it didn't have an entrance to the Underground we didn't know about. We didn't find any supplies, or an entrance for that matter, but there was a kid tucked under a mattress in the bedroom upstairs. He was little, no more than four at the time. He was unconscious, and I thought he was dead when I found him. There was a body, just skin and bone, really, on the floor next to him. Whoever it was probably starved trying to keep him alive. We called the car to come back, and I carried him home. His name is Drew. My parents adopted him, so I get to see him for holidays and everything. He's the baby brother I never had."

"You can adopt kids?"

"Well, yeah," she says, shrugging. "It happens pretty often, actually. Our line of work creates a lot of orphans."

"Huh. That was never a thing where I grew up. People always had at least one parent, usually two."

"What Border town are you from?" she asks, tucking a flyaway hair behind her ear. It's a gesture I recognize from Ava, yet Ruda doing it is... different.

"Carcera. Noah and Ava are from there, too." I refrain from saying her name, even though it bubbles up in my mouth.

"What was it like?"

I think of summer barbecues, evenings spent watching stars on the roof with my father, medical classes with my favorite teacher. Nights by the fireplace where the four of us would fall asleep in a pile of arms and legs before we got too old to be so close. Mel teaching me how to cook when my father died and my mother was too tired to get out of bed.

I'm taken back to Katie's father teaching me how to catch with a glove, both of us pretending it didn't rip out our hearts and it wasn't someone else's job. Noah offering to spend the night after my father died even though he knew it was completely against the law and knocking on my door at 3AM anyway. Climbing through Katie's window in the middle of the night to learn about the world before the Border. Trying on my father's only suit when I was finally big enough, realizing how much I looked like him, how well it fit me. Running through the snow like I had never run before. Bandaging Katie's arm in the woods. Hearing my mother scream as I left her behind.

"It was a lot different than here, I'll say that."

"Do you ever miss it?"

I nod and try to smile, but fail. "Every day."

<hr>

We sit in the coffee shop for a long while, until we're the last ones there and realize we should probably head home.

Ruda checks her watch on the way out. "Hey, we still have forty-five minutes to kill. Wanna head up to the library? There's some cool astronomy stuff up there, you'd like it."

I think of the girl with shorter hair, the one who showed me the library for the first time. Then I blink hard and see the girl in front of me, with long hair, and black eyes, not hazel. They're different people—they never even met—so it should be okay to go to the library with her. And she's right, I *would* like the astronomy books.

"I should probably be heading back. Noah's gonna be, ya know…" I trail off, kicking myself. Why can't I just enjoy this night with her?

Her face falls a little, but she tries to hide it, which I appreciate. "Oh, yeah, okay. No worries. See you at breakfast?"

I smile. "Yeah, see you then. This was… I had a lot of fun, Ruda."

"Me too, Chris." She gives me a quick hug, and I wonder if she can feel my heart thundering in my chest. When she pulls away, she smiles. "See you later."

"Bye."

We part ways, taking different routes upstairs.

I mull over this sort-of-date on the way back home, almost laughing, almost crying.

Inside, Noah immediately knows something's up. He's sitting on his bed reading, glowing in the soft light afforded by his new lampshade, dented though it is. He closes the book as soon as he sees my face. "How'd it go?"

I lean against the door for a moment to catch my breath. "It went well."

"Oh, c'mon," he groans, leaning forward in anticipation. "'It went well?' That's all I get?"

I nod and laugh a little, somewhat giddy. "Yeah, that's all you get."

<hr>

CECILIA PULLS me aside during warm-ups the next day. "Ashborrow, there's something I need to speak with you about."

I wipe my sweaty forehead and frown, watching my friends jog away. "Is everything alright?"

"Recently a crew of techs went to hack into some security cameras to inspect an area of the Underground we lost control of a few years ago. I want to show you some of the footage they found."

I follow her quietly to a laptop placed on a folding table, heart beating so loud it's a wonder no one else can hear it. My knees feel ready to collapse at any moment. *Please, no more surprises.*

"This isn't necessarily good news, but I thought that you should know."

"Should the others know, too?" I ask doubtfully.

She catches my eye as she spins the laptop for me to see. "Not yet."

Somehow, I know what I'm going to see before I do. In that moment of moving my eyes, I finally let myself hope for what I've been wanting for weeks. I expect soul-crushing defeat, but there she is, right there. She's skinny and soaking wet, tied to a dentist's chair and screaming her head off, but she is *alive.*

I glance up at Cecilia, choking on my own tongue. *Katie.*

"Is that... that's really...?" My voice dies out.

"Yes. This footage is from about two weeks ago."

It is impossible to breathe, but I force the word out anyway. "*Why?*"

"We're preparing a rescue mission for her and other missing soldiers. We're going in three weeks. The Head Trainer is allowing you to go, if you'd like."

My pulse skyrockets, and my lungs seem to implode upon themselves. Oh my God, *Katie.*

"Noah... Sam?"

"They can't come with us, but I will be there. Do you want to go?"

It's hard to hear above the ringing in my ears and difficult to see past the darkness clouding my vision. My stomach bottoms out of my chest with every breath. I nod fervently. "Yes, yes, of course I'll go."

She actually smiles, just a bit. "Good. I'll go tell the others."

I laugh with the most genuine happiness I've felt in days, weeks, a month and a half. My legs finally buckle, and I collapse onto the bleachers with my head between my knees. I am vaguely aware of Cecilia gathering the rest of my squad, of the silence following her voice.

I will hear her laugh again in three weeks, and be able to touch her face and her hair and her hands, oh, God, I will be able to hold her hands. Her cool fingers will be wrapped up in mine, and I'll throw heat into her the way I always have. She'll be right here, not just a wish, no longer a dream. Katie.

Then Noah is in front of me, hauling me to my feet and pulling me into the tightest hug I've felt in years. I cling to him like letting go will kill us both, and we laugh and sob together.

"She's coming *home!*" he shouts directly into my ear.

For once, I do not flinch. "She's coming home."

NOAH REGAINS his composure far more quickly than I do, so Cecilia sends me out for a walk. I wander the halls for a while, entrenched in memories so thick they're like walking through syrup. I pass a few people and pretty much ignore them until someone touches my arm.

"Hey, Chris, you alright?" Ruda asks, breaking me out of my sweet, hazy head.

I blink hard. "Yeah, I'm okay."

Her face blossoms into an expression of gentle worry. "You sure? You don't look so good."

"I have to tell you something," I say. "There was a girl I... cared about, before she... Katie, her name's Katie. She's still alive."

Her face falls for just a second before it transforms into a smile, black eyes lighting up with stars. I stare at her as she pulls me into a hug that I am too shocked to return. "That's amazing, Chris, oh my God! I'm so happy for you."

"You... you are?"

She pulls away but leaves her hands on my shoulders, studying me at arms' length. "Of course I am, how could I not be?"

"I just thought..." I don't know how to finish the sentence without insulting her, so I don't.

"Oh, Chris, no," she says softly. "I'm happy for you, and that doesn't change just because something almost happened between us. Getting her back is going to be amazing and, as your friend, I want to share that happiness."

"You do?"

She nods reassuringly. "Of course, if that's okay with you."

I am too choked up to tell her yes, absolutely, I want her to be a part of my life because I can't stand to lose anyone else, not even a girl I just met.

This time, I am the one to close the gap between us, draping my arms loosely around her back and resting my head on her shoulder. She stands tall and wraps her arms around me, rubbing my back as my breath stutters in my chest.

"I'm really happy for you," she murmurs.

"Thank you."

"When is she coming home?"

"Three weeks."

"That's good."

"I don't think I'm ready."

She hesitates before asking, "Why not?"

"Do you think we'll still recognize each other? Do you... do you think I'll still know her?"

She pulls away, and I feel cold where she was. "I do. You've known each other so long that it'll be impossible not to. You'll fall back together, I promise."

My throat is tight. "Okay."

She smiles. "Where are you guys working today? Can I walk you back?"

"I'd like that."

We meander through the halls, and Ruda tells me about her running regimen. I half-listen, thinking mostly of Katie. Her hair must be longer now, and she looked so small in that video. I wish we had a kitchen; I wish that I could cook for her.

We stop outside the door to the main gym. "Do you think she'll be scared of being touched?" I ask in a voice so small I want to kick myself for it.

Ruda pushes her dark hair away from her face. "She might be, for a little while. It depends on how touchy you were before, and how safe she feels around you, and what they did."

I think of all the times we came close to holding hands, all the nights we would lie entangled on the couch before we were old enough to know better. I think of falling asleep tucked against her on our first night here, and again the same way on our last. I remember how cool her skin is, how my hands always seem so big in comparison to hers, how I can feel my warmth spreading into her fingertips. I *remember*.

"Thank you," I say, opening the door to the gym. "For everything."

"Coffee tonight? You can tell me about her," she offers.

"Okay. I'll pick you up."

She waves and salutes me as a joke.

CHAPTER EIGHT

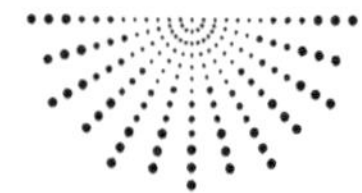

THERE IS nothing I want less in all this world than to go to the Summer Festival, but Ava begs me, and I can't say no to her. It takes me ten minutes to get ready; I don't feel like myself in this suit, made for both funerals and festivals, but then again, I've never felt like myself without Katie next to me. Ava seizes control of the bathroom, banishing Noah and me to wait outside.

"Thank you for coming with us," he says quietly, fiddling with his collar. "She didn't want to leave you alone tonight."

I nod. "Thanks for inviting me."

The air seems to thin out just then, as if there isn't enough oxygen for the both of us. I miss her so much that I can't even breathe; thinking about her being here in a few weeks only makes it harder.

Ava steps back into the room before I can suffocate, the bathroom light glowing softly behind her. Her dress is a pale yellow, dark hair curling gently around her makeup-softened eyes.

"Damn, you're really trying to kill me here, aren't you?" Noah says, standing in front of her. I can almost see the way she fills his lungs with air, the way his chest expands at the sight of her.

"Is that a compliment?" She grins at him, shining like the sun.

"Maybe." He smiles so hard his face might shatter, and presses a quick kiss to her lips. "Yes."

They remember me, then, and look back at me.

"You look good, Chris," Ava says softly, taking me in.

"You look lovely." I press a kiss to her cheek. "You ready to go?"

They walk down the stairs side by side in front of me. I can feel the empty space next to me as if she were here, as if by turning my head to look, she might appear. I glance over to see no one, just air. What did I expect?

I expected her. No, I *wanted* her.

The dining hall is decked out once again, this time with a summer theme. Paper palm trees and ocean waves—things most of us have never seen—decorate the walls, and the music beats in my chest.

We meet up with the rest of our squad, and they laugh and dance and chat while I hover in the background. Ava pulls me aside when everyone goes to the bar to get a drink. We step into the hallway, leaning against the wall opposite one another. My chest fills with air.

"I miss her, too," she says quietly, staring at the mismatched linoleum beneath her black flats.

"I need to tell you something, Ava," I say. My guilty conscience is too much for me to bear. "You have to promise me you won't tell Noah."

Her brow furrows, and she looks back up at me. "What's wrong?"

The words tumble from my mouth before I can stop them. "I almost kissed that girl, Ruda, out in the forest. On our Scouting mission. We almost kissed."

She chews on her bottom lip for a moment. "Why can't I tell Noah?"

"I feel horrible," I say, voice cracking. I clear my throat and try again. "I feel so awful about it, Ava. She's here tonight, and she's beautiful, but I feel so *sick*. She... *she's* still alive, and I nearly replaced her."

"Oh, Chris," she says, coming to stand next to me. "You didn't nearly replace her. Get that outta your head. She changed your life, and she'll always be special to you. And we're getting her back. It's okay to care about someone else, even for a little while. It doesn't... it doesn't minimize how much you care about Katie."

"Thank you, Ava."

She leans on me for a moment, and I lean back. "Of course. I'm not gonna tell Noah if you don't want me to."

"Thank you."

"Of course. Now c'mon, there's dancing to be done, and I took some painkillers before this that I am *not* wasting."

I follow her back into the dining hall and dance, even though I'm terrible, for a while. When the slow song kicks on, everyone pairs up—even Grif and Kela dance as friends—but I stand alone and sip a beer. It's disgusting, but it warms my stomach, and I can breathe a little better.

"Hey," a smooth voice from behind me says.

I turn to face the brunette to find that her tiny blue dress shows her off completely. I don't know if I'll ever be used to seeing so much skin—sure, sometimes the girls work out in their sports bras, but that's different. The dip in the baby-blue fabric nearly reaches her belly button, and her skin there is tan and smooth.

"Hey," I say placidly, keeping my eyes carefully on her face.

"You okay back here?" Ruda asks, leaning on the bar. She's so close that I can smell fruit and wine on her breath.

I nod. "Yep, just sitting this one out."

She extends a hand. "No one should have to sit this one out."

I follow her reluctantly onto the dance floor, trying to ignore how warm her hand is, how hot my stomach is now. I am engulfed in flames, as if I'm burning at the stake.

"You ever danced before?" she asks, finding us a space. I place my hands on her waist as if I've done it a thousand times, but my heart is thundering. I can't even see her dress in my peripheral as I keep my eyes trained on her face, just soft, amber skin.

"Just once," I say quietly.

She nods. "Just hold me there, like that"—she positions my hands lower—"and turn. You don't even have to pick your feet up."

She is staring at me with such intensity that the flames reach into my face. I don't want to look away from her, but I don't want her to be the one I'm looking at.

"I can't be with you. You know that, right?" I say quietly.

"I know," she murmurs. She is playing with the hair on the back of my neck. Her fingernails scratch me ever so delicately, and a shiver runs up my spine. "Did you ever play pretend, when you were little?"

I think back to the days I spent with my friends as doctors and teachers. We were knights in shining armor who took turns rescuing one another, all of us. Noah would get stuck in Katie's tree, and sometimes her father would have to save him for real.

"All the time," I reply.

"Let's play pretend." Her dark eyes are fixed on my mouth, filled with sniper-like focus.

"Are you going to kiss me?" I whisper.

"Do you want me to?"

I hesitate. The song ends, miraculously, and the trance is broken.

"Hey, I'll see you around," she says as if nothing ever happened. How does she do that?

"Coffee sometime this week?" I ask. "I'll pick you up."

"That'd be great," she says, and disappears into the crowd.

I find Grif, and we grab some cocktails and sit in a dark corner, watching the lights flash and bodies dance.

"The papaya is really good. You should try it," Grif says quietly. My drink has a bunch of chopped fruit in it, which helps it burn my throat less. "It's the orange one."

I stare at my drink, wondering why I have it, then remember how Ruda touched my neck. I take a sip before replying. "What even *is* papaya?"

"It's just this fruit we only grow every once in a while," he explains. "Just try it."

"You want me to eat something I've never even heard of?"

"Oh my *God*, you're fine. Eat the fruit."

I spear a piece with my small straw and tentatively bite it, and while it's good, it's not the best thing I've ever tasted. Griffin explains to me the history of the papaya, different ways people use it, and why he loves it, while I pick the other alcohol-soaked fruit out of my drink. I didn't know you could know so much about a fruit.

"My ancestors came from Thailand, and it can be really hard to express our culture here," he says. "My parents loved it whenever we had anything even *resembling* Thai food. That peanut noodle stir fry dish? They went nuts for it."

I settle for one question at a time. "What are ancestors?"

"They're the people that came before you. Like grandparents, but older."

The music changes to something with even heavier bass, so I have to shout my next question even though he's sitting right next to me.

"What happened to your parents?" I ask, trying to ignore the guilt biting at me for asking something so private, so loudly.

He looks down at the ripped blue tablecloth. "They're still alive; we just don't talk."

I think of how I would give anything to talk to my parents again. "Why not?"

"Chris, look, don't tell anyone, okay?" he shouts, looking around before continuing. "I was born a girl, but I've always felt like a boy. I'm transgender. When I told my parents I wanted to change my name, they kicked me out. I started going to a support group, and that's where I met Kela. She was one of the peer counselors, there for moral support, as an ally. When her parents found out I was homeless, they took me in; I haven't seen my parents in three years. My whole family moved to Level 7, which is pretty much all agriculture and farming stuff, since now they have no children to keep them here. I'm an only child."

"No siblings?" I think of how lonely my life would be without Mel. How lonely it *is* without her, now. The thought turns my stomach so much that my throat burns.

"Nope, just me. I don't mind though."

"So, biologically, you're..."

"Female."

"Is that why you don't change in the boys' locker room?"

"Yeah, that's why."

"Okay."

We go back to sipping our drinks; the heat licks down my throat and into my stomach, making me feel bolder.

"I have a question," I say after a few moments. "If you don't mind."

"Go for it," he replies.

"Why'd they kick you out? Like, why is it so bad that you're a boy?"

He pauses again, searching for the right words. "Well, they didn't believe I was being honest. They didn't understand why I didn't feel like a girl. I didn't want to do girl things, didn't like girl clothes. It just wasn't me, but they didn't—*couldn't*—understand. It's not their fault, really, although they didn't try very hard. I love my family, but I'm glad for how it worked out. I don't think I would've had the courage to leave on my own. Not at thirteen."

"I'm sorry."

He shrugs. "I'm not. It's past, and I have a family who calls me by my name, calls me 'son.' It's just not the one I was born into."

We go back to our drinks again, enjoying the silence. I eat all the papaya out of mine.

———

I GET coffee with Ruda four days later. I tell her what life was like in Carcera and what it was like to run away. She tells me what it was like to grow up here, how she learned to understand the war, and what it was like to visit the Surface for the first time. She makes me realize how much I took for granted.

"When are you going up there?" she asks during a lull in our conversation.

"A couple of weeks."

"And how long has she been gone?"

I take a sip of my water. "It'll be almost three months."

She nods. "It's summer now. It'll be warm up there."

I think back to sweltering days we spent lying in the shade by the lake, sweating half to death but with nowhere to go to escape the heat. "Yeah, it'll be hot. It used to get pretty brutal back in Carcera." I have to catch myself to avoid saying 'back home.'

She laughs a little even though it wasn't funny. "So, what did you think was outside of the Border?"

"What did I think was outside?" I echo. "That's a tough one. When I was younger, I thought it was outer space. The planets, the sun, you know. I thought there was no land outside, just emptiness."

She laughs again, and again I miss the joke. "What changed?"

81

I take another sip of my drink and pause, thinking about whether or not I want to tell her this. I'll never be close to her. She'll never know my favorite color (a perfect sky blue) or my favorite sweatshirt (the grey one with the toothpaste stain on it from my first day here). I'll never know her favorite stories, her passions, the things that keep her up at night. Her secrets. So, why not tell her one of mine, if it's about someone she'll never know?

"My father had this journal he wrote in every night. I found it after he died, and I read it. Apparently, he had overheard his boss talking to some guards about the forest beyond the Border. The Underground. It changed his whole life. Mine, too, clearly. But we never really talked about it."

"Why not?"

"He died a few days later."

"How?"

I nearly choke on my drink. Meliors—I'll never understand them. "The government blew up the building he worked in." The words tumble out before I can stop them, and I kick myself.

"Why?"

"I don't know." The lie is just as easy to say.

"But you think it was because of what he heard?"

My silence incriminates me more than any words could.

She is speechless, gaping at me with eyes wide as dinner plates. "Chris, oh my *God*, you have to tell someone, the world needs to *know*—"

"Why?" I ask.

"You have proof that they killed... how many people?"

"One hundred ninety-two."

"One ninety, *Jesus Christ, one ninety-two*? Holy shit."

I say nothing, wishing that we could change the subject.

"I'm so sorry," she continues, bulldozing past my unease. "But listen, you have to tell the Head Trainer about this."

"Why?"

"He can publish this, make it known," she explains. "It'll give people another reason to fight, a new outlook on this mess we're in. It's the raw, unfiltered truth that not a single Melior here could imagine."

"I'd rather not." My mother once told me that anything that comes before the word 'but' is nullified by it. Ruda is 'sorry, but.'

"Why not?" Ruda asks incredulously, eyebrows so high they're obscured by her pin-straight bangs.

"I never told anyone in Carcera. Not even my mother. I only told you because..."

"Because *why*?" she asks incredulously. "You're killing me here, Chris."

I feel the knife in my grip parting warm flesh, feel the blood pop out onto my fingers, warm and sticky. I hear him die again, and again, and again. Every night.

I stand abruptly and try not to spit the words at her. "It's not a figure of speech, Ruda. Some of us have actually *had* to kill people. Some of us don't want to again."

<hr>

CECILIA KEEPS me after training the next day for a meeting about Katie. We walk to the Head Trainer's office in silence.

"Ashborrow, thanks for meeting with us," he says when we arrive, beckoning me into his office. Ghosts float around me—the last time I was here, I was filling out funeral paperwork. Katie had long hair back then, nearly down to her waist. She would've been gold, so bright you could barely see her. But now... now we don't need that information, because we're going to get her back.

"Of course," I say. "Good to see you, sir."

"You as well, soldier," he says, shaking my hand. "Please, have a seat. This'll be very informal. Let's start by just talking about how you met Davis."

I sit, the glass coffee table separating us. "Well, we met when we were very young. Five, to be exact. We actually didn't get along at first, but Noah changed that."

He writes something down on a clipboard; I try not to be fazed.

"Noah's so friendly, he kind of brought her out of her shell. He did the same for me."

Again, something scrawled on the clipboard.

"The four of us have been friends since then, so about twelve years. We've always done everything together, including ending up here."

"And how *exactly* did you end up here? Forgive me, I don't have your intake paperwork."

I clear my throat. "Well, sir, when we were thirteen we had, kind of illegally, looked through an old diary that belonged to Davis's great-something-grandmother. We learned about what the world was like outside the Border, and I think from then on, we were all curious. Just after our Matching Ceremony, Ava and Katie tried to find out some information about Ava's uncle, who'd been arrested for preaching about what was outside the Border. I think he knew about the Underground, but I'm not sure how. They were found out, and guards tried to arrest Ava, who ran to my house. I ran to find Katie, while Ava got Noah to safety. Katie's brother helped her to gather her things and—"

"How old is Davis's brother?" he interjects, eyebrows raised.

"Uh, they're twins, sir. So, seventeen."

"Is he deceased?"

"Yes."

"Did you *see* him die?"

I look back and forth between them. "...no."

He and Cecilia glance at one another, a knowing look, one of both fear and epiphany.

"Is that... what does that mean?" I ask slowly.

The Head Trainer clears his throat. "Well, it could mean a lot of things. Davis is being kept at a facility near the coast. Up until now, we weren't sure why, but we believe she is being experimented on. If her brother is not confirmed as deceased, they could both be there."

The room begins to tilt, and my chest tightens. My voice seems to come from somewhere off to my left. "She's being... Lucas could be *alive*?"

"Possibly, yes."

"Why would Ankou do this?"

Cecilia shoots the Head Trainer a look, the 'I got this' expression I recognize from my own mother.

"Do you know why you were born within a Border?"

"Because that's where my mother lived?"

She nearly smiles, and then begins. "Fugent, the country Ankou rules, the country of the Surface, is an imperial one. They colonize other countries to take advantage of their resources. They need an army for that, so at birth, every child from Border towns has some DNA extracted from them to create a clone. These clones are used as a military force to imperialize other countries. Do you understand?"

"That... that's insane," I say. "You're kidding, right? You've got to be kidding me."

"I'm not," she says, voice hard but deep eyes soft as the night sky. "That's why you're kept in the hospital until your first birthdate. If there's a problem with the clone, they need a new DNA sample to create another one."

"So, there's another *me*?" I say. "Just like, walking around somewhere?"

She nods. "He's probably in training right now. When he turns twenty, he'll be sent to a permanent station abroad."

"He has my... face?"

"Yes."

"My eyes? My hands?"

"All of you."

"What about this scar on my chin?"

"Well, no. That occurred after you were born, so he won't have that."

"Does he have my personality?"

"In a way, yes. You're a product of your environment, and you two were raised very differently, but genetics do have a role in determining personality. You would recognize facets of yourself in him."

"Okay... okay," I say slowly. "So, he has my face and my soul and is in training, too. They have Katie captured because Lucas might be alive. How do those things connect?"

"If Lucas is presumed dead in Carcera, and Katie is, too, then that gives Ankou the ability to study them without anyone knowing. Everyone in Carcera believes them to be dead, so no one questions why they're gone. Ankou now has a rare opportunity to study original siblings, raised *in* a Border town, without question."

"But what if Lucas *is* dead?"

"They'll still want to study her," the Head Trainer interjects. He shoots Cecilia a semi-apologetic look. "It's rare for Ankou to obtain an original person. And they can also test her against her clone—study their personalities, physical differences, that sort of thing."

I sit in silence for a moment, trying to process it all. "How many people are out there with the same face as her? How many Katies are there?"

"Just two. Ankou only creates one soldier from each Border child in case there's a problem with one."

"And how do we know that it's her in the video? That it's not her clone?"

"Why would they torture their own soldier?" Cecilia asks, dark eyes boring into me. "Come on, Ashborrow, I thought you were smarter than this."

"*Smarter than this?*" I spit. "You just *obliterated* my worldview."

"That's going to happen a lot in your time here," the Head Trainer cuts in again. "I suggest you steady yourself, soldier."

I take a deep breath, thinking of the video Cecilia showed me. Katie, strapped to a chair, screaming. "What kinds of testing are they doing?"

"I think that's something we can discuss at a later time," he says. "This meeting is to discuss your past with Davis."

"What did they do?" I rise to my feet. I stand behind my chair, gripping the back so they can't see how hard my hands are shaking.

"Ashborrow—" Cecilia begins, but the Head Trainer holds up a hand to stop her. He leans forward in his chair, staring me in the eyes with a look of hard steel.

"There's probably a lot of psychological testing, studying nature vs. nurture. They most likely take blood samples and brain scans, and do some genetic testing. They'll also be trying to get information from her about us, and about Carcera. What she knew about the Underground before arriving here, and how she knew it," he explains, voice steely calm.

"So, she's a lab rat?" My knees tremble; I wish I'd stayed seated.

"Yes."

I nod, processing. After a few moments I sit back down, take a deep breath, and say, "What else do you want to know about her?"

"Ashborrow, you don't have to do this today," Cecilia says. She's glaring at the Head Trainer as she speaks, voice clipped. "I know this has been hard enough already."

"I'm okay," I say. "What else do you need to know?"

The Head Trainer gives me a look of approval; I feel a twinge of pride in my gut, mixed with the horror and fear. "Everything."

I DON'T TELL anyone about the meeting, not even Noah. Maybe if I don't tell anyone, it won't be true. Maybe if I keep my mouth shut, they won't do this to her, they won't take her blood or look inside her brain. The thought of white gloves on her skin makes me physically ill more than once over the next several days.

Ruda and I don't meet for coffee again for a while. I come down with a nasty cold and she goes on a brief Scouting mission. She calls after to tell me it was warmer than it was when we were up there together and that she wished I could've been there. I let it go to voicemail. I don't have a voice to talk with, anyway.

The next two weeks pass quickly. I recover from my cold but manage to give it to Grif, and he develops a mild case of pneumonia. He goes to stay with Kela's parents while recovering, and I miss him in training. Cecilia centers our classroom studies around common mental illnesses that soldiers develop, like PTSD and anxiety. I try to listen, to learn for Katie's sake, but it kills me to hear all the terrible things that might still happen to her.

The night before we're due to leave, Cecilia sits me down for a briefing.

"We haven't had any more proof that she's alive since the footage I showed you," Cecilia says. We're drinking coffee at the same table as usual.

"We're still going, right?" I ask, worry seeping into my voice and veins.

"Of course. We have recent evidence that several other soldiers are alive, but not for Katie."

"Davis," I correct.

"Right. Davis. We're still going to look for her, but there is a chance that..." She trails off, hoping I will catch what she's implying. I do, but I want to hear her say it.

"Just say it."

"I might be carrying a body out of there, and I want you to prepare yourself for that."

"But you might not be."

"Ashborrow, either way, I want you to know that you will not like what you see. It's going to be ugly. People will die; people may already be dead. This is not a simple Scouting mission."

"Okay. I can handle it." I don't even know if *I* believe that, let alone if she will.

"I know you can." Well, that's surprising.

"Any news of Lucas?"

She shakes her head. "We don't think—"

"I understand." No news of Lucas this entire time, no footage to show he's alive, even with the tech squads unveiling more and more by the day. I never allowed myself to hope for him, so this doesn't hurt so terribly. I shudder.

"How long will it take?" I ask quickly, before I can ruminate on what a calloused monster I've become. He was one of my closest friends.

"We're probably going to be out there for four or five days, transit time included. Pack a change of clothes for sleeping and a toothbrush. Some hair gel and extra socks wouldn't hurt, either."

"Do I have permission to leave my dorm before Wakeup?"

"For this, yes. Anyone stops you, just tell them you're with me."

"How long is the drive?"

"About twelve hours. They're keeping them in a part of the Underground we lost control of. It's by the coast, so they're protected on one side by the sea. We'll be camping right on the sand so we are, too," she explains.

"Doesn't that expose us?"

"We've mapped it out. There are some ruins right on the water, so we can take shelter there if necessary. Odds are they won't even know we're coming."

"Why not?"

"We've never done anything like this before."

I think about this for a moment, the severity of her words weighing heavily on me. "Okay," I finally say, nodding. "Well, let's not screw it up."

She smiles. "Cheers to that. Go get some rest."

"You, too."

We part ways, and I jog upstairs. My bag is already packed except for my toothbrush and deodorant, so I don't really have anything to do. My feet lead me to Ruda's room.

"Hey," I say when she opens the door.

"Chris, hi," she says, startled. "Do you wanna come in?" she asks.

"I can't, I'm just stopping by. I leave in the morning."

Her eyebrows scrunch together beneath her bangs, which have gotten longer since the last time I saw her, when she told me to expose my father's secret to our whole world. The thought still makes my lungs burn. "It's time already?" she asks.

"Yeah."

"That's amazing. I'm so—"

"I'm scared, Ruda." I surprise myself by admitting it.

Her face falls. "Are you sure you don't want to come in? My sister isn't home yet."

I relent, and she opens the door wide to let me in. Her room is shaped like mine, but there are green blankets on the beds and a few pictures taped to the walls. Their nightstands are different, too, and the drawer pulls are rusted—salvaged, like everything else in our lives. Like us.

"What's on your mind?" she asks gently, perching on the edge of her bed. "Come sit, I don't bite."

I sit opposite her. "What if she isn't alive?"

"Then we're gonna help you through that. Even if you bring home a body, that's better than nothing. At least we'll be able to have a funeral and say goodbye."

I nod, wondering why she said 'we.'

"They're not going to let anyone hurt you. You probably won't even have to fight."

"That's the problem. I'll have nothing to do while they're there. I'll just have to wait."

"It's better that way. I know it doesn't feel like it, but it is. If you go in there and all hell breaks loose, it would be a disaster. You'd be a mess, especially if…"

"I know. If she isn't…"

"I really hope that she is."

"Yeah. Me, too."

We sit in silence for a moment, unsure of what to do or say.

"Can I meet her?" she finally asks.

"Of course. I'd love for you to meet her."

"She sounds like a very special girl."

"Believe me, she is."

"What are you most looking forward to?"

"Seeing her smile," I answer quickly. "Or just her eyes, really. I've never met someone who can express so much with just their eyes; it's amazing. And seeing her dance. She's terrible, really is, and she says it's because she's knock-kneed, but I don't buy it. But it's *fun* to dance with her, because I don't have to be good, either. She's the only person that I feel like I can be bad at things with."

Ruda smiles. "I'm really excited for her to come home."

I grin back, only a little choked up. "Me, too."

<hr>

NOAH AND AVA give me a pep talk and two going-away gifts that night. Ava hands me two strips of the photos the four of us took one night down in the Activity Center, back when Katie was here. We barely even fit in the photo booth enough to take them. In the first one we're holding up finger-guns, in the second we're mid-laugh, in the third we're smiling, and in the fourth Noah and Ava are kissing while Katie and I stare at each other across them, happy but confused.

"I asked Cecilia to make a copy of this for all of us," Ava explains. "Can you bring Katie's to her?"

"Of course," I say, hugging her to hide the fact that she's nearly brought me to tears.

Noah quickly explains that his gift is less sentimental, more for practical use. He hands me a small portable music player and two pairs of earbuds.

"I loaded it up with a bunch of songs for the ride," he says. "Sam helped me pick it out."

"Dude, how did you afford this?" I ask, marveling at the little box in my hands.

"Turns out one of the hair salons needed someone to wash hair, so I picked up a couple shifts when you were sick. Apparently, I'm not too shabby at it, so I made good tip money, too."

"Thank you so much," I say, pulling them into a group hug. "I honestly don't know what I did to deserve you guys."

"I think it's the other way around," Ava murmurs. She is sandwiched between me and Noah, the most natural fit that there's ever been.

After either a second or an eon, we break apart. Noah is teary-eyed, although he swipes a hand across his face to try and hide it. Ava places a manicured hand on his back, surprisingly the most confident of the three of us. I think back to the whiny thirteen-year-old I once knew, and my heart swells with pride at her strength.

"You leave at 5:00, right?" she asks.

"Yeah, around then," I reply. "I'll probably be up at 4:30."

"How are you going to wake up in time?"

"Cecilia gave me a timer." By saying that, I remind myself to turn the small dial until it's set to go off.

"You should get some sleep," Ava suggests.

"I'm fine," I lie, even though my eyes are drooping. My body may be tired, but my mind is racing along at breakneck speed. I could be holding her hand in less than two days, cold or colder still.

"Go to sleep." Arguing is futile; I can see it in the way her soft features have hardened into edges of steel. "We all know what happened the last time we didn't get enough sleep before going to the Surface."

The silence is filled by memories of the two women we lost that night.

"Do you want me to wake you guys when I leave?" I finally ask.

They glance at each other and nod hastily. "Please do," Noah says.

We climb into our beds, Ava being the nice one and getting up to turn off the light. She is the first to drift off, held tightly in Noah's arms.

"Chris?" Noah whispers into the darkness.

I roll over to face him. "Yeah?"

"Are you scared?" The whites of his blue eyes are showing; he looks as if he's seen a ghost.

"No," I lie.

"You sure?"

"...No. Are you?"

"Yeah," he says quietly. "What if... she doesn't come back?"

"She's coming back," I say definitely.

"What if...?"

A lump forms in my throat. "Then... we have a funeral. Either way, it's better than what we've been living with. It's an answer." I don't know if I really believe that, but I have nothing else to say.

"Okay."

"Can you do me a favor while I'm gone?"

He cranes his head to look at me. "Sure, anything."

I crack a smile to reassure him. "Keep everyone in check."

"You got it, boss." He grins, too. "Goodnight."

"Night."

CHAPTER NINE

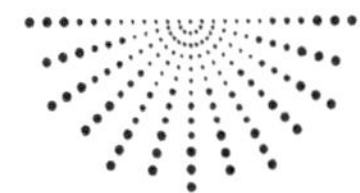

I'm walking next to Katie, and although I know it is a dream, I don't care to wake up. We're on our way to school in Carcera, a route so familiar that it is ingrained into the soles of my feet. Her hand is cool in mine, and the skin of her forearm is smooth as water.

Wanna race? she asks.

Sure. All the way?

She smiles, an expression sweeter than the first warm day of spring. *All the way.*

She lets go of my hand and sprints away, leaving me to chase her. Her hair, down to her waist again, flows down her back as we run. She makes a wrong turn, but I follow her anyway, confused now about where we're going. Trees spring up from the roads, and rotten snow banks swell against the sides of buildings. Suddenly I am blindsided by a wall of heat, and when I look towards it, she is waiting for me in front of the burning factory where my father was killed.

You're going to face a lot more than this if you're going to catch me. When I look at her face, I realize she is thirteen again, just a young girl standing in a raging inferno. My nose burns with the scent of smoke and charred flesh. I could never forget that smell.

You coming? she asks.

My tongue is cemented to the roof of my mouth; I cannot move my feet. I want to run to her, pull her away from the fire that is melting her face, at least tell her that I'm trying to save her. I can't move.

I want you to know that you will not like what you see. It's going to be ugly. People will die, she says, even as her teeth melt down her chin, ivory ink on blistering red lips. *Are you ready?*

I finally manage to break open my mouth, so desperate to reach her, but a shrill alarm sounds in the distance.

See you there.

I jolt awake and slam my hand on the timer before it can wake Noah and Ava. My whole body is covered in sweat and I'm shaking like a leaf, but I don't have time for a shower. I lie still for a moment, trying to catch my elusive breath before getting ready. I wash up and get dressed, tie my boots firmly, and glance at my sleeping friends. They are too peaceful for me to wake them any earlier than necessary, so I scribble a goodbye note on a piece of paper and slip out of the room with my bag slung over one shoulder. Guilt claws at my stomach, but I can't talk to them, not now.

The stairwells are silent as I walk down to the dining hall. I've been out during quiet times before, but never alone. It's an eerie feeling, like being a fish that suddenly darts into open water. I find myself glancing over my shoulder every few minutes.

Cecilia is waiting for me by the door to the dining hall. "You have everything?" she asks.

"All set." I hand her the timer. "Thanks for letting me come."

"Don't thank me yet, and don't make me look like an idiot for letting you come with us, either."

"Of course."

We wait for a few minutes as the other trainers arrive, men and women I've never met but who Cecilia has described to me in detail. I am introduced to Chip, Kai, Megan, Rory, Albert, Nadia, and Steven. The youngest is Steven, who still has a round, boyish face, and Chip is the oldest. His hair is peppered, and the stubble on his face is the whitish-gray of rock salt.

"We're all here?" Kai asks. Her young voice catches, but she carries her petite frame with the confidence of a decorated war hero.

Chip nods, and wordlessly, the nine of us start walking through the small side tunnel I've come to know well.

"So, you're still a soldier, right?" Steven asks me quietly. We are walking side-by-side in the back of the group. I have to almost double my pace to keep up with his long-legged stride.

"Yeah," I reply.

"You've got to be really good for the Head Trainer to let you come. What's your skill?"

I glance up at him in the half-light, still-rounded cheeks and eyes that haven't wrinkled yet. He can't be much older than I am, but he speaks as though he has decades of experience. "Cecilia didn't tell you?"

He looks at me, tripping over his own feet and cursing softly. "About...?"

"One of the prisoners was—*is*—my girlfriend, best friend, kinda..." I trail off. "It's complicated."

"Oh." He pauses for a long while before continuing. "I know the feeling. My friend and I had something similar. It was a mess. She died, of course, and I'm married to someone else now."

"Sorry to hear."

"About the marriage or her?" He laughs. "'Cause sometimes both seem like a damn shame."

"Both, then," I reply, half-laughing as we emerge into the brightly lit bay.

Cecilia and I find ourselves in a large truck with Chip, Megan, and Steven. The driver must know Chip, because he sits up in the front with her and they immediately begin chatting. From what Cecilia told me, he doesn't seem like much of a conversationalist, but they exchange pleasantries as we get settled. Phrases like "how are the kids?" and "how's Dom's back?" are thrown around.

Cecilia and Steven sit on either side of me; Steven has extra blankets and a neck pillow for the ride. I wish I'd had that idea. These bench seats are the furthest thing from comfortable (I'm also expecting motion sickness), although I'm a fan of the ample leg room.

Soon we're on our way; Megan and Cecilia make quiet conversation. They grow silent as we near the exit of the tunnel, as do Chip and the driver. The light outside is barely brighter than the darkness in here, but the world turns slightly blue, like we've sunk to the bottom of the pool. Chip is holding a gun. The only sound is static from a walkie-talkie, but Megan turns the dial down and then all I can hear is the sound of my own heartbeat and the rumble of the tires over gravel.

We emerge from the tunnel into a silent dawn. There are no birds, no trees. The wet, silver grass rustles in a light breeze, and the blueish-gray clouds puff out from the bottom, suffocating us. Humidity hits my skin like a blanket. The horizon is clear and green, and the air smells of wet grass and electricity.

Without saying a word, we all relax, thankful again for our safe emergence onto the Surface. Steven falls asleep shortly after we leave the tunnel, and I wish not for the first nor the last time that Katie was here. Blue and purple mountains loom in the distance, turning a fiery orange and pink as the sun rises and burns off the bulbous clouds. For a long while, I can't figure out how we'll cross the peaks, but eventually the truck thuds onto a paved road (a real, paved road!) and climbs steadily into the foothills.

I listen to music on my MP3 player and nibble on one of the bagels from the bag Megan brought. We weave through the mountains, and the motion makes me a little queasy, so I lie down on the floor for a dreamless nap.

My hip aches when I wake up, alone. The air hangs heavy and damp, suffocating my skin, silencing everything around me.

Immediately my heart begins pounding, and I rise slowly, taking in the state of the vehicle. Everyone's personal belongings are gone, but the guns are still here. The air is warm, smelling faintly of campfire smoke.

When I peer through the window, I relax—the rest of the crew are gathered around a small fire, roasting sausage links that are definitely not real pork.

I hop down from the car and join them, stretching on my way over.

"Good morning, sleeping beauty," Steven jokes, waving a stick with a burnt link on the end. "Here, you hungry?"

"No, thanks," I reply, trying not to gag. "How long was I asleep?"

"About an hour," Cecilia says. "It's good that you got some rest. We need you at the top of your game."

I start to ask if she's changed her mind, if I'll actually be joining the fight, but I bite my tongue.

"You alright?" Megan asks. "You look a little green."

"I get carsick," I admit sheepishly.

"Go for a walk, stretch your legs," Steven says. "It helps. Just stay within shouting distance."

I glance at Cecilia; she nods in confirmation. I wander past the trucks and think about grabbing a gun, knowing that's a good idea, but decide against it. Instead, I kick at pebbles along the road and walk until the sound of their conversation fades away.

Around the bend, the view explodes in front of me. I perch on a metal railing overlooking the valley, awed by the vastness of it all. Immediately below me is a forty-foot drop and then the river (I ignore my fear of heights as best as I can), and ten yards behind me is a sheer face of stone. The midmorning sun beats down as I stare across the narrow valley, taking in the trees and sky, jagged mountains that tear into the blue with granite fangs. I've never seen something so grand in all my life.

My fingers pry the slip of pictures out of my boot, and I stare down at them, at us, at her. She's absolutely gorgeous, even in the grainy photos that can't capture her eyes, or do her smile even a bit of justice. In the last picture, we are staring at each other across Ava and Noah. If she'd been sitting next to me, I would've kissed her. I wonder why I didn't just lean across them and kiss her anyway; I remember wanting her desperately. I wonder why two feet once seemed too far to reach for her.

I look out across the valley, west at the miles between us, and vow that no distance will ever be too great for me again.

CHAPTER TEN

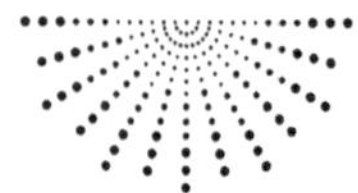

WE TUMBLE down from the mountains only an hour after our stop, winding down the cracked switchbacks with dizzying speed. My heart aches with missing the rest of my squad, but I reassure myself knowing that every mile brings me closer to Katie.

The blazing afternoon fades to a slightly-less-stifling evening, and new mountains loom in the distance, softer in the twilight. All I can do is watch the landscape fly by; it feels like a miracle to witness this.

"We're gonna keep driving through the night," Cecilia says to me when the driver turns on the headlights. Megan is asleep on the bench across from us, one arm tucked under her head as a makeshift pillow. Her long blond braid curls around her throat like a noose, but her angled features are soft in sleep.

"We'll arrive at the shore under the cover of darkness and camp somewhere hidden. Then we'll try to wait out the next day and night if we can, gather information about the area. The next morning is when we'll go in, before dawn. You'll stay in the truck."

"Aw, c'mon, let him come. It's personal," Steven protests.

Cecilia stares at him as if he's grown another head. "Which is exactly why he *can't* come with us. He'll be too emotional."

"I can still fight," I interject.

"No."

Steven and I glance at each other; I send him a silent thanks for trying.

"How long will you be in there?" I ask.

"It's hard to tell. It shouldn't be more than four hours, and no less than one. If it's longer than that, something's wrong."

"What do I do if...?"

She looks at me hard, dark eyes absorbing the night as it grows close. "The gas is on the right, the brake is on the left, and the coordinates for home will be plugged in for you. The wheel controls steering—turn it right to go right, left to go left. Don't forget to put it in drive. If we're not back after ten hours, take whatever you can and go. Understand?"

I nod, even though the thought of driving home all alone makes my throat swell with panic. I can't fathom having to explain what happened, reckoning with the idea that perhaps I am cursed to be the survivor of missions gone wrong. "Okay. How many people are you bringing out?"

"Three," she replies.

"I can be ready with medical supplies. Are they all being... experimented on?"

"I... yes. Have the inside of the cars prepped. If it's bad, then we're getting the hell out of here as soon as we're back, so you're in charge of making sure camp is clear."

I nod.

"Why'd you bring him, again?" Chip asks gruffly from the front seat. The car lurches as we climb into the mountains, and I involuntarily slide down the bench towards Steven.

"His best friend—"

"Girlfriend," I say, shooting her an apologetic look for interrupting and then leaning around her to talk to Chip. "My girlfriend is one of the captured soldiers."

"Hmph," is all Chip says for a moment. "You don't think a body would take a toll on him?" he finally asks Cecilia, as if I'm not right here.

"No, it definitely would, but they've all gotta see it at some point, right?" she replies, staring at me as the words leave her mouth.

It is at that precise moment that I realize how serious this is for everyone involved, not just me. It's one thing to take supplies from an abandoned city, but it's a lot harder to steal back prisoners from a research lab.

"Yeah, I guess they do," Chip says. "Kid, you ready for this?"

"As ready as I'll ever be, sir," I say, hoping that that's a good enough answer.

Steven elbows me and nods reassuringly when I look at him. The moon rises through the window behind him.

I DOZE on the floor for a while, hovering in the middle zone between sleeping and waking. I am faintly aware of the air itself humming with tension when the truck slows to a crawl.

The driver murmurs something to Chip, and he relays it to Cecilia. "It's a Border," he says sharply. His words drag me suddenly back to consciousness, and my heart begins to hammer against my ribcage. Even though I know we're hundreds of miles from Carcera, my gut screams *home, home, home.*

"I know, I'm not an idiot," she snaps, not one to take anybody's attitude.

"Sure acting like one." He says it under his breath, but she catches him anyway.

"What's *that* supposed to mean?"

"You brought a *kid* with us."

Her voice grows even icier, colder than I've ever heard it. "In the Underground, he's being asked to risk his life for our cause. In his Border town, he was Matched. Please explain to me how he's still a child when he's considered an adult in the only two homes he's ever known."

"He's not even a year into this."

"And he's watched his whole family die."

"All the more reason for him to be staying home."

"This is as much his war as it is ours."

"Then why don't you let him fight with us?"

"I want him to be better than we are, not to die before he gets the chance."

Chip pauses, thinking. "What makes him so special? I've never seen you ask Arthur for a favor before."

She laughs quietly. "I've never needed to. Here's the thing about Chris: he's just another soldier from just another Border town. But nothing shuts him down, and I mean *nothing*. When they got here, he was the most reserved out of the four of them, and now he's a leader. Hell, I don't need to be there half the time, even now. Remember when you lost Kara?"

He forces the words through gritted teeth. "Yes, I remember."

"It nearly killed you, right?"

"Nearly."

"And you were, what, twenty-three?"

"Twenty-two. I get it, Ceci."

She presses on, undeterred. "He's seventeen. This loss has shredded him; he wouldn't be human if it didn't. But he hasn't let it show to anyone, at least not while we're working. He's taken care of everybody else, kept the squad together when... when I couldn't. The rest of us are barely hanging on but he's still managing to thrive. PRs on everything, lightyears ahead in classroom studies. He deserves this more than anybody else I've ever met."

"And what if she dies? You're not worried that that'll be the thing to shatter him?"

The truck picks up speed again, leaving the Border behind.

"We all have to break at some point. It's part of being one of us."

He says nothing, and I'm nearly asleep by the time she speaks again, voice softer than before. "Can I be completely honest, Chip?"

"When are you not?" He says it with a hint of care, like a father to a daughter.

"I don't think she's alive. We haven't gotten anything from tech in weeks. You saw that video—she was a wreck. She's tough, she really is, but I don't know if anyone could survive much more of that."

I turn my music up to drown out Chip's response and sink gratefully back into unconsciousness.

I JOLT awake when we run something over. The impact nearly sends me rolling across the floor, but I catch myself and sit up, rubbing my sore neck.

"Just a curb," the driver says. "Sorry, guys."

"Where are we?" I mutter to Cecilia.

"We're here," she replies. "We're gonna camp out under this boardwalk. We'll be pretty hidden, and they don't come down to the water anyway."

I stare through the windshield at the abyss of blackness in front of us. "Is that...?"

"The Pacific Ocean," Meg says as she re-braids her hair. "Largest one on Earth. Only thing between us and Japan is Hawaii, but that's underwater, now. I mean, Japan probably is, too, who knows, but—"

"Meg, let it sink in. He's never seen the ocean," Cecilia says. Her voice is soft, that of a mother trying not to wake her child.

The car rolls to a halt beneath the remnants of a wooden boardwalk. I am the first to climb carefully down, unsure of the bouncy sand beneath my feet.

"Take off your shoes," Steven says, sleep resting at the edge of his voice. I can barely see him in the dark, but his blond curls act as a halo. "It's easier to walk barefoot."

I quickly untie my boots and peel off my socks. The sand is cool on the bottoms of my feet, and I dig my toes into it.

"You can walk down to the water, if you want," Kai says from behind me. The other car has parked next to ours. Kai, Rory, Albert, and Nadia all look exhausted but happy to be here.

"I can?" I ask, glancing at Cecilia, who has joined me on the sand.

She nods. "Yeah, I'm gonna come with you, if that's alright."

"Yeah, of course."

She tugs off her boots, and we begin to walk across the beach. The waves crash roughly on the shore, filling my ears with an eternal shushing sound, and salt burns in my nose.

"This is the end," she says quietly as we arrive at the water. "Crazy, isn't it?"

I glance at her doubtfully. Her silhouette is defined by the dunes and stars at her back. "There's nothing else out there?"

"Not for almost five thousand miles."

"How long was our trip?"

"Six hundred."

"Holy *shit*."

She laughs as I stare out at the horizon, which is only discernible by the end of the stars. The water laps at my feet and I jump, and Cecilia laughs again, wading in up to her ankles.

"It's beautiful," I say quietly.

"It makes you feel small."

In Carcera, I always felt too big. The Border wrapped around my life, always tightening. Now, the stars explode in every direction, so big they could swallow me whole. I wish she were here to experience this expanse, too.

We stand in silence, staring out across the water. I wonder what lies beneath the surface, where I would go if I could go anywhere. Would I try to cross this ocean, just to see what was on the other side? Would I stay here anyway, despite it all? Do I believe in this war? Am I really thriving in it like Cecilia says I am?

"C'mon, we should go unpack," Cecilia says after a long while, voice sweet and low in contrast to the rasping waves.

"Can I come back here?"

"Not in daylight," she replies. "I'm sorry."

"It's okay. I understand."

We walk back to the cars and set up camp, nestling our sleeping bags between the cars and a sand dune. Chip tells me that he's taking the first watch and orders the rest of us to settle in for the night, resolving to do a little scouting in the morning.

I lie on my back in my sleeping bag, a little too warm, a little too sandy. The stars peek between the rotting slats of wood above me, and Kai snores abrasively not five feet away. All at once I feel both too big and infinitely small, sticky and spinning.

I climb slowly out of my sleeping bag under Chip's disapproving gaze.

"Go to sleep," he mutters.

"I can't," I say. "Can I sit up there?" I gesture to the unoccupied hood of the second car.

"Fine."

I climb up carefully, trying to be quiet. The blue light of the full moon illuminates strips of sand and sleeping bags where it slides between the boards.

"Will the moon be a problem tomorrow night, with visibility and all?" I ask.

"No more than the sun usually is," he grumbles.

We sit in silence for a few minutes. I stare out at the abyss, softened by the moonlight, and try to rub the sand off my feet. I wonder how the moon could possibly be as much trouble as the sun.

"I heard you talking to Cecilia when you thought I was asleep," I say quietly. "You really don't want me here, do you?"

He sighs heavily. "Kid, that's not what I meant."

I raise my eyebrows. He won't let me go, anyway, so what's the point of convincing him to like me?

"I'm assuming you also heard that it's reasonable to believe that your... your girlfriend, she may not be alive. You shouldn't have to see that at such a young age."

I think of the silence of the ride home, her body lying still when it should be full of light, laughter. Smelling of rot instead of lavender, shroud over her face, arms crossed over her chest. If we can even retrieve her body. If she hasn't already been ripped to pieces.

I forge on, anyway. "You saw one when you were twenty-two."

"Doesn't mean you should see one at seventeen."

"Who was Kara?" I've been hanging out with Sam and Ruda too much.

He sighs again, and his previously-wired shoulders sink back into place. "She was my wife. We were in the same squad, so the Head Trainer himself advised us not to get married, but we were young and stupid and did it anyway. Never told anyone but our families in case he tried to transfer one of us. I couldn't bear to be away from her, not even for one day of classroom studies. We were married for six months before getting sent to steal supplies from an agricultural Border town. We were to take seed packets, loads of them, and fertilizer if we could find it. Now, I know you may not think you can fall in love with someone so young, but—"

"You absolutely can," I interject. He scowls at me. "Sorry."

"I did. I loved her like I never loved anyone else. But when we went to the Surface, we were caught. They opened fire and we got the hell out of there. They kept shooting as we drove away, and Kara looked out through the back window to see if they were after us. She got shot in the head, died instantly. I... uh, I held her the whole way home."

"I'm sorry," I say quietly.

He nods. "Me too, kid. Me, too. So, this girl we're rescuing, who is she?"

"Best friend, above all else. When my father died, it was hers who taught me how to be a man. Tie a tie, catch with a glove, you know, everything you're supposed to teach your kid. When we weren't Matched... I realized I was disappointed. And then we ran away, and she got hurt, and that was horrendous. And then we were here, free. I was too nervous, and we never really were together, and then she was gone."

"And what about her brother?"

I had nearly forgotten the possibility of rescuing Lucas—the guilt gnaws at my chest. "We were friends, too. But I'm sure you know there's no evidence that he's... even here. I'm pretty sure he died when we left Carcera."

"I'm sorry."

"So am I."

"How'd you lose her?" Chip asks gruffly after a moment's pause, looking out to sea.

I sigh, trying to make it sound clinical for fear of sobbing in front of someone I'm trying to prove my strength to. "We were sent to kidnap soldiers of Ankou. Probably to torture them, if you think about it. We got caught, too. Two of our squadmates were a floor below us and the helicopter was coming to extract us from the roof. One of our squadmates, Ava, was stabbed in the back. Noah had a gash on his face. I had some training in the ER, so I was trying to patch them up as best as I could, and Katie went to get the others on the lower floor. When she got there, they had already been caught, and she was captured when they tried to escape."

"And the other two?"

"Escaped, but one lost her leg. Also my fault. I was covering the helicopter and I shot before I saw who I was shooting."

"I'm sorry, kid."

"Me, too."

We sit in comfortable silence then, staring out across the moonlit beach and over the ocean. I search for the horizon, but I can't find it.

"You never remarried?" I ask quietly. "Nobody else, after her?"

"Nobody else after her," he echoes.

I think long and hard about it. They are who we could be years from now, one long dead and the other still mourning.

I remind myself that I tried to move on. I tried, but I'm not meant to.

"Do you think you can fall back in love after somebody dies?" I ask. "The same kind of love, again?"

"Yeah, I think so," he says. "If you try, if you really *want* to, it's doable. But it'll never be quite as easy as the first time, never as simple. I never wanted anyone after Kara. Still don't. I had my chance at love and that was enough. But if we don't get your girl back, you have to ask yourself if that was enough for you, or if you'll want more."

I remember Mel eating cookies fresh out of the oven. She had one, then another, then snatched a third as she walked out the door to go to her friend's house. When I complained that she was going to eat all of them before our mother got home, she just laughed and said, "It's human nature to always want one more. Don't worry, you'll understand once you've tried one."

I didn't understand back then, but now I do. It *is* human nature to always ask for five more minutes, to always want at least a little more. Except now, I don't need just a little more. I need her for the rest of our lives.

CHAPTER ELEVEN

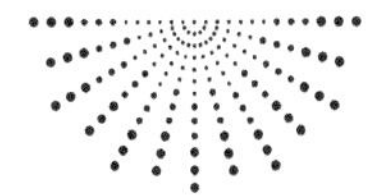

T HE NEXT MORNING dawns far brighter and earlier than I expected, at 5:17 AM according to my watch. I nearly forgot how long summer days are, how the sun hovers unflinchingly in the sky.

"Mornin'," Steven mutters, grabbing a pack of trail mix for breakfast.

I nod in greeting, too tired to form proper words. Cecilia unravels her headscarf, Kai brushes her teeth, and Rory scribbles something in a notebook. Albert puts a pot of coffee on—thank God for that battery-powered little machine.

We wake up slowly under the boardwalk, morning light streaming through the slats. Chip told me that people used to come here to see the ocean without getting their feet dirty, which I can understand, because now I have sand in some unsavory places and *everything* is raw. I'll have pink skin for weeks.

"So, we're going to scout today," Chip says once we're all gathered, sitting in the sand and clutching paper cups of coffee. "Probably split into pairs, try to find entrances and exits. We know they're underground, so let's try to map out the aboveground space."

I glance at Cecilia. She shakes her head slightly, but I speak up anyway. "Can I come with you?"

Everyone freezes, wearing the same eyebrow-raised expression. They stop eating, stop brushing their teeth—Megan even stops halfway through braiding her hair.

I scramble to find an explanation. "I mean, we're just scouting, so I won't get in the way. I can be of some real help. Just ask Cecilia—I'm good with a map. The more of us out there, the faster we can get them home."

Chip swallows his mouthful of instant oatmeal, never breaking eye contact with me. "Ceci, has he been trained properly for this?"

"Of course, Chip," she says. "You doubt me?"

"Of course not," he replies. "You really wanna come, kid?"

"Yes sir, I do," I say confidently. "I could be of some real service."

"Yeah, I heard you," he says. "I'll allow it, but you are *definitely* not coming tomorrow, understand? Don't even ask."

"Yes, sir. Thank you."

He nods. "Everybody get ready. Let's head out in half an hour."

Before leaving, Chip hands everyone a GPS unit. "Don't fuck this up," he says, showing us how to turn them on. "Log any entrances and exits you find."

We split into pairs, and I end up being the third wheel to Cecilia and Steven.

I hold my gun tightly over my chest as we enter the outskirts of the city. My backpack is hiked up high so it won't bounce if I have to run, and because I'm the youngest, I have to carry our food for the day. Cecilia explained at camp that it's a tradition, especially since I got out of watch last night, and Steven looked so relieved not to have to carry it that I believed her. The GPS is clipped to my belt loop.

"So, Chris, what's it like, living in a Border town?" Steven asks. We let Cecilia forge ahead and fall into step beside one another on the shattered asphalt, taking in the ruin. Rusted, mangled car bodies line the streets, and glass crunches underfoot.

"Not too different from the Underground, to be honest," I say, scanning the crumbling buildings carefully. "I went to school instead of training. I woke up when I wanted, usually, so that was nice. I was on track to become a doctor. Honestly, I never really thought much of the Border until we left, never realized just how much it caged us."

"If you think about it, it might not be that bad," Steven says. Cecilia stays quiet, but her pace slows almost imperceptibly as she hangs on to his every word.

"You don't have to make painful decisions for yourself," he continues. "All the hardest choices are made for you. You're going to marry who they say, so you don't have to go through heartbreak or loneliness. You're going to have two kids, so you don't end up too poor to support your family. You're going to be paid a livable wage, because they decide the prices of things *and* how much you make. Think about it: my one dollar could be your one million, but if my bread is three dollars and yours is three million, what's the difference?

"Now, I would never choose to live in a Border myself. Too boring, too mundane for me. I need adventure, but I can see why it can be appealing to some people."

"Watch yourself," Cecilia growls over her shoulder. "I could report you to Arthur and have you tried for treason."

"He's just speaking his mind," I say. "Is that...?"

"Is that *what*?" she snaps, whirling to face us. Her dark eyes cut right into me—in the sunlight, they transform from pools of ink to puddles of syrup, but her gaze is no less intimidating.

"Is that a crime?" I ask, straightening my shoulders in an attempt to be brave. She's never looked at me like that before.

"She's going to tell you no, but she'd be lying. Speaking in favor of Ankou can get you in trouble," Steven says to me.

"Of course it can. What if you're a spy?" she says. Her fingers are curled tightly around her gun, and I start to wonder if coming along was a mistake. At least if something goes wrong, I'm here to have her back. I'm a good shot.

"I was born *in* the Underground, Ceci," he says. "I'm twenty-six, one of the most successful soldiers of my generation. How and when could I have *possibly* become a spy for Ankou?"

"Will you quit saying his name?" she whisper-yells, beginning her walk again. We follow.

"It's not a bad name," he replies.

We are approaching the real city now, once-skyscrapers that have been reduced to mostly rubble. I wonder who bombed this place, if it was us or Ankou.

"Well, it is in my house, so quit saying it. Show a little respect, will you?"

"Fine," he mutters, kicking at a rock the size of a clenched fist. It skitters out of sight and ricochets off something distinctly metal, clearly out of place. The ping echoes sharply down the street. We stop dead, tense like springs.

We glance at one another with wide eyes. Cecilia raises a finger to her lips and prowls toward whatever the rock hit.

Steven and I look at each other, unsure of what to think of her and ourselves. I grip my gun a little tighter and slowly follow her, watching my back as he follows my path through the maze of rubble.

Cecilia disappears around a crumbling wall, and I follow her, a little afraid to let her out of my sight. When I round the bend, I spot the metal cellar door, and I know what it means on sight.

"Holy shit," I breathe, and she glares at me with her finger to her lips again. She circles the door as if stalking prey, gun trained on the latch. Steven pulls a map out of his bag and marks our location, and I press the green button on my GPS, like Chip told us to.

Cecilia looks up at us, placing her gun gently against her chest. *Should I open it?* she signs.

Steven and I shake our heads simultaneously.

She scoops up her gun and kneels anyway. She flips the latch gently before prying open one of the doors just a few inches. Her gun rests on her knee, and her finger is already on the trigger. She flings the door open and leaps back, gun trained. The door falls softly onto the lush grass. Steven and I rapidly scan the area for movement, guns raised. Cecilia circles the half-open hatch again, staring into it as if entranced.

"Close it," Steven whispers. "We're coming back; just close it."

"We're right here," Cecilia murmurs.

"Cecilia, please," I beg, even though I want nothing more than to climb down that ladder. "We don't know enough yet. There could be a better way. We don't even know where they are."

"They're under the south side, not far down, and the tunnels here are primitive at best. They're only under the outskirts of the city, not the heart of it. We're not going to find another access point so close to camp," she explains, still staring into the darkness.

Katie could be just under my feet, not even five yards away, and we're going to leave her for another day of torture. She could be alive today and dead when they bring her up tomorrow. We should be getting her while we can. This is my only chance to bring her back myself.

But we'll be grossly outnumbered, and we can't carry the wounded and fight at the same time. There's three of us and three people to rescue, and God only knows the condition they're in. They could be unconscious, or too ill to walk. Trying to rescue them today would ruin any chance of getting them out later. It would probably kill all six of us.

But she's *right here.*

"It's too risky," Steven says, our voice of reason. "We can't do it alone. We'll come back here tomorrow and get them out, I promise. We just can't do it today, I'm sorry."

Cecilia nods. "You're right. You marked this?"

We nod in reply.

"Good." She sighs and gently closes the cellar, staring at it sadly. "Let's go."

———

WE FIND little of interest for the rest of the morning. We break for lunch mid-afternoon, but I'm too on-edge to eat. Instead, I pace back and forth as Cecilia and Steven eat lunch on the front stairs of a house that's not there anymore. All that's left are four concrete steps and the handrail—beyond that is just grass and weeds.

"Ashborrow, calm down," Cecilia says. "We're going to get her back."

"What do you think's going on at home?" I ask.

"I left everyone else to intern with my friend Vincent for a few days," she explains. "I know the girls have a good relationship with him, and I can't leave you guys to train with random subs again. We all know how that went."

"I didn't say goodbye to Kela and Grif."

"Because you'll see them in a few days. Calm down, come eat something. You need your strength."

"Not hungry." Sweat pours down my temples and neck, coating my throat in a sheen. We're too far from the sea for the breeze to cool us off, and the sun is beating down with all its strength.

She sighs and takes a bite of her protein bar, speaking around a mouthful of synthetic granola. "Suit yourself. I'm not carrying you when you faint."

"I'm not going to faint!" I snap, turning to face her. "I'm *fine*. It'd be nice if you could actually trust me for once."

She gives me the same look my mother used to offer when I would mouth off to her, a look that was rare but impressively terrifying. God, I miss her.

"Why can't I go with you?" I ask, nearly whining. I already know the answer.

"Because of *this*," she explains, gesturing to my entire body. "Notice how the two of us are perfectly calm and you're over there losing your shit. If I let you come with us—no, if *Chip* let you come with us—you'd risk everyone's lives, including hers. You know what fear does to rationale."

I sigh, ready to continue arguing but knowing it's futile.

"Fine," I grumble, plopping down on the first step and digging a protein bar out of my bag. "Oatmeal and peanut butter, yum. Happy now?"

"Yes," she replies. "Now shut up and eat your lunch."

<hr>

When we get back to camp a few hours later, Chip and Nadia are already gearing up.

"We need to move," Nadia says quickly, shoving her helmet on. "We're going now. We found one of them, a guy, mid-twenties. One of ours."

"How did you find him?" Cecilia asks, voice sharp as she jogs to the car and tosses her bag in the sand.

"I explored what I thought was a cellar about an hour ago. Found cells, torture chambers, everything. We were right there," Nadia explains.

"What about ours?" I ask Steven.

"We go to what they found since they actually had eyes on our people," he says, adding a first-aid kit to his bag.

"Did you find a girl?" I ask. "She has short brown hair, brown birthmark on the top of her forehead, she's kinda tall—"

"I didn't stay long enough to look," Nadia says quickly.

"What should I do?"

"Get medical supplies ready," Chip says. "We should be able to extract this one and stay another day to get the others. But be ready to treat whatever we may need to."

"Why are we getting him now? Won't they know we're here?"

Everyone freezes, waiting for the answer.

"He's not looking good," Nadia explains. "We want him out, now."

I nod, struck dumb by emotion, too stupid to speak. *This is why I'm not allowed to go with them,* I think.

Kai, Megan, Rory, and Albert jog through the boards at just that moment. Chip explains the situation as they get ready. I help by refilling their canteens, feeling useless. Even the drivers are gearing up.

"You be good," Cecilia says to me.

"I make no promises," I joke, but my smile falls flat. "Please hurry."

The ten of them slip through the hole in the boardwalk, leaving me alone in the growing twilight. I listen as they go, footsteps thundering on the ancient wood, until there is nothing left but the crashing of waves and the wind whistling through the boards. I never learned the drivers' names; I didn't think they were going, too.

I set to work, hoping to keep busy while they're gone; it only takes me minutes. I prepare a sleeping bag and tarp for the patient, and set up my medical kit. Gloves easily accessible, as well as everything required for suturing and splinting. I set out a canteen and alcohol wipes, painkillers and a spare bag for vomit.

I finally peel off my shoes and socks, tucking the pictures safely inside before leaving them in the second car. I memorize the last one before I go, her beautiful face only two feet from mine. I want to believe that the gap between us is shrinking, but it still feels just as wide.

The sand is warm underfoot, the sun is just beginning its descent, and a cool breeze sweeps off the waves and through my sweat-soaked hair. I walk slowly down to the water, savoring the feeling of the sand crumbling beneath my bare feet. The water is pleasantly cool after a long day in full gear, and the waves gently caress my ankles. I want to bottle up this moment and keep it in a jar so I can show her, someday.

With a start, I remember that I prepped a medical canteen but neglected my own, so I jog back to the car and grab it. I kneel in the sand, dampening my pants, and fill it with the thought that sandy water is better than none. When I take a sip, however, it lights my mouth on fire, and I spit it back into the sea, coughing.

"Why didn't anyone tell me this was *salty*?" I groan. The realization that nothing—no one—can hear me is enough to send a shiver up my spine.

I stand quietly in the chilly water, staring out at the unseeable horizon, mouth and throat burning. Griffin told me his ancestors came from Thailand and that it was across a great body of water from where we are now. Is this the one he was talking about?

Would I have had the courage to cross that ocean, thousands of miles of water so deep it's the same distance as here to the sky? They must've been so brave. I want to tell him that; I wish he were standing here right now. I wish my parents and Mel got to see this—they would've been so amazed.

I am amazed. I am scared. I have been rooted in this spot so long that the sun is dipping low on the horizon, painting the water and sky orange.

"Ashborrow!" Cecilia bellows. I turn around to see the whole group running on the boardwalk. I can hear their footsteps pounding against the old wood; I can see an extra man, and I can see her. *I can see her.*

"Ashborrow, get back here!" Cecilia yells, and I run.

CHAPTER TWELVE

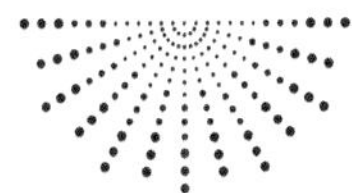

I RUN, God, I *run* to them. They slip through a gap in the boards one by one, ushering each other through and stumbling onto the sand. Albert practically drops the wounded man to the sleeping bag I'd laid out, one wrist the size of a football.

"Cecilia!" I shout, staggering in the uneven sand as I reach them. I saw her, I know I did. She must be here. My heart is hammering in my fingertips, and blood rushes through my ears.

"Ashborrow, here, here!" She shouts. I turn around, and there she is.

Katie, my best friend, is right in front of me. Her hair has grown shaggy over her ears, and her skin is so pale that her veins are traceable through her cheeks. Her hazel eyes are as wide as the ocean is deep, but they don't land on me at first. Instead, they pass right over me and find the crashing waves over my shoulder.

"Katie?" I say softly, drawing her eyes back to me.

"Hi," she says, voice hoarse. "I—"

"Oh, God." I envelop her in my arms, feeling her chest crush against mine. She's denser than I would've thought, more muscular, less fragile than she looked in the video from last month. Thank God cameras lie.

"Here," Cecilia says, laying out her sleeping bag for Katie. "Lie down, let's look at you."

Albert and Chip focus on the injured man, filling out a chart to assess his condition. Cecilia and I kneel on either side of Katie, who appears to be in much better shape.

"Katie, I mean, I—" I start, but Cecilia cuts me off.

"Davis, do you know where you are?" She asks, chart in hand.

"Above a remote facility, on the coast," Katie says. She clears her throat. "West, somewhere."

"Pretty good. What month is it?"

"...June?"

"Close. Early July. What's your brother's name?"

"Lucas," Katie says quickly.

I look at Cecilia as though she has two heads. "Cecilia, are you serious?"

"We need to assess her condition," Cecilia snaps, eyes boring into me. "Would you like to do it, instead?"

I say nothing, grabbing Katie's hand. Her skin is warmer than I would've expected, especially in the cool night air.

"Alright. Davis, is there anything that hurts right now? Worse than the rest of you?"

"My left shoulder," Katie says. "It aches."

"Dislocated?"

"I don't think so."

"Ashborrow." Cecilia nods to me, and I move to Katie's left side. The injured man howls in pain as I do so, making the three of us jump.

I spare them a quick glance over my shoulder. "I know, I know," Albert is saying comfortingly as Chip wraps the patient's wrist in a splint.

"Focus," Cecilia says sharply, and I turn my attention back to Katie.

"Sorry," I murmur, taking ahold of Katie's shoulder. I roll the sleeve of her t-shirt up and spot a dark purple bruise on her tricep. "Oh, ouch."

"Yeah," Katie says quietly.

I palpate her shoulder and the rest of her arm just to make sure nothing else is wrong. I expect my thumb to find the scar she got when we escaped Carcera, when a bullet grazed her arm, but never feel it. Maybe it was her other shoulder?

I examine the rest of her and, except for some stomach pain and a sore left calf, find nothing else amiss. Cecilia and I step away to grab her some supplies.

"She's in good shape," Cecilia says quietly as she rifles through our assortment of painkillers.

"Really good shape," I murmur. "Better than him." I take another quick peek at the injured man. He's nearly unconscious, sedated from strong medication to keep him from writhing in pain.

"Way better," Cecilia adds. The silence that follows feels as though it should be filled.

We return to Katie and get her settled for the night. Cecilia gives her some pajamas, and I kick myself for not thinking to bring spare clothes.

"Why aren't we going home?" I ask after Katie is settled. "I mean, he's in bad shape." I nod my head towards the other former prisoner, still heavily medicated.

"We aren't done here, yet," Cecilia says simply. I want to squeeze more information out of her, but the look on her face tells me I won't get any.

I set up my sleeping bag right next to Katie's, and watch her chest rise and fall as the rest of the group settles into bed. There is no debrief, no discussion of tomorrow. I've learned that that's what Chip believes breakfast is for. Steven mentioned earlier that it's so we don't stay up all night thinking about the next day, but I lay awake wondering, anyway. Eventually, I drift into a dreamless sleep, comforted by the soft whoosh of Katie's breathing.

<hr>

I WAKE in the moment just before dawn. The sky between the wooden boards is a deep blue, cloudless and already warm. Katie's sleeping bag is empty.

I bolt upright, frantically working at the zipper of my bag until it gives way. I spring to my feet and count the rest of the group—everyone is here except for Katie, and Cecilia.

Relief sweeps over me as I realize they must be together, and if

Cecilia is with her, that means Katie must be safe. I take a deep breath to calm my pounding heart, and then set off to look for them.

I find them down at the water, ankle-deep and talking softly. Katie is wearing dark athletic shorts and a grey t-shirt—Cecilia's sleeping clothes—and Cecilia is still dressed in her uniform from yesterday.

"Hey," I say above the surf, trying not to startle them.

Despite my best efforts, they both jump, whirling to face me. Katie's eyes are wide, taking me in, while Cecilia looks at her instead of me.

"Sorry," I continue, meeting Katie's gaze. It's still astounding to me that she's here. Not only here, but *healthy*. "I just wanted to check on you. How are you feeling?"

"Good," she says quickly. "I mean, better being out here. It's amazing, isn't it?" She sweeps an arm wide, gesturing to the sprawling sea and miles of clear, sandy shore.

"Yeah, it is," I say, not taking my eyes off her. She's *so* different, but I can't put my finger on why. I chalk it up to the months apart, the months she spent in torture. "Cecilia—"

"You got it," our trainer says quickly, already heading back to camp. "You have ten minutes."

Katie and I stand alone, toes in the chilly water, watching the sunlight bounce off the waves as they crest, and fall, and crest again.

"I missed you," I say quietly, itching to take her hand.

"I missed you, too," she says. "And Cecilia. And Ava."

"And Noah?"

She cracks a smile, sighing happily. "And Noah. How is everyone, back home?"

"They're alright," I say carefully, glancing over at her. "Ava is recovering, and so is Amy."

"Good," she says. "And Sam?"

Relief floods me. "Sam is good. She was unhurt."

She smiles again. "Good. I was worried."

"So were we."

We don't say anything for what feels like a long while, watching the waves crash and lighten in the rising sun. Suddenly, Katie bends down and scoops up a shell with deft, nimble fingers.

"Oh, wow," she says quietly, holding the pink shell delicately in her hands.

"It's beautiful," I say, stepping closer to her to examine it.

She runs a finger gently across the edge, pulling back sharply as it nicks her. "Ow. Shit."

She's sucking on her finger before I can look at it, pulling the blood into her mouth and then spitting it onto the sand. "Uck."

"You okay?" I ask, putting out my hand to look at it.

"Mhmm," she mumbles, spitting more bloody saliva into the sand and then returning her injured finger to her mouth. I remember being little with her, the way she would always refuse to do that because it grossed her out. I remember how she used to be scared of blood.

"Katie," I say, keeping my voice as measured as possible as I take in her strong shoulders and toned legs.

"Mm?"

"Do you remember when we were kids, and I scraped my knee, and you kissed it?" I ask. "And then we got in trouble, because we weren't Matched yet, even though we were eight?"

"Of course," she says after hocking one more blob of spittle into the waves. "Why do you ask?"

"Just remembering," I say. I look back out to sea as a chill runs down my spine because I didn't scrape my knee—I scraped my elbow. And she would never forget that. *Katie* would never forget that.

<hr>

SHE STAYS at camp with the other injured soldier, Megan, Albert, and the drivers as the rest of us go out on patrol again. Albert and Megan have more medical training than I do, and even though Katie wants to come with us, Chip truly puts his foot down.

I find myself in a group with him and Cecilia; Steven and Rory go out together, as do Nadia and Kai.

I started to protest when Chip told me I was going with them, but thought better of it. She'll be here when we get back; I have forever with her.

We're about a half hour outside of camp when Chip stops dead in his tracks, rounding to face us.

"What do you mean?" He asks Cecilia, as if they're still in the middle of a conversation.

"Ashborrow, what do you think?" Cecilia asks, looking at me with her piercing dark eyes.

"Think about what?" I look back and forth between them even though I already know. "Oh, *Cecilia.*"

"I know."

I look at her: regal posture, dark helmet encircling darker skin. Sunlight bounces off her proud shoulders and gleaming rifle, and her boots are laced neatly. A soldier and royalty, all at once.

She looks back at me, studying my face. "Ashborrow."

"It's not her." The words tumble out of my mouth before I can stop them. I gape, looking between Chip and Cecilia. They stand in front of me with years of training, of missions both successes and failures. Decades of grief between them, and I have the very thing they've always wanted—to know their loved one is alive. And it's a lie.

"It's not her," I repeat, swallowing hard. "That's not Katie."

"I told you," Cecilia says to Chip, looking up at him. The sky is cartoonishly blue behind her, so vibrant that it could easily be fake. "That's not my soldier. That girl back there is a plant."

"But we have the photo," Chip says. "And you said it yourself, that's her."

Cecilia shakes her head, looking away. "There should be an obvious scar on her left shoulder, but it's gone. Magic, poof. And *look* at this girl. She's been in training, clearly. She is *strong*, and well-fed. Our girl wouldn't look like that. You saw the videos—she should look like shit. She should look like the other guy, Callum. He's been tortured."

"And she hasn't?" Chip asks, voice rumbling around his salted beard. "She doesn't look *good*, Ceci."

"But—"

"It's not her," I interject. "I know her better... better than anyone alive right now. And that is not Katie."

They stare at me and grimace simultaneously, thinking of their lost spouses. No, no lost—dead.

"How are you certain?" Chip asks me, fighting to keep his voice level.

"When we were kids, I fell at recess," I explain, trying my hardest not to sound insane. "I cut my elbow pretty bad. Katie came over and kissed it, because it's what her mother did for her when she was hurt. Our teacher screamed at us because you can't kiss someone you aren't Matched to. She cried all afternoon, and I had this big, ugly bandage from the nurse. I asked her about it this morning and she said it was my knee, but she'd never forget that. And when she cut herself on a shell, she sucked the blood off her finger. She doesn't do that—Katie hates blood. *Katie* would never do that."

"And her scar," Cecilia says, jaw clenching and unclenching. "And the weight gain. The fitness. The lack of injuries."

Chip glances between us, eyes settling on Cecilia. "Are you sure?"

"I'm sure."

The silence that follows is absolute. There is no wind, nor birdsong, to fill the void that our words create. If we are wrong—

But we're not. Because that's not Katie.

"We have to go back to camp," I say suddenly. "We can't leave her with them."

"No," Cecilia says sternly, stopping me in my tracks. "She'll find us out. We're going to get her—the *real* Davis, for Christ's sake—right now."

"Now?" Chip asks. "With him?" He jerks his head toward me, and I flush scarlet.

"Without me, you'd be bringing home a *spy*," I hiss, enraged despite his seniority.

He stares at me, grinding his teeth again. "Fine." He rounds on Cecilia. "We're going to the same cell block. Follow me."

He starts off to the west; we hurriedly cross the cracked and cratered street in his wake.

"Why the same place?" I ask.

"Do you have a better idea?"

I say nothing, nerves taking over and turning my mouth to dust.

"The fake was planted there," Chip continues. "So, your girl is probably right in that area. They wanted the fake to look like a P.O.W.? House her with the other P.O.W.s."

"So, they know we're here?" I ask. "They *knew*? Before you went in?"

"Must've," Cecilia says, hustling to keep up with Chip's long-legged stride. He vaults a decaying fence, and we follow suit, heading off across a wide field with the remains of a baseball diamond left behind in the corner, twisted metal and sandy soil.

"But they don't know we're still here," she continues. "They would've assumed we'd rescue them and bail, not wait around. Which is exactly why we did."

"But they knew we were *here*," I repeat. "Before yesterday. They know where we're camped—they must."

"Shit," she whispers. "Chip."

"I know," he growls, striding onto the street on the opposite side of the field. The craters are worse here, and we must leap over several. "We're already caught, so what would you like us to do?"

The unspoken words are loud in my head. *We could—and should— run while we still can.* But that isn't what soldiers do. That isn't what *I* do.

But it is, the voice in my head hisses as we scramble around a pile of burned car husks. *When it was bad in Carcera, you ran. You left them.*

I wince as if struck by the thoughts in my own mind. *But I did not leave Katie,* I retort. The voice does not challenge me again, and good, because we're here.

Chip is hunched over a metal trapdoor much like the one that Steven, Cecilia, and I found yesterday.

"We—and I cannot emphasize this enough—have to fucking *hurry*," Chip whispers. He eyes me for a moment, then glances at Cecilia. "Ceci, do you have Endall?"

"Of course," she answers, then jerks her helmeted head towards me. "But he doesn't."

"What's Endall?"

"It's cyanide," Cecilia says bluntly. She shifts from foot to foot as if uncomfortable—the emotion is as unnatural on her as stoicism is on Noah. "If we were to be captured, we'd be expected to take it."

"Why don't I have it?"

"Because you aren't *supposed to be here*," Chip says, forcing the words between his teeth. "God, we need to go. Are you both ready?"

I grip my gun tightly across my chest. "Yes."

He doesn't wait for Cecilia's answer before heaving the trapdoor open, placing it down with surprising softness.

Chip is gone into the darkness before I can blink, and Cecilia follows quickly after him. I stare into the abyss as they descend hand-over-hand down the ladder, and then join them before I allow my nerve to falter.

Inside, the hallway is dark and wet. Our footsteps squelch, and my ragged breaths grate on my ears as we slink down the tunnel.

There are three doors with locks shot off their hinges on the left side of the hallway. Chip leads us past them, rifle raised should anyone come around the far corner. I look behind me to see that the ladder we descended was the end of the hallway—a dead end.

A pair of bare feet sticks out from one of the doorways. I make the mistake of peering inside and blanch at the sight of a man wearing a tattered robe lying on his back, eyes open but seeing nothing, chest ribboned by bullets.

"Ashborrow," Cecilia hisses. I look forward again; she and Chip are standing in front of the fourth door.

I nod. She must be in there, *must* be.

Chip shoots the lock without a moment's hesitation. I double over and try not to scream at the pain in my ears, but he's shoving the door open, and it screeches along the concrete floor, and I can't think about my ears anymore because *there she is*.

Katie Davis is sitting with her legs crossed on a urine-soaked cot on the floor in the back of the cell. She is staring catatonically at her bloody feet, shaggy hair covering her face, until suddenly, she isn't. Suddenly, she is looking at me.

I'm in front of her before I can stop myself, barreling past Cecilia and Chip to drop to my knees in front of the girl I've come all this way for.

"Katie," I whisper, taking in the sight of her shredded hospital gown and dirt-streaked face. "Oh, Katie."

"Chris," she croaks, throwing her arms around me despite the gun strapped to my chest. And I just know.

I scoop her up, managing to sling my gun over my back, and carry her out of the cell. An alarm blares suddenly overhead, and the slimy hallway is bathed in flashing red light. But all I see is the ladder; all I feel is her in my arms.

I trip over my own feet but regain my balance quickly; I have to keep going, I have to make it to the Surface. I can't stop, not with her right here.

Climbing a ladder with a girl wrapped around my torso proves to be extremely difficult, emaciated though she is. I haul myself up as fast as I can, but it isn't fast enough—guards flood in from the other end of the hall, and gunfire pops behind us.

Katie shrieks against my neck as Chip returns their fire, covering us as we finish our ascent. The midday air is stiflingly warm after the cool dampness of the tunnel, but the sun means everything to me these days.

"Go!" Cecilia shouts as she pops out of the hatch, looking at me with feral eyes as Chip scrambles up the ladder. He slams it closed and sets to work throwing chunks of rubble on it. "Go, Ashborrow!"

So I *go*. I run like I've never run before, but within moments, Cecilia and Chip are beside me. I let the most senior trainer take the lead, wrapping my arms as tightly as I can around Katie. The extra weight is exhausting, but there's no way she can run like this. I don't even know if she can *walk*.

We leap craters and dodge piles of rubble as we run hard and fast back to camp. The butt of my gun thumps so hard against my head I can feel a lump forming, but there is no time to stop and fix it.

"Did you... lock it?" I pant as we run down streets I've never seen before and will never see again.

"Chip threw... debris on it," Cecilia huffs. "Should... stall them... a while."

And then we're on the boardwalk, and I run the last few hundred yards all out. The surface is smooth, if pliable, and I skid to a halt by the hole in the boards that reveals our camp.

Everyone is there, even not-Katie. The other groups have returned from scouting, and they're lounging, eating lunch of freeze-dried pasta dishes.

Not-Katie looks at me just long enough for the horror to register, and then Cecilia shoots her point-blank and I swear to God her face explodes. Blood and brains spray everywhere, and Steven nearly retches.

"Ceci what the fu—"

"GET IN THE CAR!" Chip roars, dropping down the embankment into camp. It all happens so fast that not-Katie's body—the same body as the one I'm holding in my arms, alive and breathing—seems to have barely hit the ground.

And then I'm down there, too, trying to hold Katie's face to my neck so she doesn't see the carnage as I step around bits of skull and brain.

No one questions Chip.

"It's okay, it's okay," I say quietly, climbing into the nearest truck. Everything else whirls around us, but all I see is her. She winces as she lies on her back on the floor, but she is in front of me, living flesh and blood and *soul.*

I tuck a blanket gently around her despite the heat. "I'm gonna be right back, okay? I just need to help us get out of here. You *stay down.*"

She nods with a wide-eyed expression, and I jump back out of the truck, ready for more chaos. Everyone is throwing their things into the trucks even though they don't know what's going on. Not-Katie's body lies in the center of it all, and the sight makes me gag. Her wrist even bears Katie's tattoo—the Gemini constellation.

"Get IN!" Cecilia shouts, shoving me away. I leap back into the truck, and she joins me, tugging the door shut.

"Can anyone drive?" Nadia shouts. The other car is already pulling away, with both drivers inside.

"Me, I can do it," Albert says, freckled and sunburnt. "I'm not as good as Alice, but we'll get out of here in one piece."

"Let's go!" Cecilia orders from the furthest seat in the back.

Albert clambers into the front and fiddles the key into the ignition with shaking fingers.

"You better not kill us all, boy," Chip barks, riding shotgun.

"Trying not to, sir," Albert says as he puts the truck in gear and slams his foot on the gas. We peel out of camp and race down the beach, kicking up sand as we go. The sudden motion throws me back against Nadia's knees, but I right myself quickly to remain hovered over Katie.

"Where are we?" Katie mumbles, propping herself up on her elbows.

"On our way home," I say, looking down at her. "Don't worry, though, we'll be there soon."

The smallest hint of a smile graces her lips, but it falls away all too quickly. A beam of light sweeps into the car; she knows what it is before the rest of us do and flattens herself to the floor.

"We've got company," Albert says, pressing harder on the gas. The car roars even louder as armored cars seem to leap out from the city streets, machine gun turrets pointed straight at us. Gunfire pops from behind, and Cecilia crouches with her gun aimed out the back window.

"Gonna be loud for a second!" she bellows, firing a spray of bullets at the other cars. One veers off-course and heads straight into the water with a thunderous splash.

"Ceci, get the *fuck* down!" Chip roars, vaulting into the back with us and practically tackling her. Steven leaps into the front seat in his place, prepared to help Albert, while Nadia grabs the radio and tries to contact our other vehicle. Everyone takes great care not to step on us.

"Stay down, okay? Just stay down, we're okay," I say to Katie, crouching next to her. She nods with eyes so wide and shallow they might fall out of her head. I cover her ears with my hands as gently as I can, stroking her temple with my thumb. Her right temple is swollen and yellow—the last remnants of a black eye.

"I'm fine!" Cecilia shouts, elbowing out of Chip's grasp and grabbing her gun again. "I got it!"

Albert and Steven try to figure out where to go next, frantically pointing at the GPS and shouting at one another, and I settle for trying to make sure Katie doesn't bounce around too much. She stares at me with those dinner-plate eyes, sweaty hair plastered to her forehead.

"It'll be over soon," I say reassuringly, trying to ignore the chaos. "It's okay."

"Al, can you get us the hell on a road?" Chip shouts over his shoulder.

"I'm trying, sir!" he yells, veering hard to the left. We jump onto pavement and drive even faster now, weaving between buildings and careening so hard around turns I fear we may tip over. Our other car is nowhere in sight, but Steven and Kai are shouting at one another over the radio, so they must not be far.

One by one, the cars trailing us drop off. We emerge out of the city onto a flat highway, and Albert eases off the gas a little, even though we're still flying. The buildings melt away, leaving only marshland and sky. The other truck is a short distance ahead.

I slowly take my hands away from Katie's ears. "Where are you hurt?"

"I'm not," she says, so faintly that I have to read her lips.

"Are you sure?"

She nods, eyes welling with tears. The yellow skin around her right eye strains and stretches. "Oh, God, Chris."

"It's okay. We've got you."

"How's my soldier?" Cecilia asks, coming to sit next to us.

"I've been worse," Katie says, offering a smile that turns into a hacking cough. She props herself up on one elbow, gasping for air, and when she's done, she collapses onto her back again.

"I find that hard to believe, Davis," Cecilia says, squeezing her hand. "You're warm."

Katie nods. "I think I have a fever."

"Ashborrow, grab the med kit," Cecilia says. "Some aspirin should do the trick."

I oblige quickly, although the med kit is sprawled across the floor, having been hastily tossed inside as we fled the beach.

"Have you had any water recently?" I ask Katie, holding the pills in my hand.

She shakes her head. I wordlessly uncap a canteen—after checking that it isn't mine–and hand it to her. She pops back three and swallows hard, throat bulging.

"Are you hungry?" I ask.

"No," she says as she passes the canteen back to me with ghostly-thin fingers.

"Okay. Katie, I…"

"Me, too."

I can't believe we're looking at one another now, that we're both here.

She rests her head on my leg without another word and falls asleep within moments. I touch her forehead with the back of my hand. Cecilia was right, she's burning up.

"Cecilia, if she has a fever, should we take the blankets off?" I ask quietly.

"I always let... Tucker have a light blanket unless he was really hot," she replies, voice thick. She clears her throat, back to business. "Blankets help with shock, too, so I'd leave it on. Do we have a thermometer?"

"No. She feels warm, though."

She grazes Katie's forehead with the back of her hand, letting her knuckles linger. "Yeah, she does. She's flushed, too."

I glance down at her cheeks but end up staring. "Yeah, she is."

"My mom used to call that the 'mommy touch,'" she says fondly. "When a mother can just feel the fever on their baby's skin. Not that you're my kids or anything, but it's—"

"Universal," I finish. "I get it. Are those... are those other words for mother?"

"Yes," she replies. "What did you call your parents?"

"Mother and father."

She sighs. "I always forget how nitpicky Borders are. We say mom for mother and dad for father, with some variations, of course."

"I like that," I say, pausing for a moment. "I'm sorry for all we've put you through."

"You haven't put me through anything, Ashborrow. This is my choice."

"Why?" I ask, studying the way Katie's eyebrow arches across her forehead like the ceiling of the PT tunnel. She has auburn hairs growing back where Amy had tweezed them out, a lifetime and a leg ago. "Why put yourself through this willingly?"

"It's what I was meant to do."

"A real answer, please. Doesn't this hurt you, too? Aren't you collateral damage?"

"You deserve a mom," she says softly. "I can't give you one, not even close, but I can be half a surrogate."

There is a long silence, filled only by the rumbling of the truck and Katie's raspy breathing.

"Thank you."

"Don't. I don't do nearly a good enough job of it."

"You're still holding her hand."

"Yes, I am."

We sit in silence for a long while. I stare down at Katie's face, trying to memorize her. She's aged—there are lines on her forehead that weren't there three months ago. She looks tired, even in her sleep. Her hair is oily and matted. Dirt streaks her face and arms, and there's a smear of blood on her left bicep. She's not wearing pants. Her hospital gown is torn, and I can see her ribs through it. Her face, hands, and feet are gaunt, and she has bruises all over, but she's here. She's a miracle.

"She means a lot, doesn't she?" Chip asks from beside Cecilia. His voice is the gentlest I've ever heard it, gravelly soft like a grandfather's should be. I never knew mine.

"Yes, sir," I say. "She's my best friend."

"Good. That's what a partner should be."

The tears build behind my eyes, massing in a pressure that makes it hard to blink. "Yeah, it is. She is."

After a while, my butt starts to ache from sitting on the floor. Chip and Cecilia sleep on the bench seats, Nadia curls up in the corner, and Steven reclines the front seat to sleep there. I gently move Katie's head and lie down next to her, pulling the blanket over the both of us. She's shivering, so I hold her, marveling at the sharpness of her shoulder.

Albert keeps us on steady pavement as we weave through the mountains. The constant turning makes me queasy, but I refuse to get up. I want to stay with her for the rest of my life, no matter where we are, no matter what's outside.

I reach into my bag and pull out the MP3 player, picking the one quiet album Noah downloaded for me. It helped me relax on the way here, so I put one earbud in my ear and another in Katie's. I hold my breath as she shifts around, finally resting her head in the crook of my neck, and then hold it for longer, scared she'll move.

The pressure returns behind my eyes, and then the tears start to fall silently into her hair. I use my free arm to wipe them away, hoping Albert doesn't hear my sniffling.

"Hey, Chris, you alright?" he says quietly from the driver's seat.

"Yeah, fine," I reply quickly. I suck in a breath. "Really happy she's here."

It's easy to hear the smile in his voice. "Me too, man."

WHEN I WAKE UP, we're still moving, and the sky has completely darkened. Chip is driving now, a little less steadily than Albert, but we're flying across the plains, nonetheless. He has earbuds in, music playing so loud that even I can hear the screaming guitar. Cecilia is awake and reading a tattered paperback by flashlight. Steven and Albert are both out cold. Katie is asleep next to me, no longer restless, now sleeping deeply. I fear that trying to wake her would be in vain.

"I've never seen someone... die, like that," I say quietly.

Cecilia closes her book and turns off the flashlight smoothly, as if she'd known exactly when I would speak. "I know."

"Her head—"

"I know."

"I will think about that for the rest of my life."

Cecilia pauses before echoing herself yet again. "I know. It's horrible, isn't it?"

"It is."

"You know, Tomas—my husband—died the same way."

I say nothing, looking at her silhouette against a thousand stars, so big and bright they nearly illuminate her shadowed face.

"I asked to see his body," she says pensively, weighing each word before it leaves her mouth. "They allowed it. It was the worst decision I've ever made. His face—it wasn't even *there* anymore. And I've never... on *purpose*, I've never killed someone like that. No one deserves that. Not even that girl, whoever she was."

"Do you think she had a name?" I ask, straining to get the words out around the lump in my throat.

"Yes," she says quickly. "Even if it was just for her loved ones."

Loved ones. The thought nearly makes me sick.

Before I know it, my tears are slipping into Katie's hair again, soaking her temple.

"I'm sorry," I whisper, sniffling. "About Tomas, and Tucker."

"So am I," she says quietly. "And all the other people I've found just to lose. But I'm not sorry for her." She nods toward Katie, asleep in my arms. "Arthur made the right decision."

I am puzzled for a moment, wondering what decision she's talking about, but then Katie snores softly against my neck and that's the only thing that could ever matter.

"She's not out of the woods," Cecilia says quietly after a long while. "I know you know that in your head, but in your heart, you want her to be. We're not home yet. I hate to say this to you, but please try not to get your hopes up. She's very sick."

"I'm trying," I say tightly, squeezing the girl in my arms. "But it's so hard."

Cecilia clicks her flashlight back on. "I know. Now get some rest."

"You should, too," I say, closing my eyes, nonetheless. I lie half awake, committing to memory the feeling of Katie pressed into me. Her breath tickles my neck; her hip bone is poking me in the side. I revel in this moment until it is burned into my skin, until her touch feels like electricity again, until I am certain that I have made a new memory with her. And then I fall back to sleep.

CHAPTER THIRTEEN

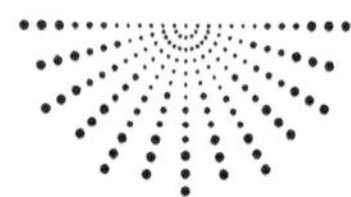

When I wake up, we are stopped again, once more nestled in the mountains. Katie is awake, leaning against the bench seat with her legs stretched out in front of her. I can barely make her figure out in the crushing darkness.

"Katie," I say, rubbing the sleep from my eyes as I take in the miracle of her. "How long have you been awake?"

"Only a minute or two," she says. "We've stopped."

"Food," I say, sitting up. "Are you hungry?"

She shakes her head.

"What about something light?"

"I really don't want to eat, Chris."

"Okay, that's okay," I say. "Can you stand?"

"I think so."

I stand first and lift her; she's lighter than I remember. We both try to ignore how her ribs and shoulder poke at me as we climb down from the truck.

The rest of our team stares at us in surprise, gathered around a small fire. They're mammals more than people, now—dirty faces and torn clothes, tired eyes. Guns nearby even as they eat, wolfing down bread and patties of synthetic meat as darkness presses against their backs.

Cecilia is the first to find her voice. "We made sandwiches. You two hungry?"

"Yeah," I say, accepting the sandwich Kai hands me. "Thank you."

Katie is too busy staring up at the stars; I remember how she would tip her head back when we were out in the woods after escaping Carcera, watching them as if they were holding answers.

"Can we take a walk?" she asks, finally glancing at Cecilia. "I feel okay. Just not hungry."

"Yeah," our trainer says, fixing her gaze on me with a 'you better watch her' look. "Stay close."

Katie sets off into the blackness, limping heavily. I shove my sandwich in a pocket and follow her, wrapping an arm around her waist.

"Chris, they'll think—"

"They know you're strong," I say quietly. "Let me help you, just a little."

She bites her tongue as we march slowly around a bend in the road. The night becomes even more prominent, crushing in as we leave the last of the firelight behind. We stop as soon as we're out of sight, sitting on the double yellow line in the middle of the pavement. The stars explode overhead, appearing by the second as our eyes adjust.

"This is what a paved road looks like?" She touches it with her fingertips, in awe.

"Yeah," I say around a mouthful of sandwich, gagging a little bit as I sit next to her. "Good call skipping the sandwich."

"What happens when it rains?" she asks, ignoring me entirely.

"What do you mean?"

"Does it dissolve?" she asks, looking at me. The fever clouds her eyes —she's only half-here.

"No, it doesn't," I say. "It stays right here."

"Why don't we dissolve in the rain?"

"Because we're people." I pause for a moment. "People can't dissolve."

"Yes, they can," she murmurs, looking back up at the stars. A gash of gray tears through the darkness overhead, and I vaguely remember Sam telling us about it in classroom studies. Something about milk, I think.

I look back at Katie and wonder where she is right now, how much her fever is burning her brain, if it hurts. She looks as if the night could envelop her and carry her off at any moment.

"I don't feel good," she says suddenly, dropping her head down to look at me. "It's beautiful but I just... I'm going to fall."

"Here, lie down," I say quickly, stretching out my legs and patting one thigh.

She lies on her side and places her head in my lap. "Thanks."

"Don't mention it. Get some rest."

She is asleep before I even finish. I already want her back.

"I missed you," I murmur, brushing her hair behind her ear. "I know you know that, but I missed you, and I'm scared you're going to... we have *you* now, real you, so please, please just hang on for me. Please. I need you."

Katie sleeps for a long while, forehead dry and burning. The night is all-consuming, but so are the stars, creating just enough light for me to see the shadows of her face. She's more beautiful than the expanse above could ever be.

My back starts to ache, but I want to let her rest, so I sit until Steven comes to collect us. He is nothing but a shadow in the darkness, looming at the edge of my vision. When I was a kid, the sight of him would've terrified me, but I'm not scared of the dark anymore. I know what true darkness is, the kind that sits in your soul.

He waves me back to the truck and turns without saying anything. I slide Katie's head off my leg, stretching before scooping her into my arms and carrying her to the car. She stirs just barely, nestling her temple against my chest, and my heart throbs.

The rest of the group stares at me as I climb into the waiting truck and lay Katie down as gently as I can, placing my pack under her head; it all makes me want to cry.

"All set?" Albert asks from the driver's seat.

Chip glances back at us, answering for me. "We're all good."

"We have about three hours left. I'm gonna try to gun it once we're on the plains," Albert says, putting the truck in gear.

"Sounds like a plan," Cecilia says, pulling out her book and flashlight. I sit on the bench across from her, staring out the window and blasting music through my headphones. The mountains fly by as the sun rises, pale and gray through quickly-thickening clouds. It seems to stop halfway, and the world is suspended in an artificial pre-dawn darkness.

The storm begins with a sudden violence. Even the music in my ears doesn't drown out the sound of the thunder and rain smashing against the windshield, pelting against our windows. I glance at Cecilia, who seems untroubled; Albert and Steven are the only ones who look worried. Albert grips the wheel with white-knuckled hands, staring straight ahead as we move slowly along the winding road. The windshield wipers fight with everything they've got. Steven taps his foot quietly, checking his watch every few minutes or so. Katie and Chip both sleep.

Cecilia waves to get my attention, book sprawled face down in her lap. She signs, *You okay?*

I nod. *Is this bad?*

She shakes her head.

It looks bad.

We'll be home soon.

I sigh, looking down at Katie. Her cheeks are a little too flushed for comfort, her breathing a little too shallow. We need to get her fluids and medicine before it's too late. We could already be too late.

The last four and a half hours home lasts an eternity; the torrential rain makes it impossible for Albert to drive as fast as Katie needs him to. We almost get stuck in the muddy plains once or twice after leaving the road, but after some wiggling, Albert gets us free. It's still raining when the tunnel comes into view, and lightning strikes not far away as we disappear inside. I want to feel sad for leaving the Surface behind, but all I can think about is getting Katie the help she so desperately needs.

The sudden quiet is unnerving as we roll downward, ears popping. Nurses and doctors are waiting for us in the bay—they throw open the doors before Albert can even put the truck in park. They're lifting Katie onto a stretcher in the blink of an eye, waiting for no one, not even me.

"Wait, wait!" I scramble to my feet, grabbing my bag off the floor and clambering after her. My earbuds are falling around my neck as I jump down, boots half on, bag partially unzipped and hanging off one shoulder.

"Soldier, we have to get her to the hospital," a red-bearded doctor explains, voice gravelly but kind.

"I know, let me come with you," I say. They start wheeling her away, but he stops me from following.

"You need to get cleaned up before you can visit," he explains. "She needs to be assessed by professionals."

"I *am* a professional," I explain, even though we both know I'm really not. "Christopher Ashborrow, Trauma Intern, Sunday evening shift. Please, sir, I need to go with her. I know her, I need to be there."

He shakes his head. "Sorry, kid. Go clean up."

They all leave me standing beside the mud-splattered truck. They wheel her away, almost running, which means she's worse than I thought. The man with the broken wrist—who, with a pang of guilt, I realize I'd forgotten about—has declined the stretcher and is walking himself to the hospital.

I'm left slightly detached from the crowd, floating unmoored. The other trainers lace their boots and clean out the trucks; Chip hands the box of guns off to a girl from the armory who looks no older than thirteen. Cecilia shoulders her bag and scans the crowd, presumably for me. When she doesn't see me, she slips through a side door, head hung low in exhaustion. I don't think she slept the whole way home.

I stand next to the truck with my boots barely on my feet, pajamas threatening to fall out of my rucksack, until Katie and her team of doctors are out of sight.

"C'mon, we can go down to the hospital together," Steven offers, clapping me on the shoulder.

I shake my head, staring at the door they took her through. "I should go be with Cecilia, find my friends."

"Cecilia needs some rest, you know that," he says quietly. "How about I walk you home?"

I shrug, not wanting to say no but really not wanting to say yes.

"C'mon, let's go. What's your address?"

"223 Cirro Hall," I say, shuffling down the rocky tunnel with him beside me. I feel as though I've jumped off a cliff and have yet to hit the ground. I don't know if the impact or the waiting will kill me first.

"Alright, cool, I know where that is," he says. "We can take the elevator, if you want. You're only supposed to do it for a valid reason, but I have a card from a few years ago that I 'lost.'" He puts the word in air quotes. "I feel like our reason is valid enough."

I nod. We emerge into the dining hall, where lunch is just being cleaned up.

"Actually, hang on." He pauses. "I'm starving. You?" I realize that I am and nod.

"How's a grilled cheese sound?"

"Perfect," I say. "Can I meet you back down here in half an hour? I'll just walk up, it's okay."

"Sounds good," he says. "You sure you don't want to take my card?"

"I'm okay. Thanks, though," I say, already leaving.

I trudge up the steps, immediately regretting the choice to walk. My legs feel like thousand-pound weights, and my eyelids are just as heavy, despite my sleep in the truck.

The room looks exactly the same as it normally does, a little messy but in an endearing way. Noah's bed is made, but the covers are rumpled; somebody left the faucet dripping by accident. It feels almost like coming home, but not quite.

I peel off my grimy, sandy clothes, wincing at the chafing between my legs and under my arms. I grab the softest t-shirt and sweatpants I own and step into the shower.

Fifteen minutes later, there isn't a grain of sand anywhere on my body. I brush my teeth and wash my face, put gel in my hair, and slip on sneakers instead of boots. I'm starting to feel like the boy on the beach was a different person than the one in the mirror right now.

As promised, Steven is waiting for me in the dining hall with grilled cheese and a bowl of tomato soup.

"I already ate," he explains. "Those meat patties were so gross, I couldn't help myself. Sorry."

"It's all good." I smile, sitting down next to him. "Thank you."

"Anytime. My niece works in the kitchen and we're tight, so it's pretty easy to get some extra food."

"You have a niece?" I ask around a mouthful of cheese. I wonder if he somehow knew this was my favorite sandwich or if it was a lucky guess.

He nods. "Yep. My wife has an older sister who was real young when she got pregnant, nineteen, I think. My niece is about your age, but she has an illness that keeps her from training, so she works in the kitchen."

"Do you think that's hard, not being able to do what everybody else does?"

"Probably. But she's mature, and she's tough. She's always gotten along better with adults than with her peers. She grew up fast, even faster than most kids do."

I eat quickly and wash it down with a long gulp of water. "That was really good, thank you," I say, standing. "I'm gonna head to the hospital and check in on her."

"You want me to come with you?" he asks.

"Go get cleaned up," I say. "I'll be okay."

"I'll check in tonight," he says, pushing in his chair. "223 Cirro?"

I nod. "Yeah. Thank you, for everything."

He tips an imaginary cap as we walk out together. "No problem. See you later."

"See ya."

As soon as he turns the corner, I start jogging to the hospital, heart already pounding in my throat. I arrive at the front desk only a little nauseous.

"Hey, Ellie, I'm looking for Kaitlyn Davis?" I ask the woman sitting there. Her mint-green scrubs are just a bit too tight. "She was just brought back from the Surface. Can I see her?"

"Chris, hey." She smiles, slowly pulling out a file. "Kaitlyn Davis, yeah, Room 310. Go right on in."

"Thank you." I offer a half-hearted smile and hurry there.

I pause before going inside, placing my hand on the half-rusted doorknob and staring at it. She's going to be there, right on the other side. She has to be, doesn't she?

The door creaks as I open it, even though I'm trying to be as quiet as possible. There she is, hooked up to an IV, fluids and medicine being steadily fed into her body through the back of her hand. She's dirty but here, alive and safe. I am home, finally.

I sit on the edge of Katie's bed, staring at her. She doesn't have the same face that I remember, although it is still distinctly *hers*. But she used to be full of life, always smiling, pouting, or showing off another vibrant expression. God, was she vivid.

Her new face is gaunt, and so pale that a dusting of freckles is visible around the acne scars that dot her nose. I remember how Lucas had them, and she was so jealous. She would sit outside for hours, but she'd always just end up tan, never freckled like him. By the time we were teenagers, she had given up.

"You have freckles," I whisper, stroking her cheek gently with my thumb. "Katie, you have *freckles.*"

I take her hand and press her knuckles to my lips, enveloping her fingers in mine. Her skin is colder than mine again; like before, my warmth seeps into her. The way it always has been.

I pull up one of the chairs to the edge of her bed and sit there with her hand pressed to my face. It's so hard not to stare at her. Even like this, she is beautiful.

A plump nurse walks in a few minutes later and jumps at the sight of me. She presses a hand to her heart, just below a coffee stain on her baby blue scrubs. "Oh, my word, when did you get here?" she asks, gold hoops jingling as she shakes her head.

"Just a few minutes ago," I say, wiping my eyes hastily. I stand and shake her hand. "Sorry to scare you, ma'am."

"That's quite alright," she says. "What's your name?"

"Christopher Ashborrow, ma'am," I explain. "Katie and I are in the same squad. I was on the team that rescued her."

She nods with a bright white, albeit chipped, smile. "Yes, you're Cecilia Adder's. She's told me all about you guys."

"You know Cecilia?"

She pulls out Katie's chart and flips through it. "Yes, I was her son's primary nurse when he was here."

I stare at her, slightly open-mouthed.

The nurse glances up at me and nearly rolls her eyes. "Yes, I knew

Tucker, don't act so surprised. He was everybody's favorite patient. All the nurses loved him; he was a fine young man."

"I'm sorry," I say quietly.

She shakes her head, hoops swaying back and forth. "No need to be sorry. It's a part of life, one of the more unfortunate and ugly parts, but a part, nonetheless. If I hadn't met his mother, I wouldn't've heard of you, and I'd be kicking you out of here right now."

"Why aren't you?" I ask skeptically.

She shrugs. "Cecilia told me you used to intern down here. It wouldn't hurt to have a trained eye on her, in her condition."

"Which is...?"

"She's severely malnourished, running a fever with a chest infection. 102.3, fairly dehydrated as well, but nothing we can't fix. Her body is being very receptive—the fever reducers are already working, and we put her on some antibiotics to clear up her chest, plus IV nutrition. She's gonna be fine, but it's nice to have some extra eyes on her. We could use all the help we can get, as you know."

"I—thank you," I say. "Thank you."

"Just doing my job," she says, popping her stethoscope into her ears. She works quickly, re-taking Katie's temperature, checking her blood pressure, and listening to the sound of her lungs.

"When will she wake up?" I ask when she's done recording Katie's vitals.

"Once she sleeps it off," she answers vaguely, closing the chart. "Could be a couple hours, could be a day. She'll be groggy and probably a bit disoriented, though. It'll take a while for her to be herself."

"Can I stay overnight?"

She makes the *eh, I don't know* face that adults always make when their children request something of them that they can do but don't want to.

"You do need rest," she starts. "But, then again, I'm sure you'd sneak in anyway. Come down at 8:00 and ask for Carla. That's me. My shift ends around then, so you might have to wait a minute or two. I'll let you in."

"You would do that for me?" I ask in disbelief.

"My son's name is Chris; he's about your age. Something about

Chrises and your good hearts, I don't know. Plus, like I said, it doesn't hurt to have somebody keeping an eye on her."

"Thank you."

"Don't mention it. Make sure you tell your squadmates you're back and get some food, too. You look a little too thin for me."

I smile. "I will."

She leaves quietly, being sure not to let the door slam.

I try to rationalize not going to find my squad. I don't know where they're training today, or even if I would be allowed to talk to them if I managed to find them. They could be in the pool for all I know, and I'm finally clean and dry again.

I don't know what I'm going to tell them, or how I'm going to sneak out tonight without accidentally insulting them. They're going to want to come down here themselves, see her with their own eyes. How am I going to explain to them that I can spend the night here, but they can't?

Overcome with exhaustion despite the ample sleep I've been getting, I decide to rest my eyes for a few minutes. I let my head fall gratefully against the edge of the bed, eyes sliding shut. When I open them again, it's 3:17, and my neck is so stiff that it takes a while for me to get up.

Katie is still asleep, but she's less flushed now. Her vitals look good on the monitor, everything humming and beeping along at a steady rate, so I kiss her forehead and begin the long trudge upstairs.

The walk up is virtually endless with my tired legs and heavy head. I pass Ruda's sister in the stairwell, and while I don't know her well enough to say hello, seeing her gives me an idea.

The pretty brunette opens the door almost before I knock. I half expected her to still be training but am pleasantly surprised she's home.

"Chris, hey, come in," Ruda says, opening the door wide. I step into her dorm, and she shuts the door gently behind me.

"When did you get back?" she asks, sitting down on her bed cross-legged.

I half-sit, half-stand next to her, very much aware of the six inches of space between us. "This afternoon."

"And...?"

I nod. "She's in the hospital, malnourished with a chest infection. She's gonna be fine, though."

"Are you alright?"

"I... yes. God, yes, but... no, too. A nurse is letting me spend the night down there, but I can't tell Ava and Noah. But I live with them, so I can't exactly sneak out."

"I think you should tell them," she says carefully, hesitating at every word. "Keeping secrets or lying never works out for anybody."

"You think so?"

"I know so. It'll be okay."

"Thanks."

"Need a hug?" she offers.

I nod and lean into her. She wraps her lean arms around me, and I cling to her, struggling to keep one breath coming steadily after another.

"I'm really happy she's back," she murmurs into my hair, lips soft against my ear.

"Me, too," I whisper. "I should get going, though."

"For sure," she says, pulling back and standing up. "I want to meet her sometime, if that's okay."

"Yeah, of course," I say, already halfway out the door. "I'll call you tomorrow?"

"Sounds good," she says. "Goodnight."

"Night." I close the door softly and start the short walk to my room, legs carrying me while my mind races.

I don't even get to knock twice before Noah throws the door open.

"Hey!" he shouts, pulling me into a tight hug. I laugh and hug him fiercely, finally home.

"Chris!" Ava says, elbowing Noah out of the way. She puts her hands on my shoulders and studies me carefully. "You look tired."

"It's nice to see you, too," I joke, hugging her tightly, careful to keep my arms high above her injury.

"Is she...?" Noah asks.

I nod when Ava steps back. "Yeah, she's home."

Noah grabs onto the door frame to hold himself up. "She's home safe? She's okay?"

"Yeah, she's okay," I say. "She's home."

"Oh, thank God." His eyes well up, and he sniffles hard.

"It's okay." Ava laughs, rubbing his back. "Noah, she's okay!"

He nods and wipes his face roughly but ends up crying even harder. I grab him in one arm and Ava in the other, pulling them into another tight hug.

"She's okay," I whisper over and over as we cling to one another in the doorway, overcome by emotion. "She's okay, she's okay, she's okay."

I finally clear my throat and pull back, wiping my cheeks with the back of my hand. "She's gonna be fine. Right now, she's sleeping off a fever and a chest infection. Once she's awake, the doctors will get a better sense of how she's doing, but she was awake on the ride home; I got to talk to her. She's gonna be okay."

"Jesus Christ," Noah says with a shuddering breath. "Can we see her? Can we go?"

I sigh. "Well, they want me to spend the night so she has a familiar face when she wakes up, and since I've interned there before, I can keep an eye on her vitals. I asked about you guys coming, too, but they don't want her to be overwhelmed. They said you can come by as soon as she's up. Is that okay?"

It's the gentlest lie I can think of.

"That's okay," Ava says eventually, even though it's clearly not. The disappointment is painted all over her face, turning her soft features into sharp angles.

"C'mon, let's get inside," I say.

My bed has never looked so good, and I plop down like a sack of flour, thankful for the soft cotton quilt against my raw legs.

"So, fill me in," I say as they get settled. "What's been going on?"

"Well, we interned with the guy who runs the K9 unit while you were gone," Noah says. He sits next to Ava and takes her hand. "The dogs sniff out bombs so we can remove them. It's pretty cool. Amy's gonna be his assistant starting next week. He kinda knows what she's going through. He lost his right leg a few years ago, so they make a good team. I—we—think it'll really help her."

"That's good," I say. "How're Kela and Grif?"

"Kela's good, but Grif still isn't feeling well," Ava says. "He's got a nasty cough, Kela says."

I wince; down here, sickness spreads like wildfire, and Katie needs to be kept as far from germs as possible. I was hoping he'd have recovered before we got home.

"No, don't worry, he's gonna be fine," she says quickly. "Seriously, he's already doing way better."

"Are you guys feeling okay?" I ask.

They look at each other and nod, a mirror image.

"How was the trip?" Noah asks. "Where'd you go?"

Someone knocks on the door just as I open my mouth.

Steven is on the other side, looking much younger now that he's shaved and dressed normally, no longer in combat clothes with a gun strapped to his chest. "Hey, man," he says. "How're you doing?"

"I'm doing alright, how 'bout you?" I ask, opening the door fully.

He steps inside. "Glad to be home."

"Guys, this is Steven. He was on the mission with me. Steven, this is Ava and Noah, my squadmates."

They exchange pleasantries, and we chat for a little while. I learn that his wife is pregnant with their first child, a baby girl.

"How's Katie?" he eventually asks, wringing his hands as if expecting a bad answer.

I fill him in on Katie's status, and there's a knock at the door just as I finish up. Ava answers it to find Cecilia, also in regular clothes, a green hoodie and gray leggings.

"Hey, guys, how's it going?" she asks. Noah and Ava fill her in on the past few days, leaving out the part about Amy transferring to the K-9 unit.

"How's Davis?" she asks me.

Noah, wondrously able to sense that I'm tired of explaining, tells her what he knows. She nods along and sighs at the end.

"It's better than I expected, to be honest," she says. "Are you guys heading down there before bed?"

"I'm actually allowed to spend the night," I reply. "Why?"

She gingerly pulls a few tiny purple flowers from the pocket of her hoodie. "I got her these."

The rest of us gape—flowers are incredibly hard to come by, not to mention expensive. We may be able to grow our food in labs, but making flowers is neither necessary nor easy.

"How did you...?" Ava asks.

"I had a bit of extra pocket money," she explains. "I think Davis deserves a little piece of the Surface when she wakes up, even if these weren't exactly grown there. They're called chicories."

"Oh, my God, I nearly forgot," I say, grabbing my canteen. "I brought water back from the ocean. Can we put them in that?"

"No, it'll kill them," Cecilia says, laughing a little. "I have a jar at home I'll bring for you to keep it in. You're gonna wanna get that outta your canteen pretty soon, or else it'll always taste salty."

"Got it, got it. Thank you," I say, taking the flowers from her. I fill the ceramic toothbrush cup with water and stick them inside.

"Don't mention it," she says. "I should get going; my bed is calling my name."

"Me, too," Steven says. "Tori's gonna be wondering where I am."

"Thanks for stopping in," Ava says.

We all say our goodbyes, and they leave the three of us alone again.

I check my watch: 5:19. I've only been away from Katie for two hours, but it feels like a lifetime. My chest tightens as I think of her alone down there, connected to machines and wires pumping medicine into her body. I know, rationally, that she's asleep, but I can't help wondering if she's scared.

"You're going, aren't you?" Ava says.

I nod. "Yeah. I gotta be there soon."

Her eyes well up, and I open my arms. She walks right into me. Her arms hang limply at her sides; she just falls against me as I wrap around her. I miss her more now than I did on the Surface.

"She's gonna be home soon," I say quietly, pressing a kiss to the side of her head. "I know it."

"Do you have to go?" she asks.

"Yeah, I do. I'm sorry."

"Tell her we love her?"

"I'm planning on it," I reply, inhaling deeply. She smells like vanilla and cinnamon, like safety, like a sister.

I let her go when she's ready and give Noah a solid clap on the shoulder, too choked up to hug him, too.

"I'm gonna grab dinner in the hospital. If I don't see you for breakfast, I definitely will for lunch," I say, grabbing the makeshift vase of flowers. "Probably gonna skip training unless I find you in the morning."

"Alright," he says. "Take good care of her."

"Of course." I jokingly salute them and head out, my stomach knotting as I leave a piece of my soul behind. I don't know how much more I can take before I'll be stuck this way, shattered.

CHAPTER FOURTEEN

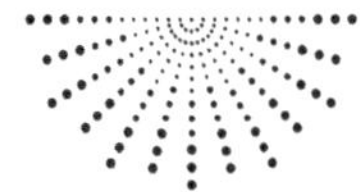

CARLA IS in the lobby chatting with Ellie, the receptionist. She leans heavily against the desk—I recognize the look of sore feet—and Ellie sips from a steaming yellow mug.

"Carla, Ellie, hey," I say, holding the flowers gently in both hands. "How's Katie doing?"

Carla frowns at me but tries to hide it—an expression shared by nurses everywhere. "You're early."

My face falls. "What's wrong?"

"I need to speak with you for a moment," she says quietly, placing a soft hand on my arm and guiding me into a small side room. Ellie gives me a look of sympathy as Carla shuts the door and takes the flowers from my trembling hands, setting them on the coffee table.

"Sit, please," Carla says, taking a seat across from me. I collapse into a chair, ears ringing, breath ragged in my chest.

"What's wrong?" I ask. "What...?"

"She's doing fine. She passed all her exams," she begins.

"Then why are we here?" My voice has a mostly-unintentional bite to it; why would she scare me like this?

She glares at me but softens again almost immediately. "We examine patients very thoroughly when they return from the Surface like Katie did," she explains. "We have to check their bodies for trackers... their *entire* bodies. Do you understand what I mean by that?"

A flicker of anger lights within me as I think of them going anywhere near there. "Yes."

"We didn't find one, thank goodness. However, Katie seems to be... lacking several organs specific to the female body."

"They're just not there?"

She nods, holding my gaze bravely. "Physically not in her body. This is not a birth defect."

I wish that adults would just explain something to me instead of making me piece it together.

"So," I say, running a hand through my hair. "She is missing... what organs, exactly?"

"Her uterus and cervix. Do you understand what that means?"

My stomach seems to bottom out of my chest; the lights dim, and I am frozen solid, stuck to my chair.

"You... she was asleep when you found this out? Did she know you were doing this test?"

"We just took an ultrasound. It was completely non-invasive, I promise you," she says quickly. "We did not violate her. She was conscious the whole time, and we were able to determine this using an external ultrasound. The kind you'd get if you were pregnant and having a routine check-up."

"She's awake?"

"Somewhat."

"Did you tell her?"

Carla shakes her head; her gold hoops jingle quietly. "The doctor does not believe that this is the right time. We're gonna call her back for a consultation in a few months. She may need surgery, just for her own comfort as she matures. This happened to her when she was young and still developing."

My stomach heaves. "Oh, my God. She had a procedure when we were thirteen. She told me it was nothing, a one-day thing, they just needed to patch something up, she'd slipped and fallen on some ice. She said it was simple, nothing like this. Oh, *God*."

"Chris, she's alright," she says gently. "She's safe and healthy. We aren't sure why, but they removed her reproductive organs, that's all."

"But she can't... she won't have kids?"

"Not biologically, no."

"Never?"

"Never."

I sit for a moment, trying to collect my thoughts. It's like trying to hold a snowball together in a warm room; everything I try to grasp melts in my hands.

A baby boy named Joshua. He would've had her eyes, my nose. His twin Evan—of course we would've had twins. They would've both had the brother I never got. I could watch them growing up together and be able to point my love in a direction, instead of it rebounding inside me and burning me up. Living here we could've had a third, a girl, Sarah or Anna or June, Katie's favorite month. Her brothers could've been her heroes, her champions. What brothers are supposed to be, instead of leaving their sisters behind to die.

"She can adopt, Chris," Carla says gently, pulling me out of my thoughts. "And that's perfectly okay. That's a very respectable way to have children, in fact, many choose it even if—"

"I was supposed to have twin boys," I say thickly, only realizing I had such a clear view of my future now that it's slipped through my fingers. "Joshua and Evan. I was supposed to be a twin, but he died, I think."

"You can still have your own," she says, thick eyebrows scrunching together. "You're fine, as far as I'm—"

"No, she's the one," I say, inhaling sharply and clearing my throat. "She's always been the one."

She nods. "I'm sorry, Chris."

"Does it hurt her?" I ask.

"No, she can't feel it. It hurt a bit back then, of course, but she's fine. If we think a procedure would help, it would just be to remove and repair some internal scar tissue. It isn't dangerous, but we want her to be as comfortable as possible in the long run."

"Why... why did they do this?"

She gazes at me sympathetically. "Honey, I wish I knew."

"Is it okay that I don't tell her?" I ask. "I don't know enough to be able to tell her like a doctor could." It's a coward's way out, but it's true; I don't know anything about this procedure. "And this surgery, what's it called?"

"It's a hysterectomy," she explains. "Now, she doesn't have a scar, so we can infer that they never made an incision during the procedure. Does that make sense?"

I nod slowly. "They went...?"

"Yep."

"I see."

She leans forward and clasps my hand in both of hers, warm and soft like my mother's. My throat swells at the connection. "Honey, you don't have to tell her a thing if you don't want to. This is a non-life-threatening condition, and she most likely has no idea. I'm sure they didn't tell her what they were doing and why, so—"

"She told me she was bleeding after she fell, and that's why they had to do it." A memory floods my mind: Katie, curled up in the fetal position on her couch.

"My stomach really hurts," she said.

"I know," I replied, putting a hand on her shoulder. "Can I get you anything?"

"Some Tylenol?" Her eyes were big like two tiny planets. We were both scared—she had pain that neither of us had ever experienced, and no one was home to help us.

"*Chris*," Carla says, pulling me back. "That happens to all women. It's part of our bodies' natural cycle every month. You do know that, right?"

I shake my head. "I... no."

She pats my knee comfortingly. "It was probably something kept hush-hush, only between girls and their mothers. It wasn't up to you to know."

"So that doesn't happen to her, anymore," I say slowly. "But it happens to other girls?"

"Yes."

"Does she know it happens to everyone except her?"

"Probably not. If I had to guess, they would've made it sound like something was wrong, instead of her body doing what it was supposed to do. And if she ever talked to any other girls about it, which is unlikely, they would've brushed it off. Nobody could've known it wasn't supposed to be this way. Honey, why don't you go see her? We can talk about this again another time, when we know more, and we can plan the best way to tell her. Okay?"

I nod, standing. "Thank you."

She rises with me and pulls me into a hug. It feels so much like being held by my mother that my knees almost collapse under me, and I choke back a sob.

She rubs my back comfortingly. "C'mon, let's get you down there. You alright?" She pulls away and holds my shoulders, studying me carefully even though she's nearly a foot shorter than I am.

I swallow hard. "Yeah, I'm alright. It's just a lot..."

"Nobody said it has to make sense right now," she says, patting my cheek. "We don't have all the answers yet. I told you because we need to start finding answers, and I wasn't sure if you had any. It's okay that we don't have the full story yet. She's home safe, and that's what matters."

I nod, picking up the vase of flowers and holding it firmly in my hands, sniffling once. "Thank you for telling me."

"Of course," she says, leading me out of the room and down the hall. "She's been asleep most of the afternoon, but her vitals look good. She just needs to rest, and she'll be good as new in a couple of days, save the weight loss. She'll gain that back quickly, though."

"How's her heart rate?"

"A little high, but nothing to worry about. That's just the fever dying down." She unlocks Katie's door. "Make sure you get yourself down to breakfast in the morning, alright? There's no Wakeup down here, but I'll give you a call at 6:15 to make sure you're up and out."

"Thank you."

She smiles at me with big white teeth. "Like I said, you Chrises have good hearts. I'll see you tomorrow."

"Goodnight."

She leaves me to enter Katie's room alone. She's still asleep, so I quietly place the flowers on her bedside table, wondering if she knows already but never told me. I wonder if she feels empty, or if her body has filled the space. I wonder how bad it hurt.

And then, without warning, she is awake.

"Mother...?" she murmurs, squinting against the light. She starts to sit up but grimaces, blinking her eyes open halfway.

"Katie, hey," I say, sitting down on the edge of the bed so she can see me. "Your mother's not here right now. It's me, Chris."

"Chris." Her smile is enough to melt the coldest of hearts. "I missed you."

"I missed you, too," I say, pushing a strand of hair away from her face. "How're you feeling?"

She frowns. "I'm a little sore."

"Do you want me to get a doctor?"

"No, no. Are my legs still here?" She lifts her head to look, but a thick green blanket is covering her lower half. The machines beep and whir as she comes back to full consciousness.

I nod. "Everything's here. You're gonna be just fine." As I say it, I realize it's a lie—not *everything* is here, after all.

"Oh, yay," she mumbles, sighing happily and closing her eyes. "Can you come here?"

"I *am* here, silly," I say, wondering if she's a little high from the pain meds.

"No, *here*," she says, bumping her head against the pillow. Yeah, she is.

"You'd have to make a little room for me. I don't really fit."

She shifts so I have maybe another half-inch of room, and I make it work. I lie down on my side next to her and marvel at how stunning she is in this golden light, where her dimpled cheeks gain a rosy hue. The round mountains of her nose and eyebrows slope into the deep valleys of her eyes, landmarked with old acne scars and freckles so faint they're nearly invisible. I am shocked that she is real, that I am blessed by knowing her.

"Stop staring," she whispers. She knows, even with her eyes closed, that I am. Does she know it is because she is beautiful, that I first glanced at her in second grade and haven't been able to look away since?

"I can't help it."

"I *will* kick you."

"You're too tired to kick me."

"I will kick you..." She yawns. "*Later.*"

"Fine, fine." I roll onto my back so we are wedged side by side between the railings. Our hips and elbows poke into one another.

"I'm glad you're here." Her words are slurred.

"I'm glad I am, too," I murmur. "Go back to sleep, now. Get some rest."

"Mmkay," she mumbles, nestling her head against my neck. "G'night."

I press a kiss into her hair. "Goodnight."

She rolls onto her side with a wince and brings one hand up to my chest. I am so scared that she'll move that I don't even breathe. She exhales through her mouth, tickling my neck.

She once fell asleep like this when we were kids, no more than seven or eight. We were lying on the floor coloring, and then when we got bored, we rolled onto our backs and made shapes out of the little bumps we saw on the ceiling. Then she said she was tired, so she rolled over and fell asleep on me. I was a little surprised, but I didn't mind, because Mel and I sometimes fell asleep on the couch anyway.

But it just felt so *different*. With Katie, I knew she wasn't my sister. It still feels different, even more so now than when we were kids.

I lie perfectly still for a long time, terrified to move. Slowly, I move my hand down to hold hers where it's tucked between us. Her fingertips are cool.

I stare down at her face, her hairline, her ears. It amazes me how she's here, how we managed to exist in the same time and at the same place. How she managed to be home when I knocked on her door in January.

I try not to think about that night, but now, with nothing to distract me except the beeping of machines, I have little choice I remember Mel, wide-eyed but level-headed, when I told her what was happening. Her hands were shaking when she helped me pack, but she helped me, anyway. I remember how thankful I was that she had stopped by with her Match for dinner so I could see her one last time, but then instantly guilty because I knew she would be in trouble. I remember kissing my mother on the cheek and telling her that everything would be alright, and promising that I would be back for them. I remember knowing, within moments, that I had lied.

And then I was standing at Katie's back door, staring inside at their flour-dusted hands and thinking, *I am going to ruin their lives.* I almost didn't knock, but there was yelling coming from Ava's house a few streets over, and I knew what was going to happen if I didn't. I had to save at least her, if no one else. They were going to kill her, Ava said, but I'd hoped they would spare my family. I know better, now.

And then we were at the train gate, and my hand was shaking just like Mel's as I swiped my father's old card. We stood with every light in the world behind us and nothing but infinite darkness ahead, and we went out into it. I never even looked back. I wish I had.

After an hour, my eyelids begin to grow heavy. I'm thankful to be back in a bed, no matter how cramped, and pull the extra blanket up with my feet until I can grab it with my free hand. I drape it over us, giving her most of it, and settle in for the night.

I glance at Katie again—she's sound asleep. I can't help but smile as I turn off the lamp, nothing but the emergency light in the corner illuminating the room as the machines whoosh quietly. And if I fall asleep, I don't know it, because finally real life is the same as my dreams.

———

THE MORNING FINDS Katie with new color in her face. The antibiotics are working—her fever is nearly gone. Even though she still feels sick, she's improving, and that's what matters. She's conscious and coherent, and she smiles at me as we talk. I even make her laugh, but it devolves into a coughing fit that has us raising both of her arms over her head to open her lungs.

I leave during breakfast so I can find the rest of our squad, but not without holding her for a long while first and reassuring myself that she will be here later, that she isn't going anywhere again. I grab my food and head to our usual table, where everyone is already eating.

"Hey, guys." I smile as I sit down, practically elated to see them all again.

Kela nearly leaps out of her chair to hug me. "Chris!" she shouts.

"Welcome back!"

I laugh a little. "Thanks. How's everyone been?"

They fill me in on everything that's happened. Even Amy is chatty today, coming back to the bubbly girl she used to be. We eat slowly to buy time.

Noah scribbles something on a napkin and hands it to me under the table. *Cecilia gave us a morning pass. Can we visit Katie?*

I nod and speak quietly to him. "Probably best to go a few at a time so we don't overwhelm her, but I'm sure she's dy... excited to see you guys."

He grins, ignoring my slip. "Cool."

We finish breakfast and head down to the hospital. Kela elects to visit Grif instead, giving me a firm hug before parting ways.

I talk to Carla about Katie, and she says it's okay for her to have visitors two at a time. Ava and Noah visit her first, while I wait with Sam and Amy.

"Where did you go?" Sam asks quietly, clutching a paper cup of lukewarm coffee.

"West," I say. "To the ocean. That's where they were keeping them."

We sit in silence for a while, staring at the cracked floor. Amy taps her fingers absentmindedly against the arm of her wheelchair.

"Why all the way there?" I eventually ask, hardly expecting an answer. "Why did they take her so far?"

"It's a research facility," Sam grumbles.

"Yeah, but why *so* far?"

"She was at the coast, you said?"

I stare at her. "Yes."

Sam sighs and says nothing. I would know the look on her face anywhere—my mother had the same one before she told Mel that our father was dead.

"Sam?"

"Chris, you have to promise me that you'll be quiet," she says, gray eyes cutting into me like steel.

"I—"

"Screw it, you can't promise that, come on." She marches from the room, and I am left to stumble after her, ears still ringing.

Amy doesn't come with us. I don't want to leave Katie, but words of protest die in my throat.

I follow Sam through winding passageways, side doors, and darkened halls. The ringing in my ears is replaced by roaring, and finally we emerge into a damp, thundering cavern. Blueish-white lights mark the bridge across the river, made of metal with a cage over the top. I wonder if anyone has ever jumped.

There is a pair of younger teenagers kissing in the shadows.

"You two, scram," Sam commands them. They scurry away, the girl tugging her shirt back on, the boy struggling to zip his fly.

"Disgusting," Sam mutters. "People die here."

So I was right—people have jumped.

"Sam, what's going on?" I ask, trying not to shout above the thundering water.

Can we sign? she asks.

I nod.

Thank you.

The mist from the river coats my bare skin and turns my hair damp. *What do you need to tell me?*

She sighs, hands raised, hesitating.

Sam. Her sign name is one of my favorites, the way it flows so effortlessly from my hands. The sign for sun, but with your hand in the shape of an 's.'

Do you ever wonder why they sent us on that mission, not some other squad?

I used to. I pause. *Not anymore. No point.*

She almost laughs. *Fair. You aren't going to like the truth. Do you want to know?*

I nod.

She raises her eyebrows.

I nod again, setting my jaw. *Please.*

They didn't know if we would survive.

"What?" Although she can't hear me, she's a pretty good lip-reader.

They sent us so that if we died, it would be less of a waste of resources. Better for the six of us to die than people who'd been here for years. Better for Avendas to die than Meliors.

"You're lying. You're lying to me, Sam." Even as I say it, I know it isn't true.

She shakes her head; the mist is turning the blond curls around her face sticky, and they cling to her cheeks.

What about you and Amy? I love Amy's sign name—moon, with an 'a.'

Still better than a Melior.

Ignavus, I correct her immediately.

A hint of a smile ghosts her lips. *Right.*

Why are you telling me this now?

I couldn't hide it anymore.

Is this... I think of her eyes boring into me in the weight room, all the meals she barely touched, the storm building beneath her skin. *Why you've been so angry?*

Yes.

We stand there for a while as I take it all in; we turn to the side of the bridge, watching the dimly-lit water rushing beneath our feet. She eventually wraps an arm around my waist, leaning her head against my shoulder and placing her other hand on the railing as if to steady us. It is then that I realize my hands are white-knuckling the railing, and I am sobbing like a little kid.

When I unwrap my hands, they ache. *We're pawns?* I sign in front of us so she can see my hands.

She doesn't answer me, but I feel the faintest nod against my arm.

Why rescue her, then? If she's not even worth the gas to get all the way there?

I don't know.

Where's Cecilia?

Sam pulls away, staring up at me. *Don't go.*

Sam.

The look on my face must frighten her, because she answers right away. *115 Strato.*

"Thank you."

I turn and walk away, one hand on the railing to keep myself steady, the other balled into a fist. If she says anything, I don't hear her above the steady roar in my ears.

CHAPTER FIFTEEN

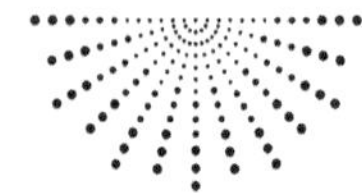

"You signed us up for a suicide mission." The words leave my lips as soon as Cecilia opens the door fighting back a yawn. Any shred of sleep evaporates from her face as soon as my words register.

"In," she commands, practically shoving me into her living room and bolting the door behind us. She wears a blue robe and matching silk bonnet and (to my shock) a pair of black-rimmed glasses.

"Who do you think you are, coming to my room and saying something like that for the world to hear?" she asks, whirling to face me once the door is shut.

"I... you wear glasses?"

"*Yes,* I wear glasses. Now what the hell were you *thinking,* saying that out there?" She walks into the half-kitchen, flipping on an electric kettle. "Make yourself comfortable. How about some tea?"

"No, thank you," I reply, taking a hesitant seat on the faded couch.

Her room is much larger than ours—she has a couch and two mismatched chairs, and even a small TV on the wall. The half-kitchen boasts a microwave, a mini-fridge decorated with Tucker's art, and the electric kettle, not to mention a table with three chairs. Behind the kitchen is one bedroom, with another off the living room. Comparatively speaking, she has a palace.

Cecilia must catch my wandering eyes, because she says, "Perks of being a trainer. We get the nicest places. I think they try to make up for the fact that we have the crappiest job."

She sets a steaming mug of tea in front of me despite my earlier refusal, and I find myself picking it up anyway as she sits in a chair across from me.

"What's your issue this morning?" she asks bluntly, blowing on her own cup. Our mugs are different, one yellow and one white, both chipped. Salvaged from the Surface, as all things are here, including us.

"Why did we go on that mission?" I ask, voice thicker than I would like it to be. I clear my throat and try again. "Where we lost her. Why not a more experienced squad?"

"I thought you were ready."

"The truth, Cecilia. Please."

She stares at the coffee table between us for a long while; her eyes trace the chipped corner and scratches in the varnish.

"I didn't choose you," she says eventually, eyes still glued to the table. "Ever. Didn't choose you for my squad, didn't choose you for that mission."

I take a hesitant sip of tea, burning my tongue.

"You have to understand that I didn't want you to go," she says, looking up at me with her warm, dark eyes. "I fought against it as best I could. Arthur was right, though."

"Don't say that. Please, don't say that what happened to us was *right*."

"It wasn't, I'd never—" She pauses, takes a deep breath. "From a numbers perspective, you guys were the ones for the job. From a human perspective... it should've been someone else."

"What do you mean?"

"You were chosen because if you died, it would mean fewer resources lost. Fewer hours spent on you, less food in your bellies. You were good enough that Arthur had faith that you'd survive, but not so good that losing you would be a significant hindrance to the war."

I stare at her in silence, waiting for her to admit that she's lying.

"So... the whole Melior versus Avenda thing..." I begin, piecing my thoughts together as I speak. "It's perpetuated by the Head Trainer, then. If Avendas are chosen for suicide missions—"

"It wasn't a suicide mission."

"Then why were we chosen instead of Meliors?" Even I can hear the ice in my voice, and she flinches. I never thought anything would be able to make her flinch.

"It was just in *case*—"

I laugh dryly. "Because that's so much better, Cecilia! That makes this okay, of course. Every day we are looked down on for being Avendas, and frankly, I don't give a shit. I think the only person it bothers is Noah. But to know that we were willing to give our *lives* for this, and then that devotion got taken advantage of? To know that we were used as *pawns*? That's the line."

"What did you want him to do?"

"*Anything* else!"

The roar of the river has returned to my ears and is now seeping into my throat. My hand is shaking so hard that I threaten to spill tea across my lap, so I set the mug down on the coffee table, folding my hands together so she can't see my trembling. I sigh and bow my head for a moment.

"Any*one* else, Cecilia. I wanted him to send anyone else. Anyone but her."

"I wanted that, too."

I look up at her, the way she's clenching her mug in both hands. Hair still in her bonnet, robe tucked tightly against her legs. I wonder if she's even brushed her teeth yet today, or if my knocking woke her.

"I'm sorry."

"Oh, Ashborrow, you have no idea."

"I just don't know if I want to live here anymore." The words surprise me, although I've been thinking them for a long time. I'm just shocked I've said them to her first, of all people.

"I've had that thought many times." She sighs, and suddenly I see who she really is: a woman who has lost too much, hurt too much, to only be in her thirties. With a start, I realize that I don't even know for sure if she is an Avenda or a Melior. That floating, faraway look in her eyes says Melior, but her conscience says otherwise.

She continues. "But what else can we do? We want freedom, of course. I could tell you all to make a go of it on the Surface, but that's no life. Eating berries and trying not to freeze every winter? We've had people leave before, but the Scouts usually find skeletons not much later. And we have a strict no-return policy. You can leave, sure, but don't even think about asking to come back."

"So, we're stuck here?"

She nods.

"Well, shit."

Cecilia laughs, and it's perhaps the loveliest sound I've ever heard. She laughs so hard that she sets down her tea, doubling over at the waist and wheezing. Her laugh is so contagious that I can't help joining her in her fit, and soon we're both wiping our eyes with the tissues she keeps on the coffee table.

"Jesus, Ashborrow, I haven't laughed that hard in months," she gasps, dabbing at her eyes. "Shit is right."

"It's... yeah." The laughter dies suddenly in my throat. "Why did we go get her? If he was willing to let her die a few months ago, why rescue her now?"

"Because we were going to assess the facility," she says quietly. "We want control of the coast."

"So, rescuing her was—"

"A bonus," she finishes.

"This is ridiculous," I spit. "How... *how*, Cecilia? How could you do this?"

"I'm not the one doing it," she snaps back. "And this is the cost of war. Of winning."

My skin bristles as I think of Katie as a cost. I think back to my father's journal, how Ankou killed so many for so little.

"How bad is Ankou losing?"

She says nothing, so I continue. "He killed my father for even suggesting that the Underground existed. We're currently looking to take back tunnels hundreds of miles away. We have funerals on the Surface and Scouting missions, and he never finds us. He must be losing. So, how bad?"

She runs her tongue over her teeth, nodding. "Very perceptive, Ashborrow. It's almost an even match. We go back and forth."

Her play on words is not lost on me. "Good one. Where are we at right now?"

"We're ahead."

I nod, taking a sip of tea. "Do you know about Katie's surgery?"

She nods and plucks her tea off the coffee table, taking a pursed sip.

"How long have you known?"

"Since yesterday. What about you?"

"Same." I sigh. "Will you help me tell her, when the timing is right?"

"Of course. I'm really sorry, Ashborrow. I know you wanted kids."

"I still do." I pause. "Is there anything else you're keeping from me that I need to know?"

Her answer comes too quickly. "No."

I hesitate again. "Is there anything else you're keeping from me that I *should* know, for my own conscience and sanity?"

She says nothing.

"How can I talk to Arthur?"

"He's the Head Trainer, to you."

"Not anymore, he's not."

"Yes, he is. I'll fucking block you at the door. Do not test me on this. We are friends, Ashborrow, of course we are, but I am still your superior, and he is still mine. Just because we don't agree with every call he makes doesn't mean we can barge down there and tell him so. Have some respect."

"I need the footage, Cecilia. That the tech squads found. Give it to me or I'll go to him for it."

"I don't have it, and neither does he."

"Why not?"

"It's not worth saving. Doesn't show us anything that we need to see."

"*Not worth saving*? She was *tortured*!"

"Trust me, you do not need to see that footage, Chris." Cecilia's eyes are damp, and the sight of that makes me recoil as if I'd been struck.

I sidestep the importance of her words. "My name's Ashborrow, Cecilia, don't change on me now."

"You don't need to see it. I won't budge on this."

We stare at one another for a minute, and then I stand abruptly, unable to take another moment.

"Where are you going?" she asks, making a move for the door before I can get there.

"Home, Cecilia," I say, embarrassingly choked up. "I'm going home."

She lets me go without another word.

AVA IS WAITING for me in the lobby. She's chewing a candy bar from the vending machine down the hall. "Hey," she says. "Noah went to take a walk after we talked with her. Where'd you go?" I think of telling her about the river, Sam, and Cecilia. The way we were sent to die, and the way the Underground is winning the war, but we are not.

"Ava, I have to ask you something."

She arches one nearly-perfect eyebrow; Sam took her to get them 'done' a while ago, but now the extra hairs are growing back in. "Okay?"

I take a deep breath. "What's a monthly?"

"A period?"

"I guess?"

"It's, uh, okay, hang on." She stands and leads me back to the side room; I hope to never see this ugly yellow paint again. We sit across from one another, leaning in like conspirators.

"Sorry, we don't usually talk about this, especially to boys," Ava says, clearing her throat. Her eyes find the floor, tracing the swirling blue lines in the cracked linoleum. "Every month or so, girls bleed, from, you know. It's because we're not pregnant. Our bodies have to get rid of the tissue and stuff it had prepared to keep a baby safe. Obviously, with no baby, it's useless lining, so it... comes out. Happens every month."

"Does it hurt?"

"Um, a little usually. Sometimes a lot. It feels like pressure on your stomach. Right here." She puts a hand between her hips, still staring at the floor. "And sometimes we get mood swings, or cravings, or headaches. I'm extra tired, usually."

"How do you not bleed on—"

"We have our ways," she says quickly, then wrinkles her nose. "Sorry. In Carcera, we didn't... Dominique told me what was happening the first time, and then we never talked about it again."

"Why?"

She shrugs. "It keeps us safe."

"I... I'm sorry. Katie..."

"She doesn't get them, does she?"

"No. How did you know?"

She looks up at me, finally. "Every month I have to get products for myself, like, hygiene stuff. She never uses mine and never buys her own."

"Oh. What do you—"

"Chris, there are some things in this world that you don't want to know. I get that Sam's been encouraging your curiosity, but—well, maybe you should ask her, instead." Her eyes are so deep that they seem to stretch before me like two bottomless wells, only now there is a roaring flame stretching up to the surface instead of the usual soft, dark water. Everything about her is cool, calculated, except that fire. I recognize it from Mel, and also Ruda and Amy and my mother and Katie.

"I'm sorry," I finally say, and suddenly find the floor quite interesting, too.

"You don't have to be," she replies. "I'm the one who's not used to talking about it yet. You'd think after all these *changes*, I would be, but..."

"Some things stick, don't they?"

I look up to see that the softness has returned to her eyes, and the wells are now filling with tears. "I still find it strange, dancing to music. I... I miss the sound of my pointe shoes on the wooden floor, miss making it as small as possible."

"I always shut off the light when Noah's done in the bathroom. I know we don't pay electric bills here, but my mother was a stickler about it."

We sit in silence, remembering the lives we used to have. A long while passes.

"She can't have children, can she?" Ava finally asks.

"No."

"Oh, Chris—"

"Please," I say quickly, voice strained. "Please, don't tell me you're sorry. She—Katie—is the one who has to live with it. With the empty space."

"Well, maybe she's lucky," she says, sitting next to me. She nudges me with her elbow. "Periods are an absolute nightmare. It's a wonder you can't tell."

We both laugh a bit.

"You always crave chocolate, and you get these headaches, and God, it always feels like you have to go to the bathroom." Ava's properly laughing now. "Literally, for like, three days a month, you constantly feel like you have to poop. And we *train* like that!"

"Jesus," I say, unable to help my own laughter. "Oh, that sounds horrible."

"Don't even get me started on the mood swings," she says, waving a hand in the air. "Because, if you know your history, men have always been the ones in power. Why do you think that is?"

"Physical advantage?"

"It's because, when you people know about our mood swings, you think we're always having one!" She wipes her eyes with the hem of her sweatshirt, then quickly sobers. "Swear to God, we're fine until you ask if we're hormonal, then that's when all hell breaks loose. In Carcera, that's why we never told you." Her face and voice both drop. "That's what Dominique said. It was so our Matches... so they couldn't hold it over our heads. And so, they couldn't tell if we were pregnant or not. If they always treated us like we were pregnant, we were safe."

"But your mother—"

"I know." She inhales sharply, lets it out slowly. Her shoulders collapse inwards. "I know."

I take her hand, small and soft, wondering how she keeps from getting the scars and calluses that litter mine.

"Sorry," she whispers. "I don't mean to paint men as the villains."

I almost laugh, it's so ridiculous. "God, Ava, no one would think that that was your point. And if men *are* villains, then they are. You shouldn't have to hide behind a fake pregnancy to avoid being... hurt."

"My mother blamed me." The words pop out of her mouth like

gunfire. "Because after your second, there's no more babies. So, he got worse once I was born, because he *knew* there wouldn't be another."

"But what if—"

"I was born via C-section. They made sure she wouldn't have a third."

"Oh."

"If she's not dead already..." She pauses, takes a shaky breath. "If she's not dead already, then he's killed her."

"Ava, can I ask why?"

"Why he beat her?" She looks at me with tear-rimmed eyes. "He didn't get the girl he wanted. And she wanted him, always did, so she was too scared to call the guards. She always thought he'd stop, that the last time really *was* the last time. And my uncle... the stigma around our family, the *shame*, it was too much. She couldn't do it."

"Noah will never hit you."

She smiles, nodding. "You're right. Wanna know why?"

"Hm?"

"'Cause I'd kill him if he tried."

I laugh a little. "I don't doubt that. C'mon, let's go see her."

We walk as quickly as we can to Katie's room; Ava matches my pace surprisingly well. Inside, Katie is flicking through the channels on the TV. Her eyes light up when she sees us.

"Hey, guys!" she says, immediately turning off the TV and practically throwing the remote. "I thought you'd left."

"No way," Ava says, grinning. She plops into the chair next to Katie's bed. "Can't get rid of us that easily."

I try not to see what's missing when I look at her, but my vision is clouded by the image of two kids sitting on the bed with her, a baby in her arms. Pain for the right reason; a hospital stay for life, not death.

"Chris, you alright?" Katie asks, pulling me back to the present. The woman in front of me is, after all, in front of me. I try to focus on that as I sit next to her and take her hand.

"All good," I say, offering her whatever tired smile I can. "How're you feeling?"

"Good, actually, just a bit bored," she says. "The TV here sucks."

I laugh, squeezing her delicate hand. "We'll get you out of here as soon as we can."

She opens her mouth to answer but is interrupted by the door opening. I turn, expecting a nurse ready to run some more tests, but it's someone much more welcome than that.

"Hey, Noah," Katie says cheerily.

"Hey." He shuts the door gently and sits on the other side of her, and finally, we are a family again. After months of being torn in half, endless nights with no oxygen, there is finally air in the room.

"I raided the kitchen," Noah says, emptying the pockets of his hoodie onto the bed. There are graham crackers, licorice sticks, packets of raisins, and even two cans of ginger ale.

"Oh, you're the best," Katie says, tearing into a pack of licorice sticks with nimble fingers despite the IV in the back of her hand. "How'd you find these?"

"Followed a nurse around and asked where I could find some ginger ale for my nauseous friend," he explains, cracking a can. "Swiped the rest when she wasn't looking."

It's the least they could do, I think, looking at the three of them. *After nearly killing us all.*

"Thank you," she says. Ava and I echo her as we dig into the snacks, sweet raisins and bubbly soda. We pass around one can at a time to make it last.

"God, that's good," Katie says after a sip. "Alright, so fill me in. What have I missed?"

"Have you seen Sam and Amy?" Ava asks, tucking her legs up under her.

"Not yet."

The three of us glance at one another; finally, I decide it's my job.

"Well, Amy lost her leg the night that, uh... yeah. She and Sam came out onto the roof, and I'd been... waiting, ready in case there were guards coming after us. I pulled the trigger before I realized who it was and it, well, it broke her knee. There was so much tissue damage in her thigh and ankle, too, they had to take her leg."

She takes a deep breath, brow furrowed. "Oh. Is she... okay?"

"Yeah." I nod slowly, thinking about it. "Yeah, she's okay."

"We've got two more squad members," Ava pipes in, trying to lighten the mood. "Kela and Grif. They're great; you're gonna love them."

"Cool," Katie says, nodding. "Avendas, or—"

"Meliors," I say with an unintentional bite, thinking about how they never would've been sent on the mission we were. I try to soften my voice when I see everyone staring at me. "They're great, though. Kela's father runs a booth in the Activity Center where you can try out these things called Surface Simulators. They show the Meliors what it's really like up there."

"Oh, cool," Katie says. "We should do one sometime, if we can."

I cut off both Ava and Noah before they can say anything. "Totally."

Katie looks between the three of us. "Okay," she says slowly. "So, what else has been going on?"

Well, we went to a funeral for a four-year-old, another girl kept relentlessly flirting with me, and Noah and I helped Ava learn to walk properly again, I think.

"Not too much," I say.

"We had the Summer Festival," Ava offers.

"Oh, I wish I didn't miss that."

"Oh, yeah, 'cause it's totally on you that you did," Noah teases. The air grows stale when no one laughs. "Sorry."

"All good," Katie says, offering him a wan smile. "I'll be here for the next one. No plans on leaving anytime soon."

It's not like we could if we wanted to, I think, immediately wishing that my thoughts weren't so bitter.

"Chris, you okay?" she asks. "You're death-gripping me, here."

"Oh, sorry," I say, quickly releasing my hold on her hand. I flex my fingers and then return them to my lap. "It's, uh, been a long few months."

"God, you're telling me," she says, popping open another pack of graham crackers. "I missed sugar."

"Hey, we're pretty sugar-deprived over here, too," Ava teases, opening her hand for a cracker.

Katie obliges, talking around a mouthful of food. "Yeah, cause it's soooo similar."

I worry for a moment that her joke will fall flat like Noah's did, but Ava picks it up in the way that only she can.

"Well, we *were* both underground," Ava says. "And we both had to run."

"You spent the *entire* time in PT instead of running," Noah points out.

"I was *stabbed!*" Ava cries, throwing her hands up and laughing. "Believe me, I'd rather be on the track with you guys."

"That's a lie," I interject.

"Yeah, it is," she admits quickly. "I hate running."

We all laugh, and despite the missing people in the room, it feels good. We may never have the children we want, but we have a family, nonetheless.

WHEN IT'S time to leave, we all give Katie the tightest yet gentlest hugs we can. I kiss her on the forehead and breathe her in, relishing the feeling of smooth skin against my lips.

In the hallway, Ava grabs Noah's hand.

"I'm glad we're all together again," she sighs happily.

"Well," Noah starts, face darkening as we step into the stairwell, prepared for the long climb.

"The four of us, at least," she hastily adds.

"What?" I ask, stopping two steps above them. I look down at the two of them as they exchange a knowing glance. "Noah, what?"

"I—" He glances at Ava, then back up at me. "Amy is transferring to Level 7. In a few days."

"What? Why?" I look at Ava, who is watching her boyfriend intently. "You both knew?"

"We found out while you were away. We've been waiting to tell you; it's been so hectic."

"Why?"

"It's been insane here, Chris," Noah says defensively, stepping towards me. "C'mon. You've been nearly impossible to find."

"No, I mean why is she going?"

"Level 7 is more accessible," Ava says quietly from the bottom of the stairs. We both look at her. "I mean, her leg is *gone*. Her life was based around her body—she ran for fun, not just because she had to. Can you blame her for wanting to get away from here, where our bodies mean everything to us?"

Her dark eyes shine with truth and tears, and I know she's right, but it's nearly impossible to accept it.

"But what about us?" I ask. "What about Sam?"

"Sam has to stay," Noah says, staring at the floor. "She's needed here more."

"Needed?" I almost laugh. "Oh, yeah, so she can die for them."

"Die for who?" Noah asks. They both look up at me.

I sigh and decide to bite my tongue, too exhausted to explain it to them. "For the Head Trainer. For Ankou. Hell, I don't know. It just seems like everyone's asking us to live for them, die for them. I'm tired of it. I just... I just want to live and die for myself. For you guys."

Noah nods thoughtfully. "Amen, man."

We walk slowly up the stairs, taking our time for Ava. Once we're home, we get ready for training, and then it's back down the stairs for a run and target practice. The only thing I think about, as my feet pound against the rubbery track, is Katie running next to me in a few days.

CHAPTER SIXTEEN

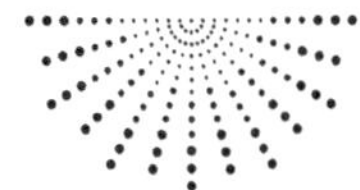

THAT NIGHT, I dream about Katie, Amy, and Mel. The three girls I've lost stand wordlessly before me in a line. I wait for them to abuse me, hit and kick me for letting them go when I should've been keeping them safe. I wait for the harsh words and piercing glares, but none come. They stand in front of me, staring. Their eyes float.

I wake up in a cold sweat at 3:43. Noah is asleep in his bed; Ava is spending the night back in her room, getting readjusted. I miss her.

I lie in bed for a few minutes and try to relax, but sleep evades me. My joggers are bunched up, and I've sweat through my t-shirt. A pit grows in my stomach as I think about Amy, so I grab the phone, tug the cord under the bathroom door, and lock myself in.

I know their number by heart, and within a minute of getting out of bed, I'm listening to the dial tone.

Sam answers, voice muddled by sleep. "Who... *why?*"

"Hey, it's Chris," I say.

"Christopher Ashborrow, it is... *it is 3:51 in the morning.* What do you need?"

"I... oh, God, Sam. I don't know. Everything's *wrong.*"

She wakes up instantly, suddenly sharp and clear. "What's going on? Is everyone alright?"

"Yeah, yeah, we're fine. I heard about Amy. I'm so sorry I didn't know sooner. Are you okay?"

"I'm gonna live."

I pause, trying to find the words. "I'm sorry."

"Don't be; this is the right thing. I want what's best for her, so if it means this... then it means this."

"How often will you get to see her?"

"Christmas, around both our birthdays, and one other time of our choice. They do trips about once a month for supplies, but they can't afford to take a ton of visitors every time."

"Holy shit."

"Please, don't remind me," she murmurs. "We picked our own birthdays when we got here. Those are July 6th and August 9th, so we'll see each other around then, and then there's the long wait until Christmas, then we'll probably pick a day in March or April."

"That's not a lot."

"No, it's not. We'll write letters monthly."

"You can't call her? There's no phone line?"

There is silence on the other end of the line. "Not for us," she finally whispers.

"I'm sorry."

"Don't be. This is what's best for her."

"But is it what's best for *you*?"

She is silent again, but the phone picks up her sniffle anyway. "It has to be."

"Sam..."

"Don't. I'll be okay."

"I know," I say, leaning against the wall and sliding to the floor. "I know. Do you want me to come over?"

She sniffles again. "No, it's the middle of the night. They could dock your credits if you get caught."

"Then I won't get caught."

"Stay home, Chris."

"We should do something for her. A party, I don't know."

"She doesn't like parties."

"Then we'll all go get coffee, or go down to the Activity Center.

Once Katie's out of the hospital, the eight of us can spend an afternoon together. We all deserve a chance to be together before she leaves."

She pauses for a moment. "We do."

Her hesitation reminds me that eight isn't enough; there should be more. They've always hinted at those who came before us, like that girl who had to run an extra mile on their first day, but they've never told us outright what happened to them.

"I'll see you in the morning?" I say softly.

"Yeah," she whispers. "Get some rest, Chris."

"You, too. Goodnight."

She hangs up, leaving me to listen to a faint buzzing sound. I hang my head and put the phone back on the receiver, wishing I could feel better. Being alone is lonely, talking to people is exhausting, and there's nothing for me in between. Only Katie, the one person I can truly rest with, but she's down in the hospital and I'm stuck up here. I could try to sneak in, but Sam is right—the punishment for getting caught is harsh, and in the hospital, I would be found for sure.

I stand in the shower and let the warm water fall over my skin, imagining that it's her pressed against me instead. When I'm done, I get dressed, then wash my face, brush my teeth, and floss. I stare hard at myself in the mirror, trying not to see her standing next to me. Short auburn hair and eyes like the beginning of fall, green and brown with that same relief that the first cool breeze of September brings.

She'd wrap her slender arm around my waist like she'd done it a thousand times, even though we were just kids the last time she held me like that. She was so shy that she would cling to me or Ava in the lunch line at school.

She'd place her head against my chest, and I'd be able to see her forehead bouncing with the beat of my heart, because she still makes it absolutely explode out of my chest, even now.

Have I always admired her like this? I remember the way we'd hug before and after school every day, back when you were allowed to hug your friends because you were little enough. I remember her tying my shoes because I couldn't figure out how. I remember scraping my elbow on the playground. I remember when she stopped holding me in the lunch line and being sad, wanting to reach out and hold her instead. I remember being fourteen and looking at her in the school library, thinking *Ankou, I hope we're Matched.* I remember tickle fights and pillow fights and even the occasional real fight, and eating lunch down by the lake on the first day it was finally warm enough to go outside every year.

I think of her slender hands on my waist, cool fingertips and the relief they bring. I think of a gold band on her left ring finger and how badly I want to be the one to put it there, to be her husband. It's the easiest decision of my life.

Even without children, she's the only one I'd choose. The ache runs deep at the thought of a life without my own, without ones that would look like me. Would look like my father.

Katie's father taught me how to tie a tie when I was fifteen. He taught Lucas and me at the same time so it would feel less weird, but it still was. Lucas figured it out before I did, so he went off to do homework, which left me and Mr. Davis alone to go through the steps again. We both pretended it shouldn't have been someone else who was teaching me. I want to teach my son to tie his tie, but the ache of a life without her is even worse.

A knock on the door interrupts my thoughts. Her hands evaporate off my shoulders.

"Chris," Noah says sleepily. "C'mon, I gotta pee."

"Uh, yeah, one second," I reply, grabbing the phone and unlocking the door. I check the mirror one last time and flatten my wild hair.

"Hey, you good?" he asks, eyeing the phone in my hand.

"Yeah, I just wanted to call Sam," I say. "Check up on her."

"Alright. You coming to the track in the morning?"

"After I see Katie, yeah."

"Alright, cool. G'night."

"Night."

I put the phone back and lie on top of the covers. Noah gets back in bed a few minutes later, immediately snoring like the sea. I miss the sound of the ocean, of the Surface, of a life I thought I'd forgotten. I want to go back; I want to go home.

I'm so groggy the next morning that Noah has to shake me three times after Wakeup and then remind me to put on shoes before walking out the door.

I head to the hospital instead of breakfast, having lost my appetite when I heard about Amy last night. I find Katie on her feet, balancing in the small hallway outside of her room.

"Hey, look at you!" I say.

She is standing with both arms out, fingertips gracing the yellow walls on either side of her. Her legs are splayed out like a foal's. She grins wide, showing one crooked tooth. "Look at me."

"She's doing great," Carla says from behind her, arms out to spot her. "She keeps improving like this, she'll be home any day."

My heart surges to think of her just one wall away—oh, hell with it, we're staying together as soon as she's home. I'm not sleeping without her ever again.

Katie and I lock eyes, and the grin spreads to my face, too.

"That being said, it's time to get you back in bed," Carla continues. "C'mon."

I help her get settled, propping her up with pillows and grabbing the coziest blanket I can find. It's green and fuzzy, and it brings out the green in her eyes as I tuck it around her.

"Thanks, Chris," she says, wincing.

"You alright?"

"Yeah, just sore. It's crazy, how much that hurt."

"What hurts?" I ask, sitting on the bed beside her and taking one slender hand in mine.

"I'm just crampy, I think," she says, shifting to get more comfortable. "After everything, I'm just surprised that that hurt so much. With what I could do a week ago, I... I didn't expect it."

"Katie..." I pause, not wanting to ask but needing to know. "What *were* you doing a week ago?"

She pauses as if she'd never expected me to ask, eyes boring a hole into my chest. When she speaks, it is in halting spurts.

"I was running, I think. I ran a lot."

I bite my tongue, wanting to let her form the narrative herself.

"They would put these—patches—on me, and I would run. On a treadmill. Sometimes I'd wear a mask."

She takes a deep, shuddering breath. Her hospital gown trembles with the force. "I would run until I couldn't. They'd do... exams. Measurements. Like getting fit for a coat at the clothing depot, remember that?"

She looks up at me, eyes sparkling for a moment.

I smile in spite of myself. "Yeah, I do."

Her eyes fall again into her lap. "I would get those every week. The measurements. Bloodwork, too. A lot of it. They'd give me weird drinks and medicines, and then take my blood. Sometimes an hour after, sometimes a few days. I never knew what they were. I asked. I got... hit. For asking."

She shakes her head, hair falling in her eyes. She pushes it away before continuing. "I was hoping you'd know why."

We look at one another, and I lie right to her beautiful face. "No, I'm sorry."

"Oh." She pauses, nodding slowly. "Okay."

"I'm sorry," I say again, taking her hand. "I shouldn't have... I pried."

"It's alright," she replies, squeezing my fingers. "It feels good to talk about it."

"Did they hurt you?" I ask.

Her silence tells me everything I need to know.

"God, Katie, I—"

"Do not be sorry," she says fiercely, squeezing my hand as tightly as she can. Her knuckles turn white, my fingertips purple. "Better me than you. Just like in the woods."

"No, Katie. Come on."

"I meant it then, and I mean it now. I'm glad it was me, and not any of you. It just would've been easier if..."

"If...?"

She takes a shuddering breath. "I saw the helicopter. On the roof. I didn't know if anyone got on it, though. If I'd known that you did, maybe it would've been, well, not easier, but... maybe I wouldn't have given up."

I think of every kickball game, footrace, impossible homework assignment that she would stay up all night to finish. Wearing herself into the ground trying to run faster than Noah even though he was a foot taller than her.

"You... gave up?" It sounds so unlike her, it's nearly impossible to believe.

She nods slowly, eyes glued to our intertwined hands. "Last week. I held on for so long, Chris, please believe me."

"Katie, of course you did," I say, wrapping her hands in both of mine. I duck to look her in the eye. "I know you did. And I would never fault you for letting go if you thought... There was no way for you to know we were coming. I would *never* blame you for a single thing you did there. You hear me? Not one thing."

"I just... I heard them rescue the others," she explains. "And not me. And then I decided it didn't matter if I lived, or if I died. Because I never thought you would've come back for me. Not a second time."

"I will always come back for you," I say, pulling her into my arms, holding her against my chest. "Always, Katie."

She hesitates and then wraps her arms around me. "Thank you, Chris."

***

KATIE and I agree that I'll go check in with the rest of the squad on her behalf, letting her rest. I go to Sam first, because I can't stand the thought of talking to anyone else, not even Ava.

She's home, which is odd, until I remember that she has time off until Amy leaves. The girl in question is out at PT for one of her last appointments in Level 8.

"Sam..." I say, trying not to choke on her name when I see the boxes. There are only two, because our lives aren't meant to accumulate possessions.

"Hey," she sighs, shoulders falling from her ears down to what seems like her ribcage. "Come in. How's Katie?"

We sit on her bed, facing each other, cross-legged like two kids about to play patty-cake.

"She's okay," I say, even though it is a lie. "She... told me about some of what she went through."

"Is it bad?"

I nod, looking up at her only to realize that I'd been looking down. "They tested her. In every way. I worry that she had to..."

"To what?"

"Hurt others," I finish. "As part of it."

"Why do you think that?"

"She's been having nightmares," I say quietly. "Talking in her sleep about hurting people. Crying. I don't wake her, because I don't want to scare her, but... I'm scared, too."

"Let me ask you something," Sam says, readjusting to sit up straighter. "Is she still Katie?"

I think of the girl we killed on the beach, who had her face and voice, but wasn't her. But the girl downstairs, who smiles at me like I'm the first sunlight of spring, that's Katie. "Yes."

"That's all you need," she says. "Amy has... she has done some awful things. I have seen her kill people without blinking, cold as stone. She has said some terrible things to me, especially after losing her leg. But she is still the woman I love. She's still Amy."

"How is she, with leaving?" I ask, thankful for the change of subject. I'm growing sick of my own pain.

"Not good. It sucks," she says, picking up her pillow and pulling at a stray thread.

"Is there anything that we can do to make this easier?" I ask.

"Yeah, cut off my leg so I can go with her."

We sit in silence for a minute, her picking at the pillowcase, me trying to figure out how to apologize for all this hurt.

She sighs. "I'm sorry. That was..."

"I'm the one who should be sorry. It's my fault."

She looks at me with eyes narrowed into two blades of steel. "Don't say that to me. You know better."

"Sam, it's true."

"I'll never believe you; you know that." She pauses. "We've all been real screw-ups recently, huh?"

"Not you. You've been doing a decent job, all things considered. Me, though…"

"You? You've been PRing on everything, and Cecilia considered you mentally stable enough to go up there. You're a star, as far as I'm concerned."

"Oh, shut up. I don't even think I can look at her right now."

"At Cecilia?"

"Yes."

Her eyes soften into thunderclouds. "What do you mean?"

"What you told me on the bridge. I talked to her after and I'm just so *angry*, Sam. It's so hard."

She swallows hard. "It gets easier, I promise. Just not yet."

I sigh. "Sam?"

"Yeah?"

"How do you know all of this?"

"Remember Amy mentioning Sasha Marse? That girl who had to run an extra mile on her first day?"

"Yeah, of course."

She runs a hand through her unwashed hair, greasy brown roots peeking out. It occurs to me for the first time that she is not a natural blonde. "She wasn't the only other member of our squad. There was Troy, and Connor, and Dom. Dom transferred out to tech after… well, after the others died.

"Sasha and Connor were killed on the Surface, but Troy died two months after we got home. He's the reason there's a cage over the bridge. They saw him jump when they reviewed the security cameras. We never found his body, so we never had a funeral, and we never talked about it again."

"Why would he…?"

"Connor took a bullet for him. They'd been inseparable their whole lives; their moms were best friends since *they* were born. He couldn't live with the guilt, no matter how many times I tried to talk him through it. I didn't know how to save him. I'm learning, now."

"Sam…" I pause, not sure what to say. I settle for the simplest words I can find. "I'm sorry about your friends."

"I know." She pauses, lost in thought for a moment. Her voice shakes when she speaks again. "The worst part, the absolute *worst* part, though, was that I understood why. I knew what he felt, I knew what it was like to hurt that bad, and I understood. I was never even mad at him for it. Everybody else was so... *angry*."

I reach out and touch her hand gently. "How do you do it, Sam?"

She sighs. "I don't..." She stops, takes a shuddering breath. "I just do."

I wait in silence for her to speak again, knowing there are words trapped in her throat.

"I've never gone more than two days without seeing her," she murmurs. "And even then, I could still call her. I can't even tell you when I last went a day without hearing her voice."

"It'll get easier," I lie. "You just have to keep busy until you adjust to it."

"What if she finds someone else?"

"There will never be someone else."

"How do you know that?" she asks after a long while.

"I just know."

"But *how*?"

"Sometimes that's the only way you ever know anything," I answer. "You just do."

CHAPTER SEVENTEEN

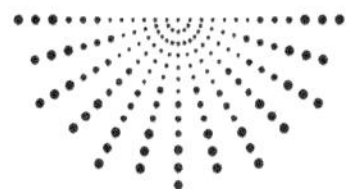

THE AFTERNOON IS SPENT in the sparring ring, trying to leave behind the chaos of the past few days. I try to ignore the thought of Katie in her hospital bed, fighting off feverish dreams or coughing so hard she brings up blood.

I nearly ask Cecilia to go down there, but I bite my tongue when I remember what she used to tell me when we would meet for coffee, back when we thought Katie was truly gone. *You have to be okay with living, Ashborrow.* She'd say it with all the sympathy of someone who once wasn't. *With doing all the things that are normal for you. You don't have to love it, but you must tolerate it.*

And so, I do. I tolerate warming up with a few laps and some time on the heavy bags. I tolerate sparring Noah, tossing him down when his feet become too rooted. I tolerate a jammed finger when Kila and I slap hands the wrong way in a messy round.

What nearly breaks me is Ava popping me in the face with her fist and then immediately recoiling as if she'd been struck, instead.

"Shit!" I hiss, bringing one hand up to my throbbing eye. "God, Ava."

She covers her mouth with both hands. "Chris, oh my God, I'm so sorry!"

Cecilia is roaring with laughter. "Oh my *God*, Ashborrow!"

"Chris, are you okay?" Ava asks, reaching up to me. "Let me see your eye."

"It's fine," I say, blinking rapidly. "I'm okay, really."

"I'm so sorry, I didn't think I'd—"

"Didn't think what, Castellano?" Cecilia asks, still wheezing. "That you'd reach him?"

Ava says nothing, only bows her head sheepishly.

"Give yourself more credit," Cecilia says. "You've got more reach than you think. And Ashborrow, you've got to come back from last week. Get your head on straight. You guys are dismissed for the day. Go see Davis, I'm sure she'd love the company."

"I really am sorry," Ava says quietly as she turns to go. "Are you okay?"

"Yeah," I lie, bristling with anger at our trainer. "I'm gonna hang back for a minute. I'll meet you guys in the hospital?"

"Yeah, of course," she says, offering me a squeeze on the arm. "I'll have an ice pack ready for ya."

"Thanks," I say, giving her whatever wry smile I can muster before rounding on Cecilia. I wait until I hear the door close behind me to speak. "'Get your head on straight?' Really, Cecilia?"

"She's back," Cecilia says simply, standing up from where she'd been sitting on a low row of rusted bleachers.

"She's... she nearly *died*," I say, bewildered. I touch my bruising eye gingerly and wince. "*You* nearly died."

"But I didn't, and neither did she. So, you need to get yourself in order again."

Her words sting like freezing rain. "After everything you've been—"

"What we've been through is *vastly* different, Ashborrow," she spits. "My husband didn't *come back*. My son will not *come back*. But Davis did, and so did Castellano. And Omenstat, despite the odds. So, you need to come back, too."

"But we nearly didn't!" I shout, voice wavering. "You... you sent us to die, just because the Head Trainer said to."

"And then I went to him and begged for two Meliors so that none of you would ever go through that again."

The silence is deafening between us, despite the roar of two box fans that desperately circulate the hot, stale air. Sweat beads in my clenched fists.

"You..." I try.

"I did. I nearly got on my knees to ask for Monroe and Hobbs. He didn't want to give them to me, but I pleaded as hard as I could. I nearly pulled the 'dead son' card, that's how bad I wanted them. To keep you safe. To keep you *all* safe, because I'd failed at that. So how about a little credit, Ashborrow? I've been pulling strings for the four of you since I *met* you."

"I... tha—"

She holds up one calloused hand, holding her clipboard in the other. "No. I'll see you tomorrow, unless she's discharged. You will have that day off, and not one more, do you understand?"

"Yes, ma'am."

She brushes past me without so much as another glance.

I SPEND the rest of the evening taking it out on the heavy bags, so consumed by it all that I miss dinner and have to trudge straight to bed with nothing but a grumbling stomach and throbbing eye. Noah and Ava manage to cheer me up a bit with some ice and a few jokes about how she managed to reach my face, but they can't do much.

I spend the night tossing and turning, listening to the clock ticking and wishing I had gone down to the hospital to be with Katie. Sleep evades me as I imagine an infection, respiratory distress, a sudden and inexplicable brain bleed that leaves her a vegetable.

I am up before Wakeup and tell a half-conscious Noah not to expect me for breakfast. Then I grab a granola bar from Ava's stash and practically run to the hospital.

I burst into her room, panting slightly. "Katie!"

"Chris?" She sits up straighter in bed. Her eyes are clearer than yesterday, and the IV is out of her arm. No brain bleed, no sign of chest pain. "Are you okay?"

The ridiculousness of *her* asking *me* such a question nearly makes me laugh. "Oh, God. I'm fine." My shoulders sag, and the lack of sleep catches up to me suddenly. "I'm so sorry I wasn't here last night."

"No, what happened to your face?" she says, laughing a little. Oh, Christ, I missed that laugh.

"We were sparring yesterday. Ava got me." I sit on the edge of her bed, offering her half the granola bar in my hand.

"Thanks," she says, accepting it and taking a bite. "How'd she even reach your face?"

I laugh. "You know, that's exactly what we've been saying."

She grins at me, and that's all I need for everything to be okay again. "So, I have some good news."

"Really?"

"Carla said I can leave." Her eyes are gleaming with hope and brightness, the orange-brown color of lake water when you cup it perfectly in your hands, in the fleeting moment before it trickles through the cracks of your fingers.

"Oh, that's amazing!" I wrap her in a hug before I remember to be gentle, but she returns it with such ferocity that I'm the one in danger of cracking.

She hangs on for longer than I expect. Her heartbeat is solid and strong against my chest.

"Are you okay?" I whisper into her hair. Screw Cecilia—I'm spending every day with her for the rest of my life.

"Yeah," she murmurs. Her lips are soft against my collarbone, and I have to suppress the shiver that runs up my spine.

"I missed you."

"God, Chris, I missed you so much."

"You don't have to anymore." I pull away and cup her thin cheeks. "No more of that, I promise."

We wait for Carla to come with discharge paperwork and clean clothes. She helps Katie change out of her hospital gown; I busy myself with reading her 'at-home care' packet, which essentially tells her to get plenty of rest and fluids. She's due back in training one week from today and has an outpatient appointment the day after tomorrow.

Finally, they are done. I help Katie into a wheelchair, ignoring the bump of her wrist bone and the feeling of her forearm, so thin I could wrap my fingers around it.

She protests slightly at my aid, but my mother raised a gentlemen, and when you know someone inside and out for eleven years, you can tell when they're tired.

The elevator ride up to our hall is silent; a thousand words bubble onto my tongue, but I swallow them all down. I wonder what must be going on in her mind—I'm too afraid to ask. I think of the rest of my squad left with a fuming Cecilia, but I can't focus on them for long before remembering who is in front of me, and then I am drawn back to the beautiful, blissful present.

The doors slide open. I move to push her, but she puts a hand up.

"It's okay. I can do it."

I nod even though she can't see me, because when you know someone for eleven years, you also know when they don't need your help.

She is strong, and because of that, we arrive fairly quickly at her door, which I unlock and hold open for her. She eyes me warily.

"We left it the same," I say. "I suppose you'll want to take a shower."

She nods again, wheeling inside with a small smile. "Absolutely. This thing's gonna get old really quick, by the way. I'll just lean on you."

I laugh a little. "Whatever you want. I'll be right out here."

She stands unsteadily but gently pushes me aside when I move to support her. "I got it. Thanks, though."

"Okay. I'll be right here," I say again.

She steps into the bathroom and smiles at me with one ghostly hand on the doorknob. "And I'll be right there."

<hr>

AFTER SHE TAKES A SHOWER, we lie side by side and spend a long time talking about what life has been like since she's been away. By the time I go down to get us some lunch, she knows about everything except for my trip to the Surface (including Ruda) and my newfound allergy to Surface Simulators. I know I have to tell her about my Surface mission; the guilt is eating away at me, but I can't risk losing her for this. On my way to the dining hall, I try to remember her favorite meal. It comes to me when I'm halfway down the stairs—a veggie burger with a side salad and unsweetened iced tea.

When I get back to her room, she's waiting for me. She stares at the tray in my hands, mouth agape.

"You remembered."

"How could I forget?"

We eat in silence, but it isn't awkward. If anything, it's like no time has passed at all. It's as if we've spent every day together, as if she's been right on the other side of the wall this whole time and I just didn't see her.

"So, we have all afternoon," I say. "What do you want to do?"

"Have you been back to the library?" she asks, wiping her mouth.

"I finished those books we were reading. And then some more, and some more."

"Can we go back?"

"Of course. We can go right now."

Her smile is enough to melt the coldest of hearts, and I can't help but smile back. At this rate, my face will be sore by the end of the day.

We head to the library, taking advantage of the elevator, although she prefers to walk rather than use the wheelchair. I push it along dutifully, reminded of Noah when Owen would insist he walk himself to daycare. He always had the stroller ready just in case, even though Owen never once used it.

The library is deserted except for the librarian, who eyes us warily. She returns to scanning barcodes when she sees the wheelchair.

Katie and I browse the fiction section, taking in the scent of secondhand books and ink much older than we are.

"I need one with a happy ending," Katie finally says, crossing her arms as she stares at the shelf filled with thousands of stories, millions of lives.

"Here." I grab one from the top of the stack and hand it to her. "An old favorite."

"I didn't know you were old enough to have 'old favorites,'" she teases, taking it nonetheless and scanning the back cover.

"Hey, I spent a lot of time here," I say, trying to keep up with her joking tone.

It's in vain; her face falls. "I'm sorry."

I shake my head. "Don't be sorry. I... all things happen for a reason. But you're standing here right now, and I get to share my old favorites with you."

She grins. "Yeah. Now, I saw a couch around here somewhere..."

I take her hand, pushing the wheelchair with the other, and lead her to the plush blue couch I discovered tucked into a back corner. I park the wheelchair and sit down, pulling her with me.

We settle into one another, and I wish I were softer for her, but it seems I've been reduced to muscle and bone, too. Nevertheless, we find ways to be comfortable; we both sit with our legs stretched out before us, thighs pressed together. I wrap an arm around her, reaching so I can still turn the pages of my book, and she curls into me.

We read in silence for a long while, and I try to pay attention, but this might be one of the first times in my life that reality is better than fiction. Her warm breath tickles my forearm, and her hair smells of lavender again.

After at least an hour, she yawns.

"You tired?" I ask.

"Maybe." She yawns again.

"Take a nap. I'll be up."

"Mmkay."

She sighs happily and leans deeper into me, so I sigh happily and lean deeper into her. I try to keep my eyes open, but sleep clouds my mind, and it becomes difficult to tell where her body ends and mine begins. We are joined together with one complete heart. Ages ago, we used to joke that we shared a brain. Maybe we do, and that's why I can finally breathe again.

CHAPTER EIGHTEEN

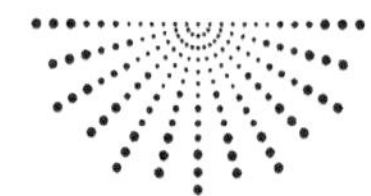

KATIE

I DRIFT between sleeping and waking, aware of Chris's blistering heat warming my skin. I've been cold for so long; it feels strange to be warm.

I missed him so much that my heart seemed to fall out of my chest with every beat. Every day when I woke up in that cell and remembered where I was, I thought I might die of the pain. And then the ultimate test—I passed, Cecilia taught me to pass—but after that I knew I was gone.

But then there she was, the woman who taught me that strength was not an option but an absolute necessity, shooting her way in to save me. And then there *he* was, the boy that made it all worth it, lifting me into his arms and carrying me away from that hellhole.

Then I was in the car, and Chris's eyes were swallowing me whole, and drowning didn't seem so bad anymore. What had once been my worst fear was now the very place I wanted to be, floating adrift in the comfort of blue, blue water.

"Thank you for saving me," I whisper against his chest, listening to the gentle rumble of his heart.

"I think it's the other way around," he murmurs.

"You're awake?"

He nods against the top of my head.

"I didn't mean to wake you. I'm sorry."

"I wasn't ever really asleep," he says, pulling away and looking down at me, stifling a yawn.

I look at his lips—they are red, the inside of a plum. I wonder if they are just as soft as they were a few months ago, when he held my cheek and kissed me like we were going to die the next day. My eyes flick back up to his, but he's looking at my mouth, too, and if he looks up again, I don't know, because I've already pressed my lips to his.

He sucks in a breath of surprise, bringing his free hand up to frame my face. He pulls away for just long enough to whisper, "*You* saved *me*," before connecting with me again.

CHRIS

SHE IS SHARPER than I remember, less muscle, more bone. Her lips are chapped, and she feels like nothing at all, like I'm kissing air. But she is safe, and she is here, and she is Katie.

"You saved me," I whisper against lips that taste like unsweetened iced tea. She feels so fragile that I might break her at any moment, that she could shatter and blow away in the wind should the slightest breeze pick up, but I crash into her regardless.

I pull away at last and bury my head into her shoulder with the hopes of inhaling her scent, searching for the familiar hint of lavender and lemon from her conditioner, overjoyed by finding it.

KATIE

I FORGOT how he smells like cologne mixed with smoke, as if our fires from the woods never quite washed out of his skin. I forgot how big his hands are, how wide and cool his eyes are, how soft the skin is at the base of his skull.

"Chris," I whisper against his hair, winding one hand in it.

"You okay?" he whispers back.

I nod ever so slightly. "I missed you."

He pulls away to look at me. "I missed you, too. You sure you're okay?"

"I've never been more okay."

He grins, icy eyes shining with tears. "Me neither."

CHRIS

We eat dinner in her room, too, joined by Ava and Noah. They smuggle up extra fruit salad, the closest thing we have to dessert, and that brings a real, genuine smile to her face.

As we finish dessert, while Noah explains what dogs look like, there is a soft knock on the door.

I get up to answer it and find the rest of our squad outside.

"What's going on?" I ask, taken aback. Even Grif is here, albeit paler than usual. I almost don't want to let him in and risk exposing Katie to another sickness. "What happened?"

Sam swallows hard—I note her red-rimmed eyes and puffy cheeks—and then drops the bomb. "Amy... is gone. She had to leave this afternoon, not tomorrow. She didn't tell us because she didn't want goodbyes to be painful. The Head Trainer told Cecilia, who told me this afternoon."

"She... what?" I ask.

Sam nods. Her grief is written plainly over her face, distorting her sharp features into gnarled knots. Grief that is all my fault.

I open the door wide, letting the three of them in.

Ava, Noah, and Katie sit on Ava's bed, eyes wide, and Ava quietly explains the situation to Katie, who blinks tears away as fast as she can.

"But weren't we supposed to be there?" Noah asks. "What about goodbye?"

"None of us got them," Kela says.

"Not even me," Sam says, voice dangerously sharp. "I have seen her, *every day,* since I was six years old. Thirteen *years* of my life with her. She was there for the birth of my children, for the death of one of them, too. I was there when her brother learned how to *walk*. We taught each other to use machinery; we grieved our families and friends together *over* and *over*. And she didn't say goodbye."

The air is still, her words hanging precariously between us.

"I'm sorry," I say.

"I know."

"Why...?" Katie asks, looking back and forth between me and Sam.

"I don't know," Sam says, voice breaking. She clears her throat, takes a deep breath, and her eyes return to steel. "I don't know. But there's nothing we can do about it now."

"You're allowed to be sad, Sam," Grif says, touching her shoulder gently.

She shrugs him away. "I know. I'll get there when I'm not so pissed at her."

We nod collectively, unsure of what to say.

She's out the door again without another word, footsteps thundering down the hall.

Kela and Grif hover for a moment, and then Kela blurts something about going to visit her parents for the night, and they're gone, too.

"Well, shit," Noah says once the four of us are alone again.

"Why did she leave?" Katie asks quietly.

Ava and I start to speak at the same time, but then I yield to her. "Level 7 is more accessible," she says heavily. "And since she's in a wheelchair, she's not coming back to training."

"But what about a tech squad?"

"I don't know," Ava says. "She made the choice that I guess she felt she had to make."

"Oh."

"I'm, uh, gonna hit the hay for the night," Noah says, standing abruptly.

"Same here," I say, glancing at the cracked clock on Katie's nightstand. I resolve to spend the night without her, to let her sleep in her own bed in some actual comfort, without me keeping her cramped. "It's getting late. See you in the morning?"

"Night," Katie says, eyes downcast.

I bend down and kiss her on the cheek, and Noah kisses Ava before standing. Once we're in the hallway, we melt.

"Shit," Noah whispers. "*Just* as things were going okay."

"That's how it goes, doesn't it?" I say as we enter our room.

"For once, it'd be nice if things *didn't* go that way," he grumbles.

"I know. I'm gonna take a shower. You good?"

"Yeah, you?"

I almost laugh. "Of course not. We literally just traded Katie for Amy, again."

"What?"

"That night, we saved Amy and lost Katie. Now it's just the other way around."

He actually does laugh at the absurdity of it all. "Holy shit, you're right."

KATIE

Ava and I get ready for bed in near silence, going about our old routine as if no time has passed at all.

"Katie," she finally says when we're both sitting in our own beds.

"Hm?" I look up from the book I'd checked out from the library.

She's pulling at the knitting of a throw blanket. "You're not going to transfer to 7, are you?"

"What are you talking about? Of course not."

"Are you sure?" She looks over at me, and all the years of sadness come to the surface of her deep brown eyes.

"Yeah, I am. I didn't even know I could."

"Prisoners of war have the option to transfer out at any point they see fit," she says, reciting as if from a textbook. "Options include Level 7 for agriculture or 9 for mechanics."

"Don't care, not going," I say, picking up my book again.

I can hear the smile in her voice when she replies. "Good."

WHEN I WAKE up with the book still open in my lap, the room is swathed in red light. There are alarms blaring louder than I've ever heard, so loud that I can't hear them, only feel them deep within my stomach.

Ava is standing at the foot of my bed, clutching a bag. I can't hear her, but I can read her lips as she screams at me, eyes wide in abject terror.

"He's here! We have to go! Ankou is *here*!"

THE END

ACKNOWLEDGMENTS

So many thanks to so many people! I could not have written this book without all the amazing people who read *Match*, so thanks to them, most of all.

My parents Cindy and Dominick supported my college endeavors, allowing me to chase summits and sunrises that inspired this book. Thank you for the grocery money and never blocking my phone calls, even when I call 3 times in a day.

To Becca, my favorite sister: thank you for freaking out over this book with me. No one knows how to match my energy as well as you (yes, pun intended).

My teachers growing up have been some of my biggest supporters. Mrs. DeMenezes read my first ever story, Mrs. Bergen introduced me to writer's workshop, and Mrs. Rigolizzo taught me to spell. Without them, I literally could not be a writer, nor would I want to be.

I am extremely lucky to know and love six grandparents. Woody, Linda, Allan, Luci, Kathy, and Jim have listened to me ramble on and on since I could talk. I can only hope they love listening to my stories as much as I love telling them.

To my amazing editor, Alexandra: thank you for asking an extremely simple (yet valid) question that led to an extremely complex (but fun) solution. This book would not be the way it is without you.

My amazing friends have inspired me time and time again. They're the ones who taught me the meaning of "found family." To Aila, Charles, Hunter, Chelsea, Genevieve, Zach, Jacob, Henry, Storm, and so many others whose names I'm blanking on right now, but I love relentlessly nonetheless: thank you, all of you.

To Jason and Miles, my northern family: thank you for keeping me warm during the coldest months of the year. I can't wait for more adventures with you.

ABOUT THE AUTHOR

Emma Grace is a lifelong novelist, student, and lover of the outdoors. She holds a B.A. in Creative Writing with a Minor in Wilderness Education from SUNY Potsdam, a combination of her two passions, however different they may be. She routinely suffers from summit fever and writer's block (often at the same time).

Emma lives in northern New York, although that is subject to change once she gets sick of the 6-month winters. She is originally from New Jersey, closer to Philadelphia than NYC, which is an important distinction. Her parents, sister, and exceptionally spoiled dog are her biggest supporters.

When she isn't holed up in a library or coffee shop, you can find Emma sunbathing on a rock like a gecko, plotting her next adventures both on and off the page.

Spark is Emma's second novel, the sequel to *Match,* her YA debut. To learn more about the Underground and Katie's future, visit her website, www.authoremmagrace.com, where you can sign up for her newsletter.